I0588846

ALONE WITH A TASMAN TIGER

A HIGH STAKES RACE. A MISSING FRIEND AND
A SEARCH FOR THE IMPOSSIBLE.

JANE ELLYSON

Copyright © Jane Ellyson 2024

The moral right of the author has been asserted.

All rights reserved. No part of this publication may be reproduced, or transmitted by any person or entity (including Google, Amazon or similar organisations), in any form or by any means electronic or mechanical, including photocopying, recording, scanning or by any information storage and retrieval system or transmitted in any form, or by any means without prior permission in writing from the publisher.

This novel is a work of fiction. Names and characters are the product of the author's imagination and any resemblance to actual persons, living or dead is entirely coincidental.

A catalogue record for this book is available from the National Library of Australia.

Paperback
ISBN: 978-0-6486607-8-1

E-book
ISBN: 978-0-6486607-9-8

Editor: Jackie Bates
Cover Design by Nabin Karna on Fiverr

www.janellyson.com

ADVANCE PRAISE FOR ALONE WITH A TASMAN TIGER

'From a compelling survival show set in the heart of the Tasmanian wilderness, to a Sydney to Hobart yacht race conspiracy, this is sure to become an Australian adventure classic.'

'A yacht appeared in the darkness, like a phantom or a tiger, stalking their prey. A totally addictive mystery thriller.'

'The biggest treat of *Alone with a Tasman Tiger* is Ellyson's mastery at weaving together a web of intriguing characters and stories into one rollicking Australian tale.'

'A winning trifecta: a thriller combining a dramatic Sydney to Hobart yacht race; encounter with a phantom yacht with terrifying technology and a competition in the wilds of Western Tasmania with incredible stakes.'

'Contained in the wilderness. Seb finds love and gets himself in a heap of trouble, and not just because of Betty.'

'I'm grateful that this one zoomed straight to the top of my gargantuan "to read" pile of books and I loved every page.'

MAP

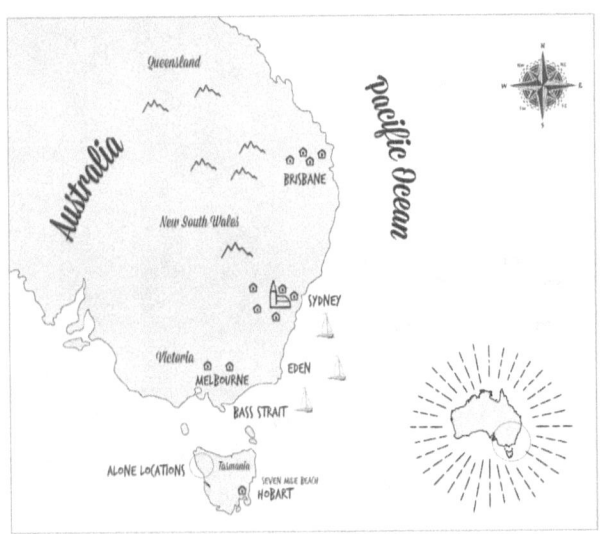

MAIN CHARACTERS

Sebastian Ward aka Seb (32). Adventure tour operator. Sailor. Competitor in *Alone* competition.

Galina-Elizabeta Ivanof (36). Drummer. Survivalist. Competitor in *Alone* competition.

Charlotte Wyatt-Harmon (22). Founder of fashion design studio, Chic Charlie. Former model (for ten days) and ASIO Information Officer (also for ten days). Wife of Scott Harmon.

Scott Harmon (26). Qualified yacht captain for water craft up to 55 metres. Keen surfer. Husband of Charlotte Wyatt-Harmon.

Jason Smith aka Smithy or Jase (30). House painter. Sailor.

Miranda Murray née Harmon (21). Married to Mason. Best friend of Charlotte. Sister of Scott.

Mason Murray (25). Journalist at *The Independent*. Best friend of Scott. Husband of Miranda.

TASMANIAN DEVILS AND TIGERS

Tasmania is famous for its many unique plant and animal species, some of which are found nowhere else in the world. The Tasmanian devil is one of these and is perhaps the most iconic animal on the island state. It is the largest carnivorous marsupial in the world.

The Tasmanian devil should not be confused with the thylacine also known as the Tasmanian tiger, which is also a carnivorous marsupial. It is widely believed to be extinct, with the last known tiger dying in captivity in 1936.

PROLOGUE

Miranda's screams were peeling paint from the walls of the birthing suite at St Christophers in London, or so Mason thought, while Scott's cries to *hold tight* could barely be heard above the thunder and lightning, as the yacht dipped and tilted in the ever-growing maelstrom in the stretch of water that separates Tasmania from mainland Australia. But it was the Tasmanian devil's manic screeches, in the deep bush of Western Tasmania, that were the most chilling of all, sounding like someone crying out from the dead.

PART 1

BRISBANE

ONE HUNDRED DAYS EARLIER

Brisbane, 15 September

'Are you sure mate?' Scott asked, as Seb scuffed the ground in front of him with his toe. 'You're taking a mighty big risk. It's highly unlikely you'll make it back in time for the yacht race briefing on the twentieth of December.'

'I've done my research and most contestants are out after forty days. In rare circumstances they make it through to sixty. I'm sure I'll be done by eighty, giving me twenty days to rest and recover before I need to turn up. This is a doddle. The chance to win $250,000 can't be ignored, Scott. I've gotta do it.'

'If you're not back by the twentieth we'll get someone else. That's as long as we can wait.'

'Understood.'

ALONE DAY 1

There was commotion at the coordination point. It was easy to spot the other contestants by their nervous laughter and scruffy backpacks. Seb suspected that by the time the competition was over there'd be a change in relationships, maybe not exactly friends per se, but perhaps more comrades, having shared a common, crappy experience.

'Over here. Come on. Gather round.' The tall, wiry man with an English accent was treating them as if they were chickens. His business shirt and jacket were incongruous in this bush setting, as was his silver name badge with the words 'Nelson Farnsworthy' engraved in a *serious font*. Seb looked at him wryly, then his eyes flickered across to an enchanting, impossibly-thin woman with gravity-defying, jet-black, spiked hair. Each strand seemed to exude untamed energy, reflecting a wild spirit. Her porcelain skin was adorned with vivid tattoos depicting slithering snakes. They were intertwined around her arms and travelled up her neck, suggesting a dangerous nature. Their sinuous forms seemed to come alive as she moved. He was fascinated. Clasped between her fingers was a cigarette she'd rolled herself. The smouldering tip seemed to illuminate her features, casting a haze around her, like a veil of rebellion. The curious punk looked back at him, observing his sleeve of green and blue peacock tattoos and gave the barest of approving smiles.

'OK,' continued Farnsworthy, 'this is what will happen. First, you'll have a medical. If you pass, you'll undertake the orientation test to ensure you've the physical stamina and wherewithal to be in the bush, by yourself. Finally, you'll be asked a number of questions to give us a sense of your psychological disposition. It's a bit like the Hunger Games, in that only six of the twenty here will be selected. Any questions?' No one said a thing as their eyes darted around their competitors. 'Good.'

For two hours, the twenty participants lifted, pushed and grunted their way through a series of physically demanding obstacles, which also tested their mental limits. After one hour, six contenders had called it a day, one weeping unconsolably as they left. Three sustained injuries, including a twisted ankle, bruised tailbone and a broken nose, which were considered too serious to allow the contestant to be left unaccompanied in the bush. Two others started fighting when one accidentally kicked the other in the head as they crawled through a mud trench. And one person passed out after the ice bath.

The final stage was the psychological assessment, which resulted in the removal of a further two candidates. Questions asked included:

Who are you?

What are your strengths?

What are you most afraid of in the bush?

How do you relax?

Why have you entered this competition?

Sebastian listened intently to the other surviving candidates' responses.

Archie: 'Twenty years of age. Jackaroo from the Northern Territory, from Dagoman land. I'm not a great talker. More than a little nervous. My strengths? Well, my history, my culture. I have bush skills, although in drier situations than here. And I know how to avoid trouble. To relax, I spend time in the bush, on country. I entered this competition, well, because I have the time – and because of the money.'

Janelle or Nellie as she quickly introduced herself: 'Forty-six. Retired captain from the military after losing half a leg in Afghanistan'. (She tapped her leg as if to prove that what she'd said was true). 'After what I've been through, this should be a cake walk. And a chance to recharge. I don't know what I'm going to do with the rest of my life. Maybe I'll figure it out here. My strengths – I've been in plenty of tough situations and survived. What am I afraid of? Snakes generally and the poisonous varieties particularly.' (She was staring at the wiry female competitor standing opposite as she made this remark). 'I know they're not that interested in humans, but I wish I was staying in a tent lined with gauze. I relax by spending time with friends. I've entered this competition as I've time on my hands and need to figure out what I'll do next, *you know*, with my life. Winning will give me options and bags of confidence. I'm well placed to survive in the bush given my time in more hostile places.'

Raj: 'Sixty-five. Chef. Retired chef. My children have all married and moved away and my wife has returned to Mumbai to visit her sister. I've no one to cook for. I think this is a wonderful opportunity for meditation and a little bit of intermittent fasting.'

Valda: 'Thirty. I'm Irish originally and now an Aussie citizen. I've taken unpaid leave from work as an environmental officer as I'm on the other side of a bloody, messy divorce. I know how to find edible foods in the wilderness so won't starve. I've entered because I've just lost half my assets.'

Galina-Elizabeta Ivanof. 'Thirty-six. You are unlikely to remember my name so you can call me Betty. My mother is Estonian, my father was Australian. He died. What are my strengths?' She spat on the ground. 'I've killed a bear. Does that count? Yes, the bear was protected but my dog was not. I've spent many nights in the forest in Estonia. I think that will be useful. There are few things that frighten me. To relax I smoke. When I can't smoke, I play the drums. I've entered this game because, well, why not?'

Seb was enchanted. *Confident. Tough as nails. She'd have no trouble surviving in the bush except perhaps for the not smoking.*

And then Seb introduced himself.

Seb: 'Thirty-two. Part-time sailor, part-time adventure tour operator – until the business went bust during COVID. Originally from New Zealand but my accent has faded given the twenty years I've been here. My strengths – I'm pretty good at catching fish. Most afraid of? Hoping not to bump into a grumpy tassie devil. I relax by going fishing or playing drums – and never at the same time.' (Everyone laughed). 'I've come here cause I've a hundred days free until my next job, and winning this Robinson Crusoe experience would set me up nicely, thank you very much.'

'Very well,' Farnsworthy said. 'Here are the rules of the competition.

- Your tracker must be kept on your wrist at all times.
- You must film for at least five hours each day, and no footage can be deleted.
- No killing of bandicoots, Tasmanian devils, platypuses or eastern quolls. Avoid killing any snake, even the poisonous ones, unless your life is threatened.
- Position timelapse and motion-activated cameras next to any traps, to prove no protected species have been injured.
- Do not travel further than one kilometre from your point of arrival. This will make it easier for us to extract you if necessary.
- Do not attempt to make contact with other contestants. Doing so will result in immediate disqualification.
- There will be periodic medical checks. If our doctor believes you are at risk from malnutrition or psychological distress, you will be extracted. No negotiation.

- When you want to leave, call and say *I'm tapping out.*
- You are not allowed to speak to anyone about your experience in the bush unless permission is given. All stories and media attention will be owned and managed by Channel 13.
- All contestants will attend the wrap up session in Hobart, most likely in January, where the winner will receive their cheque. This will be a live broadcast event.'

'Now. Backpack inspection.'

Two of his staff, dressed anonymously in blue jeans and black Channel-13-branded t-shirts approached the finalists. All backpacks were upturned and inspected to ensure nothing beyond the minimum specified clothing and first aid kit would be taken into the wilderness. Three chocolate bars were removed from Valda's inside jacket pocket, while a dozen cigarettes were found inside a false tube of toothpaste in Galina's toilet bag. Valda kicked the dirt, keeping her eyes low while Galina shrugged her shoulders nonchalantly.

'Now, gather round. You've the opportunity to select a further ten items. These will support your comfort and safety, so choose wisely.'

Seb was surprised and a little delighted when Galina stood beside him in the circle surrounding the cache of camping and hunting tools. Each contestant in turn was asked which ten items they would take with them. Galina selected the following:

1. knife with belt carrier
2. lighter
3. water container
4. blanket
5. sleeping bag
6. cooking pot
7. head lamp
8. tarp
9. snare wire
10. paracord (rope)

Seb's selection was much the same, except he took an axe instead of paracord, a saw instead of a small blanket (he was curious at her choice here), and a fishing line and hooks instead of snare wire.

'Good,' she said softly. Seb shook his head, and wondered at the meaning of her remark.

As they carried their chattels to the water's edge where two boats were waiting to transport the contestants to their *Alone* location, Galina whispered to him, 'They're lazy. There's no way we'll be far apart. They've been too insistent in saying we are a long way from each other, which means *they're lying.* We can help each other, OK?'

Seb nodded. 'But we have trackers to wear, *all the time,*' he whispered.

'No talking,' Farnsworthy growled. Galina raised her eyebrows, looked at Seb and mouthed 'easy'. Seb realised that together they'd have a wider selection of survival tools than if they were on their own. The thought of being in the wild with someone who seemed more than a little wild themselves, intrigued him.

One by one the contestants were transported by boat to their respective sites on the water's edge. Seb had googled maps of the area prior to departure and knew it was vast, dense and largely uninhabited by humans. There were no roads, with transportation by boat or helicopter the only options. Given the time between the departure of the boat with a contestant and their return it seemed clear that Galina's assumptions were correct. The contestants' locations could not be that far away from each other. But distance of course was only one measure. The denseness of the terrain could mean that it was difficult to move far by foot and then they could be located, on opposite sides of the water, without a boat.

It was three o'clock in the afternoon when the boat left Seb on the muddy shore of a large inlet. It was a forbidding location, surrounded by high mountains, with thick bushland behind him and a large lake in front, where many trees had died, a testament to the damming of the river at some point in the past. Still, he reasoned, he had plenty of fresh water, there was good tree canopy coverage and he still had four hours of daylight left to make a basic dwelling. That was his priority.

He chopped down a dozen saplings, and created a square structure. Given the time of year he knew there was potential for torrential rain, so building a shelter off the ground was critical. As the light was fading, he was pleased he'd created a framework with a tarp top. It was basic but it'd do for a first night's accommodation. He was already hungry and decided to try fishing. Scavenging through nearby foliage he found a cricket and threw out a line between two dead trees, crossing his fingers he'd have early success. Just as the kindling ignited in his fireplace, a splash sent Seb rushing for the shoreline. There was something on his line. It was impossible to pull the fish in, as it had done a runner, looping several times around a dead tree. He shoved his tongue into his cheek and considered his options.

Option 1. Strip and swim out to the tree to untangle the line and grab the fish. The water was cold, dark and decidedly uninviting. Still, there was unlikely to be anything nefarious in there. Not like swimming in the ocean with the prospect of sharks.

Option 2. Do nothing. He wasn't that hungry, yet. The fish might still be there in the morning, significantly weaker after a night spent trying to escape. Easier to catch. But a larger fish might have eaten it by then.

Seb chose the harder option. Indeed, this was unlikely to be the most daunting thing he'd have to do if he was to outlast everyone else. He considered the safety of a night swim, stripped down to his socks and jocks and grabbed the camera.

'Don't be afraid,' he said awkwardly, facing the camera in what would be the first of many video diary entries. 'Just about to go for a dip to get my dinner. Thought I should film the retrieval, just in case something goes amiss, and I disappear without a trace.' Seb chuckled nervously and walked tentatively into the water, the headlamp revealing a moonscape-like surface in the shallows. At waist deep, he sank into the water and slowly breast stroked out to the dead tree. Reaching down to find the fishing line, his hand stroked something soft and unfamiliar. Seb swore as a frightened platypus broke the surface of the water and swam away. Calming his breathing, he again reached down for the fishing line. It was knotted around a branch. Holding his breath, he sank below the water surface, untangled the knot and gently pulled the fish toward him. Resistance from the fish was low with a bite mark near the caudal fin revealing just how close Seb had come to losing his dinner. He roared with delight as he emerged from the water, holding the medium-sized trout high, disturbing two wallabies that could be heard thumping away through the bush.

Galina

Galina surveyed her surroundings. It would do. In fact, it would do very well. She moved her pack and camera equipment to higher ground and immediately scanned for a tree suitable for the first night's sleep. An old eucalyptus with three thick branches would be ideal. Using the rope and blanket she created a hammock high enough in the tree to avoid any grumpy Tasmanian devils or the slithering, ground-dwelling serpents that would shortly emerge from winter hibernation. Having established the first night's accommodation, she scanned the area in search of scats from pademelons or possums. A game trail was identified and she mentally listed what would be required to set a trap the next day. A fireplace was built and lit near a large rock that served as a perfect seat. She sighed, sat down and removed her boots. Pulling out her knife, she dislodged the heel from her left boot, revealing a stash of cigarettes. She sighed as she took her first drag. Using the knife on the right boot, she extracted a plastic bag of beef jerky. Dinner was ready.

Valda

Valda was excited and exhausted as she moved her camera equipment to a small clearing close to the water. This wasn't an ideal location, with widow-maker tree branches in evidence in nearby towering gums. A circum-navigation of the area identified two nestling boulders that would provide shelter from the wind. Looking skyward, she assessed that there was little chance of rain, so this would be an adequate campsite for the first night. She moved her pack and equipment and created two fires, one on each side of her sleeping bag. It felt safer. The air was crisp, carrying the earthy scent of dried leaves, rich soil and the faint aroma of Huon pines. Snuggling down, she smiled as she listened to the crackling of the fire, the gentle rustling of leaves and the night cries of currently unidentified nocturnal marsupials.

Raj

Raj was in good spirits as he watched the bubbling stream, close by to where he'd been deposited. There was a large flat rock sitting on top of a group of smaller round rocks, whose shape had been developed by years of fast-flowing water. It'd probably flood during a downpour, so he'd need to camp on higher ground. However, when the sun was out it would be the most perfect spot for fishing and meditating. He set up his camera, sat on the flat rock and declared that he had arrived in paradise.

Janelle

Nellie's first impressions were positive. Amidst the dense, untamed wilderness of the bush, the sun's rays filtered through the thick canopy, casting dappled patterns on the forest floor. The air was fresh, carrying the scent of eucalyptus. The former army captain stood at the edge of a small clearing, gazing intently into the vast expanse of grey and green. With her binoculars fine-tuned, she scanned the area, ever vigilant for signs of danger or potential resources. A bees nest was spotted and the location recorded in her notebook.

The dense foliage and unfamiliar terrain presented a challenge, but she remained focused and was able to identify natural mint that she could use for tea. Delighted, she shoved a handful of leaves in the top pocket of her dark green, camo-coloured shirt. Moving further into the bush she identified a venomous snake, coiled on a sunny spot on a log. It moved off before she needed to retreat. The hum of insects filled the air. She sighed and smiled, pleased that she had managed her first encounter well. Several minutes later she discovered a small stream winding through the undergrowth. She knelt beside it, cupping her hands in the cool water to wash her face but resisted the urge to taste it. It was too risky. All water needed to be boiled, particularly given the increasing presence of animal tracks. She drew a rough map of the area in her notepad and returned to where she'd left the camera equipment and her belongings to establish a temporary camp. With the fireplace flaring, she boiled water in the cooking pot, made mint tea and turned on her camera.

'Campsite established, serpent avoided and first food source identified. It's a bees' nest so extraction will have challenges but I'm confident these can be overcome. Additionally, I've discovered a mint bush so am enjoying a soothing beverage before I settle down for the night. Nothing else of consequence to report.'

Archie

Archie loved the feel of the mushy ground under his bare feet.

'I'd wear shoes if I were you,' the black-t-shirt-clad assistant called out as he pushed the motorboat back out into deeper water. Archie waved and ran into the bush, eager to explore this place that he knew he'd come to know intimately. Using the bushcraft skills his grandfather had taught him, he located several bush tomato plants. A dozen of the ripest fruit were selected. He smiled as he listened to the melodious call of the black currawong. Several dusky robins, darting around lower tree branches, were a sign that insects were present. Pausing to listen for the distinctive sound as they rubbed their leathery front wings together, he identified and pocketed a dozen crickets. With enough snacks in hand, he returned to an area, not far from the water's edge where a tree had landed between the fork of another. He knew it was a perfect site for making a humpy, a traditional shelter used by his ancestors.

Archie cleared the ground of debris and spent the next hour gathering long, sturdy branches, flexible vines, and bundles of tall grass. Branches were arranged in a circular shape around the fallen tree, forming the foundation of the humpy while the vines were threaded around the branches, binding them together. Tall grass then filled the gaps between the branches, providing insulation and a natural camouflage.

Archie threaded two of the crickets on fishing hooks, cast out and tied the lines to a dead tree. Maybe there'd be fish for breakfast? He wasn't worried. He already had a backup plan based on the scats he'd observed. Roasted cricket was one of his favourite meals and he knew that there'd be spectators, high in nearby trees, now that darkness had fallen. The bush tomatoes were sitting on a flat rock that served as a plate. He ate them one at a time between each crunchy cricket. When the fire died down, he moved into his humpy, leaving four tomatoes on the plate, wondering how long it would take for them to disappear into the night.

ALONE DAY 2

Sebastian

Seb was awake before the sun filtered through the trees surrounding his campsite. While he'd been woken several times by the unfamiliar sounds of rustling in the bushes, he'd slept well. He mentally noted major tasks to be completed for the day. These included finishing his camp, throwing his fishing line out, and beginning his chat with people unknown. Frankly, the thought of having to film for five hours was fine – it was the commentary that made him uncomfortable. He wondered what he would talk about. On a whim he decided to call his camp Sailing Siesta, as this was what he should be resting and preparing for, the Sydney to Hobart yacht race. He recognised he needed to note the number of days passing so he could determine when he needed to get out in order to make it to Sydney for preparations prior to departure. He turned on the camera.

'G'day. Hello from the Sailing Siesta camp site. Errr...' He turned the camera off again, suddenly lost for words, while he considered what to say next. 'You'll be pleased to know that I enjoyed barbequed trout last night and again this morning. A little cracked pepper and butter would have complemented it beautifully but, well, don't have any. I need to collect fire wood and ferns and stuff, you know, to finish my hut, but first I'll put my lines out. A busy day ahead of me.' He turned the camera off and checked the time stamp. Two minutes recording had elapsed. This was crazy. He'd have to set and forget it. He pointed the camera at his camp and tried to ignore it.

His fire had gone out hours earlier so he left to collect kindling and thicker logs. He recognised this would be a daily activity so he mentally created a route plan and then identified a dry place to store the wood in preparation for the rain that would inevitably come. He then went in search of materials for his dwelling. He was building for the long term, at least ninety days, so it needed to be strong enough to withstand the rain and wind. His thoughts flickered to his companions. What were they doing? Looking across the water then into the mountains behind his camp he wondered where they were. There were no human-like noises to provide a clue. He particularly considered his Estonian competitor. What would she be doing now?

. . .

Galina

Galina had woken well before dawn. She hadn't slept much, but then she didn't need much. Slipping a knife into the lining of her jacket, she removed her stash of quinoa into a t-shirt that she then tied in a knot. It'd be a wonderful accompaniment to the meat she intended to catch in her trap. Firing up the kindling, she cooked a small portion of the precious seed with a piece of beef jerky and considered what she would film today. This was the part of the process she knew she'd enjoy least.

The hammock in the tree had worked well but was not a long-term solution for a dry and secure dwelling. Looking at the sky she assessed there'd be no rain today. Her shelter could wait. Setting her traps was a priority. Scooping up her snare wire and cameras she returned to the scat spot she'd identified the previous day as being the most likely trail where the edible and allowable marsupials would pass. One camera was a small movement detection device that would provide valuable information on animals passing through the area at night. The second was a more substantial piece of equipment with which she was supposed to film herself or her activities for five hours each day. She turned the big camera on, said nothing and set to work making two traps.

. . .

Valda

Valda had spent an unsettled night. In choosing her camp she'd not noticed a nearby ant hill. The small black critters had found their way into her sleeping bag and she was now covered in flaming red bites. She spent the first twenty minutes of her day applying antiseptic cream to her wounds with the camera on, facing the unknown people she imagined watching her from the comfort of their leather reclining chairs, while sipping a glass of wine.

'As you can see, I've had an eventful night. Well, the ants have had an eventful night.' She held up her arms, then lifted her t-shirt to show them her back. 'Lesson from being alone day one. Determine if there's an ants' nest near your camp, before settling down. It's not as bad as it looks but does mean I need to find a new camp, as soon as I can. As you can see it's a beautiful day and if not for the ant bites, I'd be in good spirits. Not sure what I should start with as I'm hungry and I need somewhere else to camp. I think I'll go looking for food first. That's all for now, folks.'

Raj

'Good morning everybody. I hope you're doing well. Hello from my new home. I made a temporary but imperfect shelter last night. I now need to find somewhere else to set up, somewhere a bit quieter if possible. There were two dogs arguing rather viciously last night, or maybe they were devils. Quite a fuss. Would hate to have gotten between them. I need to get my fishing line wet as I'm a little bit hungry. This is however a beautiful place and I intend to spend an hour or two mediating on this wonderful rock as soon as my new camp has been established, and while I wait for those fishes to bite.'

Janelle

'Morning people. Today's main task will be retrieval of the honey from the bees' nest. I estimate this task should take no longer than thirty minutes. I've spent the night considering the safety aspects of the retrieval process and believe I've a sufficient plan to avoid injury. As you can see, I've established a more than adequate camp, although further work will be required to ensure it's animal proofed and comfortable. I'm again enjoying a morning cup of mint tea and look forward to complementing this beverage with honey soon.'

Archie

Archie turned on the camera and then turned it off again. He was dumb struck, unsure what to say to the persons unknown out there. Reflecting on the rules he recalled that they only had to record for five hours a day; they did not have to talk for five hours and indeed there was no requirement to talk at all. Archie picked up a camera and turned it on. He pointed it to his humpy and provided viewers with a peek inside before coming out to walk the camera to the water's edge and along as far as was practical before the bush became too dense. Returning to camp he pointed to the small rock where he'd last night left the bush tomatoes and where there was now nothing to see, and then pointing to tiny scats a few metres away.

'Possums,' he said, believing no further explanation was required. He moved the camera over to the water's edge, threw out a line baited with his last cricket and sat down on a broken stump to take in the view while waiting for the fish to bite.

Later the same day

Sebastian

Seb had enjoyed a productive morning. Not only had he gathered enough materials to complete the shelter, he'd also spotted a koala with a joey, high in a tree, making him smile.

Returning to camp to check his fishing line he was

delighted to discover another fish on the hook. Baby trout again for dinner. He turned on the camera as he gutted and scaled the fish, then took his knife and marked a slash in a stump he was using to mark the days since he'd arrived.

'This is day two and my second fishing excursion is going well. I'll probably be bored of trout if that's all I catch, but that's OK. I do wonder what else there is to eat here. I'm really more of a creature of the sea than of the land so maybe I should go swimming again to see what other foods are beneath the water line. Maybe tomorrow. Anyway, you just watch me cook and eat this fish. Bit boring for you I think. More exciting than watching me throw my lines out.'

Galina

Galina had created a solid ground-based shelter. Even without an axe, she'd managed to gather enough branches to build the framework that was secured together with the paracord and snare wire. The leftover branches went into a pile that could be used for firewood. In collecting kindling, she had spooked a quoll who'd been asleep in a burrow she'd intended to use for keeping her kindling dry. He was small and rather adorable and definitely did not possess enough meat on his frame to provide any value beyond an afternoon snack. And he was of course listed as a protected species. She chastised herself for forming an attachment to a potential food source and then corrected herself, as she was confident that her traps were well-set, perfectly-placed and that there would be something bigger for dinner the next day.

Valda

'While the day didn't start well, waking up with these annoying bites, it has improved. I've managed to find some mountain pepper that will provide wonderful flavour for any meat I manage to find, contain and cook. And there's good news here too. While I was resting on a rock, I heard the distinctive sound of a hen, a Tassie hen. Sorry the camera wasn't running so you'll just have to believe me when I say I jumped it and broke its neck.' She held the carcass up to the camera. 'For those of you at home uncomfortable with my actions, this is not on the DO NOT EAT list.'

It had been a while since she'd plucked and gutted a chicken but the memory of how to do it came back quickly. She washed the fowl, fired up the kindling, threaded pieces on green sticks and sat down smiling in anticipation at how delicious her roast bird with mountain pepper would be.

Raj

The fishing line was flickering. Raj was initially

delighted but this morphed into mild disappointment when he pulled ashore a medium-sized eel. They were a tricky animal to skin and only ordinary eating, but he was hungry and any food was welcome. He was delighted that on his walk through the bush that day he'd found native currants and lilly pilly, both of which could be used to hide the greasy flavour of the slithery eel now boiling away in the cooking pot on the fireplace.

Janelle

Nellie set up the camera and turned it on. She was certain she had a workable plan for removing the bees from the tree without serious injury to herself. Her risk-management plan involved wearing her white long-sleeved shirt, camouflage trousers and leather gloves. Climbing a eucalyptus tree adjacent to the one hosting the nest was challenging, but doable. Morally she would have preferred to leave the hive undisturbed, but it was not listed as a protected food source and would be a wonderful sweet addition in her food larder. The task took longer than anticipated as she had to carry her sleeping bag up the tree with her as an additional shield against any bees not happy with her attempts to relocate their queen and hive.

Securing herself on a branch adjacent to the nest, she wrapped the sleeping bag around her shoulders, broke a branch from the tree hosting her, tentatively reached across and poked the stem of the nest connected to the branch. This was more difficult and precarious than she'd imagined, and it took several prods before the hive swung and fell, by which time several hundred bees had spotted her and sent out an intruder alert. She quickly dropped the stick and wrapped the sleeping bag tightly around her shoulders, holding firm to the tree branch. Several bees spotted her exposed arms and let her know, in no uncertain terms, of their displeasure at her actions. She needed to hold fast and not attend to the bee stings for at least an hour, by which time the bees should have headed off in search of a new home. Time passed slowly. Climbing down the tree was harder than ascending, and her prosthetic leg came loose and dropped to the ground. She shimmied down the remainder of the tree and was delighted to discover that the leg was intact. Her stump sock however, was now filthy and would need washing. Hundreds of bees were still hovering around the nest so she made the strategic decision to leave the extraction of the honey for a few hours until the remainder had left to join their colleagues in the search for a new home.

Archie

The fishing lines sat quietly in the water. The fish were no longer biting. Archie's thoughts flickered to the possums that had taken his bush tomatoes. Roasted possum was his backup plan if he couldn't secure another food source. Confident that he knew where to find more crickets and bush tomatoes, he spent an hour carving a pointy end on a straight branch to use as a spear. Target for the spear at this stage unknown.

LATER THAT AFTERNOON

Sebastian

With the recording button pressed, Seb walked over to the water's edge and doubled the number of fishing lines in the water, experimenting with different insect baits and a lure he'd fashioned from bird feathers and berries. He also tried a better place for casting a line, which was difficult to find as the shore was littered with snag-potential debris from fallen trees. He turned to the camera sitting on its tripod on a boulder covered in lichen and moss.

'I wanna explore this place,' he said sweeping his arms in an arc. 'Well, a one-kilometre perimeter around my camp only, of course. Gonna start by following the water's edge in this direction.' He pointed inland, away from the direction the boat had brought him. 'Don't really want to carry the camera, but can't see how I'll get an extra three hours of recording in today, well unless you want to see me sleeping. Hmmm. Hope you don't suffer from motion sickness. I can already see from here that the path is going to involve a bit of ducking and squeezing.'

He removed the camera from the tripod and put it into his jacket pocket. Looking at his location tracker he wondered how accurate it was, and indeed what would happen if he walked beyond the stipulated, but impossible to measure, one-kilometre boundary.

Movement through the thick bushland was both challenging and slow-going as he was often climbing through long branches reaching out parallel to the ground in boggy conditions. His noisy movements gave several snakes advance notice of his arrival. Well, that's what he assumed he heard moving quickly through the leafy floor litter. His reconnaissance trip failed to identify a more suitable camping or fishing spot, which he reasoned was a good outcome. Curiously, someone had been here before. Maybe a year ago. There was a highly valued, Huon pine tree on the ground that had been cut into several pieces with a chain saw. Seb suspected that the cutting was illegal, and the chainsaw owner had been disturbed and departed quickly, without this precious timber. His thoughts again turned to his fellow Robinson Crusoes and he kept alert for signs of other human activity.

Walking back to camp he remembered that he had to set up a camera close to any trap within the first week. He'd only ever caught animals out of the sea and had no experience in setting a trap for land-based critters. Still, now was the perfect time to learn a new skill.

Galina

Strengthening her shelter was Galina's priority for the day. She momentarily regretted not having chosen an axe and her thoughts flickered to the scruffy, ginger-haired sailor who did. *I wonder how far away he is?* Nibbling on beef jerky she planned a route for firewood collection and tossed around an idea she'd had in her head for a while. A rustle of leaves drew her attention to the right of her shelter where the quoll was standing, watching her intently.

'You live dangerously, buddy,' she said as she surreptitiously turned on the camera. 'Darn lucky you're the most interesting thing here.' The quoll continued to assess her and twitched his nose. 'You could be a little *suupiste*.' He wouldn't know that he had been referred to as a snack in Estonian. Ei. (No) 'You are protected. I will protect you.' A sudden chorus of kookaburras spooked him and he bounced quickly away through the undergrowth. Galina looked at the camera in her shelter, raised her eyebrows with disdain and scooped up her contraband before placing it in her sleeping bag. The camera was hastily set up in the clearing in front of her shelter. She unconsciously ran her fingers through her hair and then chastised herself for caring about her appearance. The red record button was illuminated, and she strode in front of the camera and stared out towards an unknown audience.

'So. I go now collect wood for fire, for trap, and ferns for hut and bed. You can watch me check my trap later. I'm good at this.' She leant across and turned the camera off, noting that this recording lasted nine seconds. Her biggest challenge would clearly not be sourcing food or keeping warm. It would be finding a way to burn through five hours of footage each day.

Valda

It was only the second day, but Valda was already feeling alone and indeed lonely. She wondered what her friends were doing. Gossiping over cake and coffee? Catching the train home from work? She hated commuting but at this moment, she missed it; watching the throng of people and wondering what their lives were like. Were they happy? Were they wishing they could get away from it all? Just like her? She turned on the camera.

'Hello. Nice to have someone to talk to. Found a replacement campsite and have created a temporary structure. No ant or termite mounds nearby that I can see. But I'll test that tonight and then tomorrow decide if I have to move again. That's OK. Gives me something to do. My bites are no longer bothering me and I've enough energy after consuming roast chicken to do anything. Perhaps I'll go dancing.' She hesitated a bit surprised at what she'd blurted out. 'Wonder how long it will take for the birds to spread the word that there's a new predator in the area and take flight, well figuratively that is, as these guys don't fly. Can see it's going to be a bit of a challenge not having a fridge for storage.' She paused, looking out across the water and thinking about what to say next. 'You know, it's funny. I thought that getting away from it all was just what I wanted, and I'm not a big user of social media. But I keep reaching for my phone in my pocket to check what's going on, far more than I thought I would. And then I spend more time than I'd like dwelling on my new reality as a *divorcee*. I need to keep busy. Perhaps I should have thrown myself into my work rather than running away on retreat to get over the death of my relationship.'

Raj

'Good afternoon all. I expect you're wondering what I thought of my culinary creation. Well, to be honest, it provided sustenance but there is little chance that my lilly pilly, native currant and eel stew will ever appear on a restaurant menu. However, the gremlins in my tummy have been quieted and I can now sit and meditate.'

Raj took a deep breath and closed his eyes. With weathered but gentle features, his deep brown eyes held a depth of experience and his salt-and-pepper hair, neatly tied back in a loose bun, bore witness to the passage of time. On his wrist, a strand of wooden beads aided him in his meditative practice, as he gently fingered each bead in a rhythmic cadence. Sitting cross-legged on his weathered rock with his spine upright and his hands resting peacefully on his knees he concentrated on his breathing. Those watching from TV land could see the raw beauty of the Tasmanian bush, a canvas of rich and earthly tones and lush eucalyptus trees. They could also hear a symphony of sounds from the native wildlife. The murmur of the nearby creek blended into a harmonious type of background music, and in the distance, a wallaby could be heard gently bounding through the bush.

Janelle

Nellie approached the honeycomb carefully. Now that the bees had departed, she was able to admire its beauty. Its hexagonal cells, crafted by the tireless work of the bees, glistened with a golden hue under the dappled sunlight, filtering through the canopy of trees. She used her knife to cut the honeycomb into pieces before wrapping them in a clean t-shirt and placing them in her cooking pot for transportation back to camp, where she crushed the comb with her hands and then strained the honey. Storing it was going to present a problem as she was regularly using both her cooking pot and tin mug. Hopefully she'd continue to catch fish that could be skewered on a stick or cooked through on a thin rock. But her thoughts turned to what she could find in the bush to create a storage vessel or a mini larder; something that wouldn't be a magnet for ants and other critters.

Archie

The day passed easily. Archie circumnavigated every inch of the land that had been temporarily assigned to him. There were plentiful food sources and he knew he wouldn't go hungry. As the evening began to draw in, he practiced his spear throwing technique, moving like a ghost around his humpy. Holding the weight of the spear in his hands he wondered if he should make a woomera or spear thrower, to increase the strength and distance of his weapon. A new experience which he'd only observed once when staying with his grandfather. What did he have to lose and it should increase his hunting success? He sniffed the air, breathing in the scent of eucalyptus and pine and enjoyed the feeling of the strengthening wind on his face. It was picking up, giving advance notice of stronger things to come.

ALONE DAY 3

Sebastian – 6am

Seb woke to the rustling of leaves and the creaking of branches. He'd slept well after his exploratory walk the day before. As he lit the fire for a morning beverage of hot water, he wished he had mint leaves or lemon grass or better still, a tea bag. He leaned over and turned on the camera.

'Slept OK last night. Bed quite comfy. Getting used to the different sounds and smells. Wind picked up in the middle of the night, revealing places I need to plug and reinforce today.' He stopped talking as he thought about what he needed to gather. 'Interested in exploring a different area today. Going inland a bit. Well, after I've updated my daily marker, checked my lines and hopefully enjoyed something fresh for breakfast.' He dragged his knife roughly across the timber stump, marking his third day *alone*.

On checking his lines, he was delighted to see that he'd caught three medium-sized trout and an eel. He turned to the camera beaming.

'You beauty. What a haul. Of course, my success creates a bit of a health challenge as I don't have a fridge to keep them cool. I could probably build a smokehouse if I can find suitable timber. So much easier if I could have a squizz on YouTube.' He stopped talking, considering the options, placing his fingers on his lips. 'And the other problem I've got here is storing stuff. All sorts of thieving critters around. Probably watching me now.' He scanned the trees above. 'If I continue to catch a fish a day, I'm set. But, you know. Fishing is fickle. I'll probably end up doing the feast-famine thing.'

For the next hour the camera recorded the skinning and boiling of the eel and the hot rock frying of the three trout. Seb felt like a snooze after his trout banquet but forced himself to his feet and picked up his axe, turned the camera off and headed inland. He enjoyed the birdsong that emanated from every direction. The distinctive calls of lyrebirds echoed throughout, interspersed by the melodious warbles of kookaburras. His feet, breaking twigs with every step, sent two wallabies darting through the underbrush. Every step revealed a new perspective, as the dense vegetation opened up to reveal hidden clearings and sunlit patches. Huon pine trees, with their distinctive aromatic scent, stood tall and majestic, their trunks weathered by time. In the distance, he could see one that had been split by a lightning strike, serving up the perfect material for the smokehouse. He crunched his way through the scrub and assessed the task ahead. It was going to be hard work. Still, he was fuelled up and grateful for the energy the breakfast trout had provided. An hour later he had trimmed enough timber for two small smokehouses. Neither would be a solid build, only having a limited life, without the screws and neat finishes typically required. But he only needed it to last eighty days. With the timber required piled neatly he moved further into the scrub, sourcing vines and supple branches to keep his smokehouses together. Two hours later he was back at camp with his raw materials.

'As you can see, I'm back at camp. Collected stuff to build a smokehouse.' He swung the camera around to his pile of raw materials, then put it back on its tripod. 'It's a bit of an act of optimism 'cos I'm assuming my fishing luck run will continue. I've only built a smokehouse once before, with a mate, and with wire and screws. Still it'll give me something to do to kill the time. That's it for the chat. Enjoy the movie.'

Seb used the axe to dig a shallow pit for the fire close to

the shelter. He then selected a straight, dry piece of wood for the main frame of the smokehouse and then used smaller branches for cross supports. He gathered clay from the water's edge to construct the base and walls of the smokehouse and rocks were also selected to enclose the fire pit. Additional smaller rocks were combined with clay and water to form a primitive mortar to hold his construction together. The vines were then used to bind the timber pieces, with large leaves and bark carefully placed to water-proof the roof. The sun was beginning to set as the smoke-house was completed.

'And there you have it folks. I'll go throw a few lines out and hopefully tomorrow you'll be able to watch a working demonstration. Bye.'

The camera was packed back in its case and placed in the shelter and the fishing equipment scooped up. Seb cast out three lines and sat back looking up at the sky with its shifting yellow and orange hues, splashed across chalky coloured clouds. The noises and atmosphere in the bush changed as well, with the daylight giving way to the soft glow of the descending sun. Shadows grew longer, and the textures of the terrain became more pronounced. As the sun began its descent below the tree line on the opposite shore, he noticed that there was a ribbon of small grey clouds ascending from the tree tops. Seb jumped to his feet. Someone else had a fire burning. Maybe they'd built a smokehouse too? The shapes of the clouds were curious, as they were orderly and symmetrical. Like the smoke signals the Native Americans used to communicate. But none of the other contestants had American First Nations heritage, as far as he knew. And what could they possibly be trying to communicate? Then he remembered that one of the contestants was Aboriginal. Yes. That was the most likely explanation. They were cooking their dinner. Seb wondered what they were eating. Proof of nearby human companionship felt comforting.

Galina – 6am

Galina yawned. There was a rock on her sleeping bag. It wasn't that windy last night, she thought. She opened her eyes slowly and looked towards the opening of her shelter. The quoll was asleep on her bedding, leaning against her feet. Detecting movement, he stood up, momentarily looked at her and bounded off into the bush. *Guess it's payback time for using his burrow to store firewood.*

Branches were strewn across the campsite clearing. She kicked them to the edge, making a mental note to break them up later for firewood. Her immediate priority was to check her traps. She could feel the vibrations of an animal struggling against a restraint. A cobweb was laced across the top of one of her boots and she wondered at the occupant, who – like her – had set a trap to catch an unsuspecting victim. The spider with the red back was quickly brushed aside and flattened, before the boots were inspected and pulled onto her feet. Galina stomped off through the bush in case there was anything else living inside her boots that needed eradication.

A medium-sized wallaby looked up nervously as she approached the trap. The kindest thing to do was to end the animal's suffering, so she leant forward and snapped its neck. A quick check confirmed it was male. She was pleased about this, as she was uncomfortable with the thought of finding a joey in a dead female's pouch. Sitting on a nearby log, she lit a cigarette from the fire, took a long drag and considered everything that needed to be done in the next two hours. Her eyes flickered to the camera attached to a nearby tree and focussed on the trap. She extinguished her cigarette and chastised herself for potentially revealing her forbidden pleasures. *Damn stupid to lose this competition through carelessness.* She leant down to fast-forward the overnight footage. As suspected, the wallaby had jumped into the first trap, heard the device begin to fall, bounded quickly away and hopped directly into the second one. She was rather pleased with her foresight. Remembering the requirement to record five hours a day, she returned to the shelter to collect the main camera and tripod and positioned it with a direct view of the carcass.

'Morning. You can see, I am successful. This may be gruesome for some. Turn away now if you find it so.'

It was messy work skinning the wallaby and partitioning the meat. There was many days' worth of food from this one animal and it was important that it was well preserved. Dried or smoked wallaby jerky were the best solutions and she'd need to work quickly while the weather conditions were favourable. The animal was quickly dissected and a rough smokehouse constructed.

Hours later, she turned off the camera, lit a cigarette and admired the results of her efforts. It was a veritable feast that should be shared. But how to do this? She knew who she wanted to share it with. Galina lit her campfire, and took the small blanket down to the water's edge. Seated in the shallows, she scrubbed her blood-soaked face and arms while enjoying the serenity of her surroundings. Her circumstances felt surreal. After drying herself off with the blanket, she dipped it in the river and returned to her camp to take a seat on a small boulder near the fire. She then placed the damp blanket across the fire, removed it, and then repeated the process several times, sending puffs of grey smoke into the air, all the while wondering how smart the sailor was, or if he'd even see the smoke.

Valda – 6am

Rather than dancing, which was hard to do without music, Valda threw her energies into shelter-strengthening activities. The strong winds needed to be accounted for with additional interwoven branches and ferns.

Expecting rain at some point, she created an awning out front to ensure that the fire could stay burning. After her exertions she was aware of her body odour and that her clothes were feeling rather *lived in*. Experimenting, she boiled mountain pepper in the cooking pot, and soaked her clothes one by one, before wringing out excess water and throwing the garments on top of her shelter. It was a process she'd read about in an Australian Aboriginal Studies journal. The sky was cloudless and there was a gentle breeze providing reasonable drying conditions. With nothing more needing to be done at camp, she headed off into the bush with food foraging as her objective. This really was a lovely setting, and she wished she had someone to share it with.

Two hours later Valda returned with the corpse of another hen. She turned on the camera.

'I'm back and you have another opportunity to watch me pluck, gut and cook lunch. Not a varied menu but a sustaining one.' She subconsciously made a clucking sound. 'What I'd really kill for is a Toblerone chocolate bar. Just one mountain would be enough.' Her focus returned to the hen.

After removing all the unwanted parts of the bird, she boiled the chicken, again using mountain pepper, and put the eggs aside, for a rainy day. She looked up at the changing skyline; thickening clouds covered the blue, and pinks and purples began to merge into grey. As the colours of the bush intensified, so did the creep of loneliness. She shook her head to chase the demons away.

Raj

Raj yawned and stretched after sixty minutes on his rock. With his tummy rumbling, he knew that finding food was a higher priority than meditating. There was an off-odour in the air this morning. As a chef he recognised the distinctive scent of something deteriorating. As the smell intensified, Raj's attention shifted from the picturesque surroundings to the pungent aroma that surrounded them. The scent was powerful, a combination of rot and decay, making Raj's nose scrunch up involuntarily. He pulled his boots on and headed inland. As he ventured deeper into the bush, the source of the odour became apparent. Just ahead, partially concealed by foliage, lay the lifeless body of a Tasmanian devil. Its fur was matted and dishevelled. Flies buzzed around the carcass, and the ground beneath was teeming with wriggling maggots. Raj felt a mix of revulsion and sadness at the sight. The Tasmanian devil was an iconic creature, and seeing it in such a state was a stark reminder of the natural cycle of life and death. This fella had clearly come off worse in the battle he'd heard, two nights previously. Taking a step closer, Raj watched the maggots moving with an almost hypnotic rhythm, squirming and wriggling over the creature's body. Flies landed on the carcass, intermittently taking off and landing again. The whole scene seemed like a macabre dance of life and death.

Though it was a disturbing sight, Raj recognized the importance of these scavengers in maintaining the delicate balance of the ecosystem. The maggots were also a rich source of protein, and he was hungry. Steeling himself for the task, he leant forwards with one hand over his nose and the other scooping up the wriggling white critters.

He returned to his camp and lit his fire. He grimaced as he skewered the maggots on a green twig and nestled it between two forked sticks. The snack was surprisingly delicious but not sustaining. He was still hungry.

Janelle

Her pencil moved lightly across the surface of the journal. This first map was just a draft and she'd redo the measurements and redraw the lines later. She'd chosen a compass as one of her ten items. It probably wasn't necessary as the one-kilometre boundary of her life was limited. But she'd always loved maps and had completed a degree in surveying, with an intention to be a cartographer, before joining the army. Drawing maps made her feel grounded. Maps told a story and she wondered what story there'd be, once this mission was over. She closed the journal, moved the rubber band around the pages and placed it in her backpack. There was an hour of light left before she'd need to return to camp.

There was more wildlife about as she walked through the bush. Birds high in the trees sounded warnings of approaching danger as she picked her way through the undergrowth and overhanging branches. Her military training had her immediately identifying bushes that could act as camouflage or a hideout. But she no longer needed to hide. She was safe here.

Returning to camp she made a warming beverage of honey and mint before turning on the camera.

'I'm enjoying my tasty tot. Thank you, bees.' She took a sip. 'Sorry I didn't bring you along on my wanderings. Bit hard to hold a camera and a journal and pen. I plan to create a detailed map of my home territory for the next, however many days I'm here.' She unconsciously glanced around her surroundings. 'Should we go and see if I'm having anything for dinner tonight?' The tripod was placed on the shore and each of the four lines pulled in, in turn. 'Nope, nope, nope and you beauty,' was announced in turn. 'Honey flavoured trout for tea. If only I had a bit of butter and few almonds.' She winked at the camera before turning it off.

Archie

Archie shimmied up a towering gum, located one

hundred metres from camp. It was the perfect place to survey the land from the tree line to the water, and to ponder his options. He needed to manage his food supply. Possums were an easy potential protein source, with wallabies coming a close second. He'd need a spear to immobilise a wallaby. It'd been years since his grandfather had taken him on country to look for the faintest of animal markings in the soil and broken branches and to show him how to cover his scent, while he tracked his prey. He was looking forward to applying what he'd learnt.

The cry of a wedge-tailed eagle caught his attention. There were a pair of these magnificent birds gliding on the warm air currents with outstretched wings, like him, surveying for food. He felt a kindred spirit as he watched them cross the water and fly high into the canopy of trees on the other side. Their flight path had drawn his eye to a few puffs of smoke rising high in the breeze.

He descended and returned to camp to collect the camera, tripod and knife before venturing deeper into the bush, where he set up his filming equipment before selecting several branches suitable for carving additional spears. He didn't talk, as he cut and trimmed, letting his actions illustrate the process used by his mob for generations. An hour later, with several weapons created, he gave a demonstration of his spearing technique, knowing that he would need to travel light when he went hunting later as dusk was arriving. There'd be no cameras carried.

To pass time until darkness fell and to provide something of interest for those on the other side of the camera, he gathered a selection of vines, grasses and reeds and started weaving different widths of cordage. He made a fishing net as well. It was good to have an in-water as well as an on-land plan for food sourcing. He switched off the camera, picked up a spear and disappeared into the fading evening light.

ALONE DAY 4

Sebastian

Seb woke up, sniffed the air, pulled his t-shirt up to his nose and breathed in. *Yep. That smell is me. I'll need to de-pong and figure out where to hang my stuff. He looked at the sky. Lovely day for a dual-purpose dip, but first I should...* He grabbed the tripod and walked down to the water's edge, plonking the equipment on the ground. He pressed record.

'Morning everyone. Welcome back to paradise. Planning on taking another dip today, but first I need to see if I'll be having something fishy to eat.' Hoots of laughter were emitted as each line was pulled in with a medium sized trout. 'These guys must have been in school.' He grimaced at his joke that was of the *daggy* genre his father loved. He missed his dad at that moment, but shook the thought away.

The three fish were gutted, and placed inside the smokehouse. He decided not to have the camera recording his clothes-washing activities. No one needed to see his smalls and bathing rituals. So, the tripod was placed near the smokehouse. Those in TV land could watch the flickering of the flames instead.

Seb stripped his clothes except for his tracker watch. He knew it was waterproof as he'd been swimming on the first day and it was still working perfectly. He also knew that it wasn't meant to be removed as a safety measure, so he, or his body, could be located if needed. It felt 'Big Brother' and he unconsciously pushed the device against his hand. It wouldn't easily be removed. Maybe a little left-over eel oil would do the trick? *Later. I'll check that later. Gotta get the washing done.*

His clothes were dragged through the water several times, wrung tightly to remove excess water and then thrown on one of the dead tree trunks. He recognised it was more of a refresh than a proper clean. The water temperature was delightful, both crisp and refreshing and he enjoyed ducking and diving as he'd done as a child at Opoutama Beach in New Zealand.

A crashing sound from his campsite broke his reverie. *What?* He raced to his shelter to discover his smokehouse on the ground across the fire. There was no breeze, so a thieving critter must have been the culprit. But which one? He'd need to rethink the design, and more realistically stay closer when food was cooking. He pulled the timber pieces out of the fire, dusted them off and retrieved two partly smoked fish. The thief had been successful and was likely to be back. He then noticed the camera and smiled. The thief would have been captured in the act, providing valuable insight into how he had both collapsed the smokehouse and removed the fish. The footage was rewound and the young possum identified. He had scaled the smokehouse and tried to retrieve the fish through the chimney, with his weight causing the structure to fall and break apart. He'd been tipped into the fire, burning one of his thumbs, but this had not deterred him from stealing a fish. Seb was horrified to note that his arrival at the shelter, in all his nakedness, had also been caught on film. He remembered that there was a 'no deleting of footage' rule as well as one relating to not injuring protected species. *Possums definitely not on that list. Doesn't matter that the thief has been hurt. He could well end up in the pan if the fish stop biting. And being filmed in all my glory. Oh well. What can I do?* Seb reached across for his small saucepan and placed the two remaining fish inside. Eel oil lined the bottom of the pan which would make it easy to fry the fish on the fire. Dipping his finger into the greasy substance, he wiped oil around the inside of his wrist and the tracker watch band, and pulled it off. Success! Seb smiled as he pondered the possibilities of how far he could travel now he wasn't being tracked. *A celebratory breakfast is called for, but first I need to hang out the last of my washing.*

Finding somewhere to hang his clothes, where they could catch a breeze or occasional sunshine, proved a little challenging and he momentarily wondered if he should have chosen the paracord. *Nah. The axe is better. Been the right decision.* He used the axe to dig holes in the stony ground and cut down a few saplings with y-shaped forks before making two washing lines in the open space between his shelter and the water's edge. One of the structures was so well grounded that he wondered if he should make a swing. It was a great viewpoint for sipping beer. His thoughts turned to his sailing buddies, who could well be cooking breakfast sausages around a BBQ on the beach and discussing race strategy at this very moment. He missed their joking and teasing. As he threw the last of his clothes over a branch, he looked up and again spotted the same small grey puffs of smoke he'd seen the previous day. *No more than two kilometres. Once you cross the river, you're no more twenty minutes away by foot – whoever you are.* As he cooked his remaining fish, and considered the day's planned activities he could hear a familiar sound. He smiled. It was the soft beating of a drum and he knew it was the tattooed Estonian inviting him to visit.

Swimming was the only option, as he'd not yet made a raft, a canoe or even a floating device. He'd need to be away for no more than three hours so he could safely swim back in the light of day and still have time to record a few hours of 'his story'. His tracker also presented a problem. If he wore it, he would definitely exceed the one-kilometre perimeter. He could leave it on his bed, but there'd be no movement and that might arouse suspicions. Watching his trousers flicker in the breeze, an easy surveillance foil was found. He tied the tracker watch to a vine and hung it from his newly created washing line. The limited circumference of movement could be explained away on the evening's update as time spent repairing the smokehouse. It was worth a try.

He looked across the water to identify a *reasonable place* to land with reasonable being a shoreline limited by obstacles such as dead trees or boulders. From where he stood, he could only spot obstacles that were revealed above the water line. Like icebergs, he could only speculate at what lay beneath. Looking back to camp he could see that his red t-shirt was now flapping frequently in the breeze and would provide a valuable marker for the return journey.

He took a few tentative steps down the riverbank and pushed out into the still water with a gentle breaststroke. A fish jumped, causing his heart to leap. Moments later his arms hit previously unseen chunks of floating driftwood. They were from a Huon tree and he was pleased to note their buoyancy. A platypus surfaced and then deep dived. Twenty minutes later, as he came in closer to the riverbank on the other side, he stuck a large moss-covered tree trunk in the water. He pulled himself along it to the shore line and then walked up the river bank feeling victorious. Shaking off the water, he looked back to his camp on the other side. His washing was barely visible and indeed the water line had few features that made any area easily discernible from the other.

He'd planned to walk along the coast but could see this would be slow-moving because of the rocks on the shoreline so turned and walked inland, hoping he'd find his way to the camp fire sending out the smoke signals. His squelching boots would ensure that it would not be a quiet arrival. *Should I take em off? Nah.* But then they knew or hoped he was coming, as indicated by the gentle beating of a drum. Lizards scattered and birds squawked with each step towards the familiar sound. A feeling of being watched came over Seb and he intuitively looked around and spotted a quoll sitting motionless on a log, regarding him carefully.

'Hello.' The animal immediately jumped up and disappeared into the bush. Seb kicked his boots against the log to dislodge the mud that had clung to them on his walk from the river. Only some of the clay fell, with his kicking motion disturbing a copperhead snake that'd been hiding inside. The serpent slid under the leaf litter and all thoughts of removing his shoes and walking barefoot evaporated.

Climbing a small rise and skimming over a large

lichen-covered rock Seb arrived in a clearing where he could finally see Galina beating her makeshift drum.

As he walked into camp she looked up.

'You took your time, sailor.' Seb was stunned into silence. 'Take your clothes off.' Seb had preconceptions about the openness of Nordic women to sex, but this direct-ness took him by surprise. He stood mute, unsure how to respond. 'I've an excellent washing line if you want to dry those clothes.' Galina pulled down the paracord which was holding her own washing high up in the treetops. Seb looked up and started laughing, relieved. 'Here you go.'

She gave him a sarong, and a pair of dry socks and invited him to sit on a log near her fire. He checked for snakes before sitting down and when he did, she wrapped the small blanket around his shoulders. It smelt of smoke. 'Don't think I'll get these boots dry before you go, but at least your other clothes should be more comfortable for the trip back.'

'Until I get back in the water again.'

'No canoe?'

'Give me a break, Betty. We've only been in the bush four days and I hadn't planned to go off on an illegal, contrary to the rules, exploratory mission.'

'Hmm,' she replied. 'You hungry?'

'Watcha got? Fish?'

'Wild animal stew.'

'That'll make a change? What type?'

'Jumper.'

'Jumper? Not rat I hope.'

'No. The animal on your Aussies' emblem.'

'What? There's an emu and a kangaroo on the Australian coat of arms. I don't believe those animals are in this area. Emus are certainly not. Think they're extinct on Tassie.'

'There's your proof. Skin of the animal that's now the skin of my drum,' Galina said pointing at a skin stretched across a nearby tree. Seb glanced at the skin pulled tight with several pieces of snare wire.

'Ahh. A wallaby...'

'Was wallaby. Now stew. You should eat.' She passed a bemused Seb the saucepan and her only spoon. He tentatively took a sip.

'Cor. This is fantastic. Where'd you get those little white squiggly things from?'

'Like the kangaroo, the quinoa probably does not live here.'

'So, you're a magician as well as a hunter, able to procure, or dare I say, hide things well.'

Galina smiled, enjoying the compliment. 'Perhaps,' she replied coyly.

'If you come to my camp, I'll cook you trout,' Seb offered.

'I don't swim.'

'Well, it's reassuring to know there's something you

don't do.' Seb looked at her admiringly and was again captivated by her tattoos. 'I'm guessing you know a bit about serpents.'

'Maybe. What do you want to know, sailor-boy?'

'Which ones are poisonous?'

'I'd treat them all as dangerous.' Seb couldn't help but think that she was self-describing. He scooped out another spoonful of stew.

'This is fantastic. Will you show me how you set your trap?'

A clap of thunder interrupted her response and a gust of wind blew leaves across the camp. Seb looked up at the sky that had previously been a canvas of blue. There were an increasing number of dark clouds forming low.

'I'll need to go. I've washing on the line.' Seb couldn't help but smile at the domesticity of his remark. Galina didn't understand.

He took another mouthful of stew, wiped his mouth with the back of his hand, before throwing off the small blanket and sarong. He stood up, naked save for his undies and hastily pulled his not-yet-dry clothes from the line before shoving his feet back into his still-sodden boots. Now fully dressed, he picked the blanket and sarong off the ground and folded them. He looked around for Betty who was strengthening her shelter in preparation for the storm, a cigarette dangling from her lips. A grin swept across Seb's face.

'I'll be back.' Galina nodded as she took a drag on her cigarette and reached out to receive her things. 'Thanks again for the stew Betty, and...' he hesitated 'and for inviting me across the...'

'I had too much food. If you had a canoe, I could give you some to take back.'

'Next time.'

'Okei.'

A low and foreboding growl before a lightning strike signalled an impending deluge. Seb looked at Galina, who flicked her hand in farewell. He turned and ran through the bush. The return journey was easier as there were glimpses of water through the swaying trees. He emerged at a different spot on the riverside to where he had arrived and noted that the tide had changed direction. It would be a longer swim back and he'd need to be careful of the drift-wood now bobbing up and down in the water. Tentatively walking into the mud, he was aware that the birdsong had changed, the usual songs replaced by more anxious chirping. A clap of thunder sent the birds rising together as Seb dove into the water. Utilising his favourite front crawl, he counted each stroke, estimating it would take nine hundred before his feet touched ground on the other side. He regretted swimming with boots on, but he'd no choice.

It was dark when he finally reached shore. The rain was now pounding down, limiting his visibility. He'd no idea how far away he was from his initial departure point as nothing in the landscape was familiar. Moving carefully, he weaved his way through the scrubby bush on the water's edge. He was delighted when he came upon the illegal timber logs he'd discovered on the first day and knew that he was now less than a kilometre from camp. He could see a small, bright light rotating like a spaceship as he made it into his home clearing. His tracker watch had been experiencing some wild movements at the end of the vine on the washing line and he'd need a good story before he turned the camera on. He slipped his tracker watch on and picked his washing up off the ground. Luckily, the wind had flung one long-sleeved t-shirt into the heart of his shelter. He put it on and slipped into his sleeping bag, and then remembered that he needed to record for another three hours.

'Wow what a day. It feels like midnight, 'cause it's so dark but it's only threeish I reckon. I've had a mad day starting with the collapse of my smokehouse and the theft of one of my prized trout, as you know if you saw the previous footage. This meant the rest of the day was spent rebuilding it, only to have this storm destroy it again. And I made a washing line and washed my stuff. That was a waste of time. Well maybe not. The sun will come out again. I'm doing OK. This place has a wild beauty.' He was thinking of his Estonian competitor across the water. 'And if I'm able to build a watercraft I'll be able to fish further out. Bet I've lost my lines.' He scratched his chin. 'No worries. I'll throw new ones out tomorrow.' He looked across the land to the water and breathed in the aroma of rain-soaked soil. It was noisy inside the shelter, and he wondered if anyone in TV land had heard a word he'd said. He looked back at the camera. 'Sorry I forgot to share my day's activities with you. Was rather distracted after the possum incident. There's not too much else going on around here,' he lied looking around his shelter, avoiding eye contact with the tiny porthole to the wider world. Now, if I have this camera in ninety-eight days' time, I'd be talking to you from a yacht in Sydney Harbour just before we race to Hobart. I'm hoping to be back. I promised my mate Scott I'd be back.' He paused, lost in thought. 'It'll be a fantastic race and we'll quite possibly encounter storms like this. Well...actually, worse. Much worse.' Seb's thoughts automatically stepped through what was involved in sailing through a tempest. How you need to be tight as a team, be nimble, and be OK operating with limited sleep. 'My bedding here is actually luxurious compared to the hammock on the yacht.' Seb noticed his greasy pan and again thought about his fishing lines. 'So people, tell me. Should I go and see if I have anything for dinner or should I wait out the storm?'

Galina

Galina stared down the path Seb had taken when he fled her camp. It'd been nice having company. She was slightly nervous about his safety. He'd said he was a good swimmer. The journey across the river would've tested this. Would he send her a message when he was back? *A smoke signal would be impossible in this deluge. So would a drum message if he had the wherewithal to make one.* She shook her head, picked up her saucepan and covered the fire before retreating insider her shelter. The quoll was asleep on her bedding and didn't wake as she sat down.

'I'm clearly a very frightening person, Suupiste. You fear for your life.'

Valda

Valda had not slept well. As she woke, she wondered what her friends were doing. She forced her boots on and headed off into the bush in search of food. While the flight-less birds remained hidden, their eggs did not. She felt miserable thinking about the next generation lost. She shook the thought away. This was an excellent and easily available source of protein. Her focus needed to be on the bigger prize. When she returned to camp an hour later, she turned on the camera, and forced a positive tone in her voice.

'My day started well. Got a few more eggs, and will make tasty scrambled eggs, of sorts. Also collected fire-wood. Might do a few Pilates stretches as I'm a bit stiff after a not-great night. Feel free to join in at home.' She placed the camera at the water's edge, took a deep breath and pulled the kinks out of her shoulders and back. Her mood improved with each movement, and she found herself enjoying the peaceful setting.

'I'm going for another walk now. Talk later.'

Raj

Raj woke early and turned on the camera.

'Bit embarrassed to admit how much I enjoyed my roasted maggots last night. Truly delicious and I feel I may need to visit my dead friend again, if my fishing expedition is not successful. I'm trying my new bait of, you guessed it, maggots, in the hope that my fishy friends might enjoy this little nibbly morsel as much as I did. So far, nothing, but I can wait a little longer.'

Raj sat on his rock and occasionally dropped off to sleep in the filtered sunshine. A tug on his fishing line half an hour later woke him instantly and he slowly stood and walked backwards. Another eel jumped and squirmed as it was pulled onto the shoreline. A heavy rock to the head stopped the wriggling. Raj tutted. It was food. He needed to be grateful. The slimy meal was gutted, washed and thrown into the pan on the fire, before Raj threaded another maggot on the line and cast it out, all the while saying positive affirmations about the size and colour of the trout he hoped to hook.

. . .

Janelle

Nellie could not believe her luck. Not one, not two but four fish on the line. However, her success presented a problem; how to keep the next few days of food edible. Working quickly, she constructed a walled rock pool at the water's edge in which to keep the fish alive and contained. Unfortunately, one of the fish jumped onto the rock wall and flipped into the river before swimming quickly to the bottom. Moments later, a hawk swooped and snatched her dinner from the pool, reducing Nellie's food stock to two. Nellie took off her jacket and threw it across the top of the pool, to limit further departures while chastising herself on her short-sightedness. Several rocks were placed on the jacket to stop it floating away. She turned to the camera which had captured the morning's achievements and mistakes in all their glory and tragedy.

'That's it. I'm eating them both now. Aye. Can't risk losing another one and I really need that jacket dry.' The two fish received a quick rock punch to the head and the jacket was thrown across a low hanging branch to dry. 'Probably should have chosen a fishing net among my ten things, but then I'm not sure what I could've given up.'

Her problems gave her focus. How could she create a more secure fish corral? She hummed while her fish, now drizzled with honey and threaded on a thick, green twig, sizzled. The wind started to whistle through the branches, creating an eerie melody with the increasing creaking of branches adding a haunting undertone.

Archie

Rising before light, Archie moved silently through the bush, noticing subtle signs such as broken twigs and fur threads on tree bark that provided insight into animal movements. His bare feet hardly touched the ground and when he stopped to survey his surroundings, he was able to feel the distinctive vibrations of animals and particularly of a large wallaby or small kangaroo, bounding towards him. He crouched low in the tall grass, blending invisibly into the scrub. Waiting patiently downwind of his prey, he held his spear tightly in his hand, ready to spring release it when the moment presented. Two small kangaroos bounded in his direction, then stopped. They looked around furtively, before deeming it safe to eat, lowering their heads to the bush floor. The kangaroos continued to graze, occasionally lifting their heads, perhaps sensing a presence but unable to pinpoint the exact location. One kangaroo bounded two steps closer to Archie, looked around and then resumed grazing. Archie seized the moment and sent his spear soaring through the air. Both kangaroos looked up quickly and started to move, but the nearest marsupial had moved too close to the hunter and was now hit with the full force of the spear. Birds screeched a warning and rose rapidly. Archie moved quickly with a quick strike to the head, halting the animal's suffering.

Archie threw the carcass over his shoulders and returned to camp to butcher it. *There's meat that'll go to waste.* His thoughts turned to family members he'd love to share this feast with. His grandfather would be particularly proud, with kangaroo tail being his favourite part of the animal.

With his clothes now covered in muck and blood, his thoughts turned to washing. He remembered seeing a Tasmanian pepper berry tree near to where he had set up his film equipment the previous day. Scooping up his basket, he returned and pulled two dozen berries. The fruit could be added to the meat to add a unique spicy flavour and would also assist in removing the signs of carnage from his clothes.

Later that afternoon as he washed himself and his clothes in the river, he sniffed the air and looked up. The quickly darkening sky and the nimbus clouds were giving notice that there was a storm coming: a big one.

ALONE DAY 5

Sebastian

Seb listened to the storm crashing around him and wondered how Galina was faring. He chided himself. She'd be managing very well. He turned his small saucepan upside down and started drumming Phil Collins' song 'In the Air Tonight' with two sticks plucked from the firewood pile. *No. The noise wouldn't travel far in this drenching.* However, he'd like to think that she'd hear it and know that he was thinking of her. He finished the song, sighed and turned the pan right-side up and put it outside to catch rainwater. Unconsciously his hands continued to tap the rhythm of the song on his thighs as he listened to the water furiously hitting his pan. He looked around thinking about what to do next. Sleep? Nah. He spied the camera and leant over to turn it on.

'It's raining. A bit of an understatement as you can hear. Feels a bit set-in.' Seb looked around his shelter looking for inspiration on what to say next. 'I've been doing some drumming and been thinking about making something that'll float. A canoe was my first thought, but I've decided that I can't do it with an axe alone. A raft maybe, but I'm not sure how long the vines and or fishing line would hold the craft together. I really should've taken the snare wire.' He smiled remembering that Betty had some. 'I'll have a go, what've I gotta lose. Mind you. Not sure if I have the inclination to head up river and collect those logs in this weather.' He picked up his drum sticks and a large piece of wood and started drumming the Collins classic again. Two verses in he stopped. 'Sod it. Gotta get out of this place.'

Fifteen minutes later Seb was back in front of the camera, with plasters on his face and arm and wrapped up tightly in his sleeping bag.

'That was truly a stupid decision. And bloody dangerous. Branches flying everywhere. Only made it a short distance, before I nearly came a cropper.' Seb turned his face and held his arm up to the camera revealing three nasty gashes. 'And the stupid thing is I'll end up with pneumonia if I'm not careful. The only dry thing I have left is this sleeping bag and there's *no laundrette* nearby. I've had enough to eat so I'm gonna hunker down. Apologies in advance for the snoring. Night all.'

. . .

Galina

Sitting cross-legged in her bed Betty brushed the quoll with a small branch while admiring his white-spotted, ginger-brown coat. He lifted his hind leg and scratched his belly, making a soft clucking sound. She reached into her pot and pulled out a piece of meat.

'I'm only giving you this to keep you close in case I need to eat you.' The quoll gobbled the morsel, impervious to the danger he might be in and then looked impatiently at her, expecting more. 'No. No more. Off you go. Need to do television and don't want evidence you've moved in. Skit!' She clapped her hands twice and he jumped up and raced out into the rain.

'Morning strangers. It's raining, but I'm not wet. I have your jumping animal in my belly and in the pan. Enough for many days so I'll just sit and watch. You can too.' She turned the camera outside of her shelter and reached inside her sleeping bag for another cigarette.

Valda

Boredom was setting in. She lay on her bed listening to the rain fall and the wind howl while counting the number of twigs threaded together on her roof. Then she counted the number of beetles taking cover. She didn't need to go out for food as she had enough although her kindling was damp so cooking was impossible. If the rain eased, she'd go scavenging. Sooner was better than later, as dry twigs would become increasingly difficult to find. She turned on her camera.

'I wish I'd brought a book, or cards or maybe even a jigsaw. I'm feeling a bit crazy this morning. Didn't think I'd get bored; thought I'd enjoy being alone.' She sighed. 'This tempest is relentless. It has power and I, so little; I feel so small. And alone,' she said softly looking at her hands and her dirty finger nails and then back to the camera. 'I need to wash my hands. Luckily, it's not too cold. Fingers crossed the rain eases as I must get out and find some dry firewood. If there's any. Otherwise, I'll be eating raw eggs. Yuck.' She stopped talking and looked outside again. 'Wanna watch the storm?' She turned the camera around and looked out into the pouring rain with unknown others, imagining they were eating chocolate in front of their screens.

Two hours later the rain eased a little and Valda seized the opportunity to get out in search of kindling. Her strategy was to find large pieces of bark that had fallen on the ground before the storm and which may be covering dry timber or kindling. More often than not, the bark was providing shelter for lizards and snakes that slid or scurried away when their hideout was revealed. After an hour of limited success, she changed her approach to collecting slightly damp timber which she would bring under cover to dry. It wasn't until she returned to camp and dropped the branches in a pile that she felt a number of leeches crawling around inside her clothes. They were also cocooned between each toe and gorging on her blood. Tears flowed as she flicked each sucker away.

Raj

Raj put his head outside his shelter and opened his mouth, relishing the taste of fresh rain and the soothing feel of heavy drops splashing on his face. A deep belly laugh followed along with a wild thought.

I need a shower. He stripped naked, save for his boots and rushed out into the clearing. He imagined he could hear the Phil Collins song, 'In the Air Tonight' which he thought was entirely appropriate, so sang out loud while he jiggled and twirled. Surveying the ground, he noticed that several earth worms had also come out to dance. He rushed back to camp to collect his mug, and scooped them up. Worms were perfect for fish bait, and afternoon snacks if the fish weren't biting.

A warning crack sent him scurrying to his shelter, moments before a large branch fell to the ground and splintered. The dancing would need to wait, and he was pleased he'd managed a partial body splash before his retreat. His socks were now soaking and uncomfortable so he removed his shoes revealing three enormous leeches. Delighted with this easy capture of fish bait, he popped them into his mug with the worms, dressed and went back out again into the rain to throw out his fishing lines. Returning to camp he turned on his camera and sat back cross-legged.

'A different sort of day today, but one with many blessings. The rain is nourishing the earth and providing fish bait. There is nothing else to do for now. You are welcome to join me while I visit another place.' Raj closed his eyes and gently joined the tip of each thumb with his index finger, while the other three fingers stretched out. After focussing on his breathing, he began to Om, a deliberate vibration, morphing into a meditation.

Janelle

Nellie lay motionless in her bunk listening to the rhythmic sound of water falling into her saucepan. Her thoughts drifted off to earlier years when she was running along the beach with her dog Kevin, listening to the waves crashing against the shore. Her reverie was interrupted by a large drip on her face and for a moment she imagined it'd come from Kevin. Bolting upright she noticed that one of the corners of her tarp had flapped open and water was now running across the inside of the tarp. She wrapped her bedding up into a tight ball and placed her jacket across it recognising that survival required her bedding staying dry. Focussed on her task she didn't notice a sinuous form slip into the shelter. Indeed, the first indication that she was no

longer alone was a subtle rustling of leaves and a soft hiss-
ing. She froze and slowly turned her head towards the
sound. As the snake moved closer inside the shelter its
forked tongue flickered out to taste the unfamiliar environ-
ment. Its scales were glistening from the rain. The black
and yellow banding on the serpent made identification of
the tiger snake instantaneous. As its namesake suggested,
this snake was venomous; highly venomous. Its movements
were both cautious and deliberate. Suddenly, noticing the
eyes that were fixed on them from the large unknown
beast, the snake rose up, adopting a defensive posture to
more carefully observe Nellie. She wondered if the serpent
could feel her thundering heart. A snake bite would be
lethal in her isolated circumstances. She'd be stone-cold
before any rescue team's boots hit the shore. Her only
option was to remain still, as if she was dead already.
Seconds felt like centuries as the standoff continued. The
sound of a branch cracking broke the snake's focus and it
lowered it's head and left the shelter, the same way it'd
entered.

Nellie sank to her knees in relief. This was too much.
Should she call in and say those two words which would
spirit her home? Was it time to surrender? No! She'd stared
danger in the face before and survived. *Not today*.

Archie

The heavens opened again before dawn. Archie was pleased he'd eaten well the day before and had a food store for the days ahead. He pulled a large branch, thick with leaves, across the front of his humpy and secured it.

Sitting cross legged on his kangaroo mat, Archie looked around his shelter. He'd not yet caught a fish and did not wish to lose his trap, which was now sitting in the corner of his humpy.

There was nothing else to do for now so he settled back and went to sleep, not at all disturbed by the branches falling around him.

ALONE DAY 6

Sebastian

Seb was deep in problem-solving mode as he lay in his sleeping bag listening to the rain. He couldn't see how he could craft a canoe out of a log with the equipment available. Or not one that would float. But he could make a raft, and while he didn't have snare wire, he knew Galina did. His most immediate challenge was getting the small logs he'd seen on the first day back to camp. They'd be a pain to drag back through the bush, and it'd be near impossible in this deluge. He looked out at the river that had risen a foot in the last day. There was no urgency for getting the raft made, apart from his curiosity in visiting his neighbour. The river had more debris in it that normal and was moving quickly in the wrong direction. It'd be five hours until the tide turned. There were also risks in being outside with the storm flaring up. He wished he had access to a weather reporting channel so he could better plan his activities. For the moment, the best use of his time would be in rebuilding the smokehouse in his shelter, and occasionally popping out to see if the fish were biting. He turned on his camera and provided a brief update on the incessant rain and his limited plans for the day.

Four hours later, the smokehouse had been rebuilt, three fish had been caught and Seb's frustration at being inside his shelter had reached breaking point. He turned off the camera. *I feel like a swim. And I've bounty to share. It's only fair I reciprocate after she fed me. And I'll be able to collect the wire.*

He looked at his clothes, all still damp and hanging from sticks in the walls of his shelter. He chose his long trousers with deep zipped pockets where he could store the fish, and his long-sleeved woollen t-shirt. *If I had a raft, I'd transport my jacket and be warm on arrival. Next time.*

He tied his tracker on the swing and ran down to the water's edge. Taking a deep breath he plunged in, gasping from the initial shock of the chilly water. He swam purposefully to the other side, reminding himself that he needed to be back in the water in an hour's time in order to avoid swimming against the current. Something nipped at his leg, obviously aware of the fish in his pocket. The rain continued to pour and he put his head down and rolled into his front crawl, fingers tight together, to ensure the fastest journey to the other side.

Galina

'Back so soon, sailor? Galina offered as he walked into her clearing. He smiled. 'Guess you were hungry.' Seb was mildly irritated by her assumption that his only interest was food.

'No. I've come to trade fish for snare wire.'

'Ahh. Good to see that you've become a true frontier man. Would you like to come in and warm yourself by the fire?'

'That'd be great. I'm soaking wet.'

'Obviously. Give me your trousers and we'll dry them a little, near the fire.' Seb reached into his trouser leg pocket to retrieve the trout, when he heard a low-pitched hiss from the back of the shelter. He froze. Galina grinned. 'Not for you Suupiste. Out!' She whistled through her fingers and a quoll darted out into the rain.

'Why do you call that large rat Super Star?'

'I do not call him Super Star. I call him *Suupiste*. It means "snack" in Estonian. I want him to know not to expect too much from me, and that hanging around here is a little hazardous.' Seb who was now in the process of removing his trousers, tripped on the waist band and fell over, laughing.

'I guess that message applies to me too?'

'Perhaps.'

Seb studied her face while passing her his trousers. It was hard to read. With the trousers hung, they skewered and cooked the trout together, with Suupiste looking on grumpily from a distance.

Galina regarded Seb as he turned the gnarled twig roasting the trout. *You are a strange man. Did you really cross that river just to bring me fish?*

They sat in silence watching the fish cook, listening to the crackling of the fire and the thundering of the rain. Galina's eyes flickered across to the sailor.

'You've been fighting a tiger?' It was more a statement than a question. Seb looked back at her wide-eyed.

'What?' She pointed at the slashes on his arm. He laughed.

'No. No. There are no tigers here. Died out many years ago. Just an altercation with a falling branch.'

'Good.' Seb was unsure how to respond. 'I think our lunch is cooked.' Galina passed him a piece of trout which he took from her with a smile. She didn't react and then tilted her head back to drop a morsel inside.

'*Jah.* Tasty.'

'Have more,' Seb implored.

'No, you need more. Energy for swimming.' She reached across with another piece, this time directly to his mouth and he felt her fingers on his lips as the fish entered. She looked back to the fire, unaware of the impact she was having on him.

'I should go,' he said.

'Of course.' Galina watched him put his wet trousers back on again.

'Next time I'll come on a raft.'

'Perhaps.' Again, Seb was confused by her response.

Galina watched him walk down the hill until he was out of sight. She picked up her makeshift drum and Suupiste scurried back into the shelter.

The tide had already turned. Seb hit the water hard and was surprised by the strength of the current. He battled the river with each stroke, dodging debris and inadvertently swallowing water. The torrent was dragging him downstream and he knew he'd not make the previous landing point. Seb thought someone had hit him with a hammer when a small log careened into his cheek. In agony, and recognising the dangerous situation he was in, he rolled onto his back to catch his breath and let the current pull him further downstream. He crashed into a fallen tree still attached to the shoreline, and held tight. His back ached, but he realised the log had probably saved his life. If he'd been swept further away it was possible that he'd drown and that his body would never be found. Fighting against the pain in his face and back, he inched his way along the log until his feet touched the river floor. Moments later he collapsed on the shoreline, his face in a puddle, with the rain continuing to slam down.

Valda

Valda stumbled into her shelter, dripping wet. When she'd left to relieve her bladder, it was dark. The faint light from the crescent moon had been blocked by murky clouds so her journey was guided solely by the light of her head lamp.

'Damn. I wish I was a bloke. I've never said that before.' She peeled off each piece of clothing and threw it angrily into a pile. There was nowhere obvious to hang anything else to dry and she wasn't feeling in a creative house-keeping mood. Shivering, she suddenly became aware of a large drop of water slithering down her back. But it wasn't water. It was another leech. And it had a mate, which was now leap-frogging across her buttocks. She grabbed her wet shirt and lashed her back until it looked like candy-cane and her demons had tumbled into the dirt. Wrapping her sleeping bag tightly round her naked body, she curled into a foetal position, gently rocking. *Should I tap out?* As her body warmed, she calmed down. Breathing deeply, she assessed her situation.

My fire is burning and my shelter has survived its first storm. There are likely to be others. Leeches are creepy, but not life threatening. I need to find food. But I've been pretty good at this so far.

She boiled water in her saucepan, added mountain pepper, and cooked two of her eggs. With her hunger sated she sat back on a pile of rocks, thinking about how to spend the day. The camera stared at her. She was a little afraid that if she spoke openly about how she was feeling, she might talk herself into leaving. Still...

'Day two of the storm and it's still raining cats and dogs or rather *lecherous leechers*. My fire's still going and I've a store of dry twigs. I've eggs to eat but I'll need to go out to get something else soon. It's been blowy, but my shelter remains solid. So, all in all, not too bad. I've nothing else to say. Wanna look at the rain again?'

Raj

Raj stared at the crescent moon and wondered who else might be looking skyward. It felt special seeing the moon in the morning. He sighed and his tummy growled. This phase of the moon did not bode well for fishing. He was best to consider other food sources. But what? Maggots?

Leeches? Worms? They were easy enough to find, *or to be found by*. Wanting to keep his clothes dry, he stripped naked, picked up his tin mug and went out into the rain. As he dipped and jived, he scooped up worms from the ground. Several minutes later, his teeth began to clatter so he abandoned his dance and retreated to the shelter. He placed his thin cooking rock on the fire, and dressed. Moments later half a dozen worms were roasting, joined shortly by a similar number of leeches pulled from between his toes.

Janelle

Nellie had spent the early morning repairing her plug for the hole in the tarp. Her fix from the previous day had failed and what should have been an easy task was frustrated by the constant fogging-up of her glasses. She left the glasses behind when she braved the rain to check her lines. The fish were also taking refuge. She walked back past her failed fish holding pen, and could see that she'd need to build a much higher wall to accommodate the changing tides and now, flooded river.

Returning to camp she managed to light the last of her timber in the fireplace and make a cup of mint and honey tea. Feeling warmer, her mood lifted. She pulled out her journal, documented the morning's activities and listed the jobs still to be done once the rain lifted. Feeling more in control she turned on the camera.

'It's day two of rain. It feels never-ending, but I know that at some point, it will stop and the sun will come out. The rain appears to have spooked the fish and sent the serpents heading for dry cover. I had my second encounter with the subject of my nightmares yesterday. There's not a lot to say. As you can see, I'm still alive. We both checked the other out, and it decided it would rather not share a dry shelter. On this we concurred.' She smiled at her humour. 'I'm hoping the fish come out today. While I wait, I'll write. Bringing my journal was a smart decision. Like yesterday, there won't be much activity for you to watch. What would you prefer? Watching the rain fall and the river rise or me sitting here scribing my musings? I suspect watching the river would be more interesting.' She poked the camera lens out through a small break in the branches that formed the wall of her shelter, and lay down on her bed with her journal, pen in hand.

Archie

Archie loved the rain: the sound of it; the smell of it. Raindrops drumming on leaves, branches rustling and then crashing to the ground. An earthy scent rose from the soil while the perfume from the eucalyptus trees intensified. So different to the dusty cattle station where he worked in north Queensland. He suddenly missed the warm winds carrying the aroma of wild grasses, the sporadic whistles of the cattlemen and the gentle lowing of the cattle. Another world away.

He'd no need to venture outside his humpy for now. There was enough food. There was enough time.

ALONE DAY 7

Sebastian

Seb reached for his medical kit, shoved three painkillers in his mouth and crunched down. The taste repulsed him, but he didn't have the energy to reach for his water. His teeth were chattering, his head was throbbing and there was a repetitive beat thudding through his body. Forcing his eyes open, he realised it was mid-morning. *How did I get back here? Think Sebby.* He remembered thinking he was drowning, but not in the river, in the puddle he'd collapsed into on reaching land. Realising this was a dumb way to die and with a risk of never being found, he forced himself to his feet. One step at a time, under and over logs, and through the haze of the unrelenting rain. He tramped back to camp in a semi-conscious state, like an animal hit by a car.

He sat up, and took a swig of water. His giddy head took a moment to adjust. Looking out of his shelter and through the rain, he could see his tracker on the ground. Damn. Yesterday's high winds had broken the vine and flung his nemesis towards the river. As he scrambled to put his tracker back on his wrist, he wondered how long ago it had swung free. Would those monitoring his movements be suspicious? He stumbled down to the water's edge to check his lines. An eel was wriggling on one. Not a favourite food. Still, it would provide much needed sustenance. As he pulled it in, he caught his reflection in the water. A red and purplish mark was splashed across his left cheek. Something else to explain.

He returned to his shelter, changed into drier clothes, threw the last of his kindling onto the fire and repositioned the camera. After he'd skinned, skewered and started roasting the eel, he turned the camera on, and took a position staring into the fire, so that those at home could only see the non-bruised side of his face.

'Morning all. A bit of luck overnight catching this fellow. As you can hear, the weather conditions haven't changed so I've been staying close to home. More than a bit bored. Hoping to build a raft once the rain lets up.' *Damn. I forgot the snare wire.* 'Nothing else to do but snooze, so you're going to be treated to more falling water. Sorry.' The camera was turned towards the river and Seb crawled back into his sleeping bag, exhausted.

. . .

Galina

A wispy trail of smoke preceded the two smoke rings. The wind quickly erased her smoke art and Galina took another drag on her damp cigarette, still staring down the path Seb had taken during his hasty retreat. Had he heard her drumming? A little anxious, she chided herself for forming an attachment to the red-headed Kiwi. The storm had been intense, and she hoped he was as good a swimmer as he'd claimed to be. She scanned her shelter. The quoll was asleep on her bedding. She reached across for her knife and sharpened it on a stone. The critter awoke in fright, regarding her carefully, before scampering out into the rain. Lifting the knife up to her head she hacked at her hair. It didn't need cutting, but she needed something to do.

Valda

'No. Stop,' Valda screamed when she woke the next morning. 'Enough!' Thunder immediately rumbled in response, or so it seemed, and lightning struck a nearby eucalyptus tree, sending several branches spiralling to the earth. Valda again spontaneously curled into a ball, pulling her knees close to her chest. It was as if the universe was replying in-kind.

Yes. You've had enough. Go home.

'How long have I been here?' Valda whispered softly to herself. She knew the answer to the question and wondered why she'd even posed it. *Just a week. I've only been on my own for seven days.* But it was enough. It was too much. She wanted to go home. Tears welled up as she reached for the handset.

'Hello. Yes, it's Valda. I'm tapping out.' Relief surged through her body as she listened to the instructions on what she needed to do next. She placed the handset back in its case and turned the camera on. There was no need for words. The folk at home would watch her quietly pack while she waited for the boat to come in. It was too wet and dangerous to dismantle the shelter. Someone would have to do it later. She quivered with excitement when she heard the distant sound of a boat's engine. Running out into the rain, she raised both arms high and waved furiously. It was unlikely they would miss her but she wanted to be sure. She didn't want to be alone anymore. The camera equipment and her back pack were passed to the smiling guy with the black t-shirt, who then held out his hand to help her climb aboard.

As the boat pushed off, the skies began to clear.

Raj

Raj sat cross legged on his sleeping bag and stroked the

stubble on his chin. His stomach rumbled, reminding him of the priority for the morning. *Surely the rain will stop soon?* Raj shook his head, chastising himself for his self-talk, delaying tactics. He rolled onto his feet, zipped up his jacket, pulled his plastic hat down over his ears and stumbled out into the rain. His shoes slushed in the puddles and he wondered how many squidgy travellers he'd collect this morning. They were OK roasted and a backup option if his own gathering efforts failed.

His curiosity prompted a return to the carcass of the Tasmanian devil. It was now a white bony shell, devoid of flesh. Something large had eaten it, and the bugs and maggots had finished off what remained. The rain had long washed away any tracks of a predator. He offered up a prayer for the departed devil and headed inland in the only direction he'd yet to venture. Food pickings were again limited, and he returned to camp, two hours later, with a handful of bush tomatoes and half a dozen leeches squashed between his toes, destined for fish bait.

Janelle

Still? The skies continued to weep, or so Nellie thought as she lay under the covers. Her stomach rumbled and she knew she'd have to get outside to find or catch food. *What's that?* Nellie lay motionless as she concentrated on listening to the distant unfamiliar sound. *Was it a drum beating or perhaps a boat engine?* It was hard to tell against the back-drop of the thundering rain. Maybe she could hear nothing at all and that her sense of frustration at her containment was causing hallucinations. She knew how easy it was for that to happen. Her mind drifted back ten years previously to when she was patrolling the outskirts of a remote village, in the mountainous region south of Kabul in Afghanistan. It'd been a long, hot day, not unlike any of the thirty days that had preceded it. Her mind played tricks as she surveyed the scorched earth, seeing mirages and listening for any signs of something out of place. The crackling of the radio made her jump.

'Mulligan Over.'

'Unusual activity over to the left. Can you investigate? Over.'

'Roger that. On my way. Over.'

Nellie signalled to her partner in the bunker that she was moving out. She double-checked her rifle and took several cautious steps in the direction of the bombed-out stable. It'd been given the all-clear three days ago, and her troops had good visibility on all approaches to the dilapi-dated building. Ducking behind a stone water well, she strained to hear anything unfamiliar. There was just the bleating of goats and the distant sound of gunfire. Maybe the animals had moved inside the structure to escape the heat? Heart thumping, she ran ten steps to the corner of the building, waited three seconds, and peered around.

Nothing. No one. Not even a goat. She inched along the wall until she came to the gap created by a previous explosion. She paused and signalled to her partner that she was going in. And that was the last thing she remembered before her world exploded.

Staring at her artificial leg, she picked up her journal and noted down the return of memories that would haunt her forever. Taking risks was part of being a soldier. She needed to eat and keep warm now, so taking calculated risks was essential for her success in this competition. Her fire was nearly out and the last thing she wanted was to sacrifice precious pages from her journal as kindling. She pulled on her leg, grabbed her coat and went out into the rain.

Archie

Archie had been awake for hours. Listening. Thinking. Wondering where the animals were taking shelter. He knew the rain would make it difficult to track anything moving through the scrub. But the camera set near his trap gave him eyes, and the rain covered the sound of his feet on the earth and his scent in the breeze. It was the perfect time to go hunting. He picked up his spear and woomera and moved invisibly into the bush.

ALONE DAY 10

Sebastian

In the three days since the rain had stopped, Seb had floated four of the already cut timber pieces back to his camp. It'd been five days since he'd last visited Betty. One part of him put the delay down to his previous near life-ending swim during the storm. Another part put it down to the raft not being ready. But then it wouldn't be ready without the snare wire. And then there was her apparent disinterest in him.

He was providing a one-sided face, fish-catch update, when he heard a drum start to beat. Coughing loudly, he feigned a need to sip water and turned the camera off. He looked across the river and could see two smoke rings floating above the tree line. The message was unmistakeable. It was time to visit his intriguing competitor again.

The river was moving slowly and appeared devoid of debris. Seb knew that he couldn't see all that was beneath the waterline. He wondered if he should freestyle it again or swim with a single log, acting as a safety float. *Nah. I'll swim.* He returned to his shelter and turned on the camera.

'I've decided to go out on another scouting expedition. Won't be back for a couple of hours. Hoping I'll have something interesting to report to you then. He hesitated. 'Probably not.' He ran out past the site of his not-yet-working animal trap and through the bush to the limit of his one-kilometre boundary. There'd be a trail created on the tracker that would *nearly align* with his story. He then slipped off the device and tied it to the vine. The wind had dropped so *his movements*, would be very local. He walked down to the water's edge and walked in slowly before pushing off with breaststroke for the other side.

Galina

'Morning Betty,' Seb offered cheerily as he walked into Galina's camp.

'My God. What happened to your face?'

'An altercation with a log.'

'Are you OK?' she asked with uncharacteristic softness.

'I am now. I've been reminded to treat the river with respect.' She regarded him carefully and neither spoke for a moment.

'You forgot the snare wire.'

'Indeed. That's why I'm here.'

'It's over there. Don't forget it this time. Did you bring any fish?'

'Of course.'

'Give it to me.' She held out her hand. Seb pulled the large trout from his pocket. She stuck out her bottom lip approvingly. A rustling in the bushes made him look to his right. The quoll had stepped tentatively into the clearing. He passed the fish across to Galina. When the fish was thrown onto a thin, cooking rock, he remarked with a sigh,

'You and your rat.'

'*Jah*. So what?'

'There won't always be enough food to share.'

'Says who?'

Seb hesitated. 'No one of consequence.'

'A drummer is someone of consequence, unless of course they are lacking drum sticks.'

'That would be me,' he replied cheerily, pleased the tension had lifted a little.

'Will these do?' She passed him the sticks she had carved the previous day with her knife. 'You can now let me know when you make it safely back to your camp.'

Seb examined the intricately carved sticks, then leant over and tested them on the saucepan. 'They're perfect. Thank you Elizabeta. May I?' he asked pointing to her wallaby skin drum. She nodded and Seb moved closer to her and the makeshift drum. He started playing his warm-up routine to get his wrists used to the movement. Galina occasionally tapped an accompanying sound on the saucepan and Suupiste stared at them both, a little bewildered. The quoll's eyes moved to the fish that had momentarily been left unattended on the fire.

'Ei Suupiste. Wait your turn,' Galina said firmly, anticipating his next move while continuing to beat along on the saucepan. Suupiste yawned and stretched, feigning indifference.

Sitting around the fire felt familiar. Seb reflected on the many times he'd sat with his mates Scott and Jase on a deserted beach, cooking sausages. It was typically at the end of a long day's sail. They'd anchor the yacht, take the dinghy to shore, and spend the hour before daylight disappeared playing beach cricket. They were such fun times, spent with easy company.

'What you thinking about, sailor-boy?'

'Evenings spent around a fire, just like this, with my friends.'

'Not your family?'

'Not so much. I've only my sister now and she's off sailing near Guatemala. Lucky thing. And you, your family?'

She shook her head. 'My mother met someone new

after my *isa* died. Not sure where she lives now. I've been independent since I was fourteen. It's better for me. *Much better.*' Seb was surprised at her openness and wondered at what was not being said. He watched her light up a cigarette and inhale.

'It's three months today until Christmas.'

'So what?'

'Three months 'til I'm back with the boys, making final preparations for the big race. You should come and see us off.' Galina shrugged her shoulders. 'Or, if you're here in Tassie, come to Constitution Dock to watch us cross the finishing line.'

'You assume we'll no longer be here.'

'I'm counting on it. I'm hoping that...'

'Shhh.' Galina interrupted. 'Can you hear that? Seb turned his head and concentrated on separating the birdsong from the new rhythmic sound bouncing across the water. 'It's a boat,' she whispered. Seb stood up and Galina threw him the snare wire. She flicked her hand, giving him the signal to run.

Treading as softly as he could, he moved quickly over tree roots and sprinted down to the river's edge. Water lapping on the banks provided evidence of the recent passage of a boat. If they were visiting his camp, they'd quickly spot his tracker and his return to prepare for the Sydney to Hobart yacht race would be happening today. But they had no reason to visit him. He hadn't *tapped out* and surely ten days in was too soon in for a medical checkup. Filling his lungs with air, he took a long dive and swam under the water emerging a third of the way across where he stopped to scan the river in both directions. Nothing. No one. But then he heard an engine fire up. He gently dropped below the water line and breast stroked as best he could, still holding the wire, until he was a football field away from the other side. The boat was approaching at speed and there was no longer time to get to shore and hide in the bushes. He inhaled and sank down to the riverbed's murky floor, listening to the boat's motor as it approached and then passed over the top of him. As the sound moved further away, he floated up and gasped for air. The occupants were all facing forward, but he didn't want to risk discovery so dropped down again below the waterline and swam for shore.

An hour later, back at camp, he'd changed into dry clothes, put his tracker back on and moved the camera closer to his fishing lines. Luckily the fish had been biting and he had two trout to display for his daily *show and tell*. As he pulled them in, he could see his reflection, noting that the bruise on his cheek was changing in colour but still prominent. Another attempt at speaking with one side of his face concealed might attract suspicion. He remembered the murky river water and reached for some mud, applying it generously to both cheeks.

'Hello listeners. You wouldn't believe the day I've had.

Two wallabies came into camp and I chased them without success, falling over in my efforts.' He pointed to his muddy face and partly obscured bruise. 'Catching marsupials is clearly not my thing. Luckily the fish have been biting so I've something for dinner and something for the smoke-house. I'll get you to help me keep watch to ensure that pesky possum doesn't return and take tomorrow's break-fast. I was thinking I might...' And then he heard the distant beating of Betty's drum. She was checking in on him. Smiling, he picked up two sticks from his kindling pile. 'I was thinking I might get in some drumming before dinner.' He tapped away enthusiastically until he could no longer hear the drum beating across the river. 'These sticks are rubbish,' he said throwing them on the fire. Might carve myself some new ones. You'll really hear the difference. Time to watch me cook dinner.'

Raj – Two hours earlier

Raj patted his stomach and wondered how much weight he'd lost in the last ten days. His tummy growled as if an independent being from his body. *I know, I know.* He turned on the camera.

'Morning all. We've made it to day ten. Well, I have. Don't know about the others of course. Why don't you accompany me to the shoreline while I check the lines to see if I will have anything fishy for breakfast?' The camera was repositioned and Raj pulled in his first line. 'No fish, but no bait, so there's clearly something biting. Let's look at line number two.' Raj jumped to the next rock but could tell from the slackness of the line that there was nothing on the end. Line number three and four were also bait-free. *What to do now?* 'With no bait I need to go foraging. With no food in my tummy, I'm lacking energy and motivation. I'm fed up. I don't even want to catch a fish. I'm sick of fish and eels and worms. No. I want a feast. A proper feast. I want to eat rice. I want to eat rice until I'm so full, I burst. And for these reasons, I'm tapping out.'

An hour later, Raj smiled when he heard the sound of a motorboat. He'd already dismounted his shelter and his backpack and camera equipment were packed and stored together on his favourite meditating rock. As the boat came into shore, Ralph waved while holding a camera to record the moment. The boat hit the sand, Ralph jumped into the shallows and passed Raj a small insulated food bag.

'From your wife. Emergency provisions. Biryani and a few samosas.'

'I love my wife,' he cried out, scooping his hand into the still warm dish and shoving it into his mouth.

'I'll get your things then. Enjoy.' Raj sat down on his rock and concentrated on identifying each flavour, every one even more delectable than he remembered.

.   .   .

Janelle

Nellie was determined to build a fish corral. And not just any corral. She wanted to build one that would be impenetrable by birds, land creatures and safe from rising tides. The challenge was constructing something secure with the limited materials available. She sketched half a dozen ideas and then went out foraging, relishing the sense of purpose the day held. By early afternoon her fish holding yard was constructed and she toasted her success with a mug of mint tea. She turned to the camera.

'Here you go folks. Whaddaya reckon? Not engineering perfection nor a piece of art, but scoring highly on functionality. Well that's the theory. Needs to be tested of course so I'll turn you over now to the fishing channel.'

Three hours later Nellie had secured a brown trout, a black bream and a long-finned eel. She realised she'd no knowledge of how the three would co-exist together in a small space and was suspicious of the underlying strength of the eel. So that was hit on the head with a rock and the trout and the bream placed in the new enclosure. She returned to camp to skin and cook the eel. Sitting close to the fire she felt content. The leaves were rattling in the late afternoon breeze and the sky was turning red-orange, boding well for a clear day tomorrow. She started to hum, enjoying the tranquillity until she heard the distinct plopping sound of a rock falling into water. Racing to the water's edge she saw what looked like a large cat moving slowly away from her corral with a fish in its mouth.

'Come back here you rascal. Drop it now and don't you mock me with that limp.' She hesitated. *Or is that genuine?* Indeed, it appeared to have a damaged paw and now Nellie felt overcome with sympathy. She stopped chasing it and returned to the corral to ensure the last fish was still there. It wasn't. *Damn.* The disabled possum had moved a large rock from the fish wall creating an easy escape route. She'd have to rethink her design tomorrow.

Archie

Archie was enjoying listening to the sound of his kangaroo fillet fry while he reflected on his hunting success. Kookaburras, yellow-tailed black cockatoos and magpies belted out a noisy chorus as sunlight filtered through the trees. Two kookaburras swooped down low and landed close to the fire, their presence a statement of their trust in this new creature in their territory and their optimism. He smiled and carved two small pieces from the slab which he threw to them. They scooped up the offering and flew high up into a nearby eucalyptus tree. Archie had taken his first bite of the meat, relishing the flavour when he heard a new and unfamiliar sound. It was a low guttural growl. His eyes scanned the surrounding bush. There was no movement other than the long grasses bending gently in the morning breeze. He heard the sound again and noticed a lone magpie watching him. The magpie chortled out the unmistakable sound of a kookaburra, followed by his own distinct and melodious warbling. *You clever mimic.* Archie threw the bird a piece of meat and it flew away.

ALONE DAY 12

Sebastian

In the two days since Seb had last visited Galina, he'd finished his trap and built a raft. The small camera was carefully positioned beside the device to ensure it would capture footage of any animals passing. *Hopefully they won't be passing – they'll be caught.* Seb tied the raft together with vines and snare wire left over from his trap. He'd hacked out an oar and a quant pole from a felled Huon pine. The construction activities had all been recorded on the main camera, along with commentary about the snare wire he'd *found in the bush*. He tested the raft to see if it would float, which it did, although navigation was challenging.

'That's a wrap for Day Twelve. Pretty successful day all round. Might do a bit of fishing while I wait for something land-based to stumble into my snare.'

He turned off the camera, picked up the quant pole and paddle, and punted his way across the river.

Galina

'You're not wet, so...'

'Yes. I've got watercraft. Wanna have a look?'

Galina offered the barest of smiles. 'Of course.' She followed him down the path and nodded cautiously as the raft came into view.

'You know what this means?'

'That I'll no longer be your laundry lady when you visit?'

'Yes, and, more importantly, you can come across with me to the other side.' She regarded the raft carefully.

'I don't think so.'

'What? I built this raft for you. It's called *Betty's Boat*.'

She laughed. 'Nice try sailor-boy. Again, I don't think so. But you can show me how it works.'

Seb picked up the paddle and pushed the raft out. It wobbled unevenly, before settling and he paddled in a loop before returning to shore. Seb looked at Galina, her face was pensive.

'I've got you Betty. I'll keep you safe.' He held out his hand and she hesitatingly took it. He placed his other hand on the small of her back and their eyes met momentarily, before she stepped onto the floating platform.

'Suggest you sit down to minimise the potential for an afternoon dip.' A flash of fear crossed her face and Seb knew she'd taken a huge step in trusting him. He pushed the raft smoothly out from the bank. It was a perfect day for boating. The deep blue sky highlighted the puffy white cumulus clouds, and several eagles were flying high, moving from one vantage point in the tree line to another on the opposite shore. When they reached the middle of the river Seb turned the raft around to return. Galina was trailing her fingers in the water, enjoying the tranquil experience that felt like floating on a carpet. Suddenly the raft was rammed by a floating log which sent them spinning.

'Noo,' she yelled, before falling backwards into the water. Panic gripped Galina as the icy water soaked her clothes and dragged her down. She thrashed about in the water and floated away from the raft. Seb could sense the fear in her frantic movements and dived in.

'I'm coming Betty. Don't panic. Don't fight the river.' She continued to flail, constantly dropping beneath the surface and swallowing water. 'I'm here, but I need you to be calm. You'll need to float. I know it's not intuitive, but roll onto your back and push your head down in the water. Trust me and then we can swim back together.' Exhausted, she stopped fighting the water and followed his instructions. He then placed his arm over her shoulder and across her chest, using side stoke to swim her to shore.

They were both exhausted when their feet touched the

river bed. Seb sat in the shallows and looked out across the water. The raft was nowhere in sight. He turned to Galina who was walking up the hill back to her camp.

'Betty, are you OK?' he called out

'You should go.'

'I don't want to leave you. You're upset.'

'I want to be alone. Go.' Seb's heart ached as he watched her walk away. *I'm an idiot. A stupid idiot. Why did I force her onto the raft?* There was nothing else he could do now. Respecting her wishes, he dived into the water and headed for the far shore.

ALONE DAY 17

Sebastian

Five days had passed since that fateful paddle on the river. Time had moved excruciatingly slowly. Each morning Seb had checked for smoke signals and listened carefully for the gentle beat of a drum. Nothing but the wind in the trees and the ever-present birdsong. He then headed inland to see if any animals had wandered into his trap. Nothing. Rewinding the film footage, he looked for evidence that wallabies or kangaroos had been moving through the area. Again, there was nothing save for the birds, which were keeping him from being truly alone. He counted himself lucky that the fish continued to bite, and that he'd not had a single day without something to eat. He'd love to have red meat again and some human company, but wouldn't cross the river until Galina signalled that he was welcome. And he'd have to swim, unless the raft turned up. He'd been back to the site from where he'd originally sourced the cut timbers, but there was nothing suitable left. The only way that he could cross to the other side now was by swimming. The daily five hours of filming was proving difficult. His days were monotonous and he found it difficult to think of anything new to report. For the first time since arriving, he wondered if he would last the distance.

He was throwing out his fishing line when he heard the unmistakable sound of an approaching motorboat. The potential for human conversation made him happy and his mind raced with questions. *But maybe they're coming to collect a contestant who's tapped out and won't be stopping?* Five minutes later he had his answer when a boat with a doctor, cameraman and pilot pulled in close to shore.

'Hi Seb. Just wanted to check in and see how you were holding up,' Ralph said. 'This is the doctor. He'll do a few tests.'

'Nice to have company,' Seb replied. 'I'm fine. Bored but fine. This your first stop?'

'Couldn't say,' the man with the stethoscope replied. 'Breathe in slowly. Good. Breathe out slowly. Good.' He made a note on his clipboard, before wrapping the blood pressure cuff around Seb's upper arm and inflating it. No one spoke for several minutes. 'OK. Step on the scales please.' Seb looked across at the cameraman and back to the doctor before following the instruction. *Bizarre.*

'Anything interesting happening in the outside world?' Seb asked.

'Don't know what you'd find interesting,' the doctor replied. 'You've lost weight.'

'I know. Tying my belt buckle up a notch.'

'Anything you'd like to ask me?'

'You mean apart from the two questions I've already asked and you've not answered.'

'I meant about your health.'

'I'd kill for an apple. Did you bring one?'

'I think you know the answer to that.'

'When will you be back again?'

'Couldn't say.'

'Wish I could comment that it's been great having visitors, but these are words I just couldn't say.' The unnamed doctor suppressed a smile, scribbled something on his clipboard, nodded at the cameraman and headed back to the boat.'

'Bye. Come again,' Seb said as the motorboat was pushed out into deeper water and the engine fired up. He watched the boat head across the river, certain that their next stop would be Galina's camp. Not for the first time, he wondered how she was faring.

. . .

Galina

Suupiste's ears pricked up at the unfamiliar sound. Galina heard the boat too and quickly extinguished her cigarette before throwing dirt over the butts in the fireplace. She sauntered down the hill, preferring to meet whoever was visiting, away from her camp. The boat pulled in as she arrived at the shoreline.

'How're you going, Galina?' Ralph asked.

'As you can see, I'm doing well.'

'Pleased to hear it. The doctor's here to give you a once over.'

'A once over what?'

'I mean a checkup. A medical check over.'

'As you wish.' The doctor walked towards her holding up his stethoscope.

'May I?' She nodded. He placed the device on her chest and asked her to breathe in and out.

'You smell of smoke,' the doctor said.

'I've been sitting beside a fire smoking a kangaroo.'

'How did you catch that?'

'In my trap.'

'And it died instantly?'

'Not quite, but soon after.' The doctor raised his eyebrows before asking her to step on the scales and to let him measure her blood pressure.

'Is there anything you'd like to ask me, health related?'

'No.'

He turned to Ralph. 'She's good. We're done here. Let's visit the next competitor.'

'Shh,' Ralph replied. Galina watched the men climb aboard the boat and head upstream before walking up the hill and back to camp.

Janelle

Nellie was sipping honey and mint tea in her shelter when she heard a boat approaching.

'I'd offer you a cuppa but I've only one mug,' she called out as she walked down to the water's edge.

'We've already had elevenses thanks,' Ralph joked as he jumped ashore. 'Here for your first medical check-in. This is the doctor.' She looked at the medic and nodded. 'We'll be filming. All part of the process.'

'Understood. Will you hold my tea,' she said passing her mug to Ralph without waiting for a reply. Ralph passed the tea to the young guy driving the boat and signalled for the doctor to start his various tests.

'You been sleeping OK?' the doctor asked.

'Mostly,' she replied honestly. 'I sometimes remember times I'd rather forget.' He nodded and made a note on his clipboard. The remaining tests were done in five minutes.

'She's good.' The driver passed her back the mug of tea and she watched them climb aboard the boat and leave.

. . .

Archie

Archie had only just returned to camp when the boat pulled in. He had a small wallaby slung over his shoulder as he walked down to greet his visitors.

'Oh. We have another wildlife warrior,' Ralph remarked. Archie was unsure how to respond and put the animal's carcass on the ground while he waited for another comment or at least a question. 'Just here for your first medical checkup. This is the doctor. He'll do a few tests and ask you a few questions.' Archie stepped forward and the doctor reached across with his stethoscope. Ralph and the driver filmed the carcass while the doctor followed the same process he'd applied with the previous three contestants.

'That'll be more than enough food for a couple of days,' Ralph whispered. Archie heard the comment, raised his eyebrows and made no comment.

'He's good, too,' the doctor said. Archie picked up the wallaby and returned to his shelter not bothering to wave goodbye to the trio.

ALONE DAY 19

Sebastian

The banging of timber against timber woke Seb in the early morning. What? He crawled out of bed and poked his head out of the shelter.

'You beauty!' he screamed, delighted to discover that his raft had floated back to shore and was bumping up against a dead tree. He ran into the water and pulled it onto land. Some of the vines had gone, but it was still in solid condition. Glancing across the water he thought about Galina again. Indeed, he thought about her most days, and nights. It'd been a week since she'd fallen into the water and stopped trusting him. He shook his head to chase all thought of her away.

There were two trout wriggling on the lines. *My day is looking up.* He whistled as he returned to camp to skin the fish. Sitting by the fire, with one fish cooking and the other in the saucepan with a lid on top for safekeeping against prowling possums, he picked up a piece of firewood and started tapping the side of the pan. It wasn't loud, but might be enough to be heard on the other side. He stopped tapping. A single kookaburra has started a morning call and was soon joined by others in a noisy and melodic chorus. When they stopped a minute later, Seb could hear the beating of a drum.

Galina

'Did you bring fish?' Galina asked as he walked into her camp.

'Yes.'

'You're not wet.'

'You have superior powers of observation.'

'You mock me,'

'What? Never.'

'So you built another raft?'

'No. Here's your fish.' Suupiste popped his head out from Galina's sleeping bag, let out a low-pitched hiss and sniffed the air. 'Really? That rat is way too comfortable here.'

'A temporary arrangement.'

'Have you told Suupiste that?'

Galina smiled. 'Not yet. Soon. When I leave to collect the prize money.'

'I was meaning to talk to you about that.'

'Chat over kangaroo stew?'

'Thought you'd never ask.' Seb suppressed a smile as he sat down by the fire. Galina joined him and pulled the saucepan off the fire and placed it on a rock between them. They took it in turns of dipping her only spoon into the marsupial casserole which also included quinoa and salt-bush. It tasted even better than last time. They didn't talk as they ate, seated together in a companionable silence. When he was full, a feeling he'd not enjoyed in over two weeks, he turned to Galina and passed back the spoon.

'Betty.'

'Yes Sebastian.'

'We need to talk about this game.'

'Ah ha.'

I don't want to compete with you.'

'Because you'll lose?'

'Quite possibly. But more importantly, I think together we'll be invincible.'

'Go on.'

'I can fish and you can hunt. We won't go hungry, unless of course, you give too much food to that rat of yours.' Galina smiled and reached across and rubbed Suupiste's belly.

'And we agree to split the prize money fifty/fifty.'

'And who will be the winner?'

'It doesn't matter as long as it's one of us. You can trust me and I have a feeling that I can trust you.' Galina tugged at a piece of hair behind her ear. 'We must of course keep our collaboration a secret, and do nothing to arouse suspicion.' Galina was nodding. 'Every day, we must film for five hours without fail.'

'Anything else? she asked.

'If we know we're the last two, I'll tap out first so I can get back to Sydney for the race to Hobart. I could then meet you at Constitution Dock when the race is over?'

'Perhaps,' Galina said.

'If not,' Seb said ignoring her reply, 'we'll definitely meet at the awards ceremony, where we'll need to appear as if we don't have a relationship.'

'That should be easy,' she replied mischievously, 'we don't have a relationship.' Seb involuntarily twitched then glanced down at his feet, afraid she'd know what he was thinking. He drew a circle in the dirt with his toe.

'*Betty's Boat* came back this morning. That's why I'm dry.'

'Good. You'll be able to take stew back with you when you go.' Seb was again thrown by the comment. Did she want him to leave?'

'Look I'd better get back now. Gotta fit in five hours of filming fishing or whatever. I'll see you whenever.'

'Whenever,' she replied.

. . .

Galina

Galina was sorry to see him go. He was amusing and much better company than the quoll. She was pleased the raft had come back as the journey across the water would be safer now and maybe he'd come more often. But she hoped he didn't ask her to come aboard the raft again. She couldn't do it and wasn't ready to tell him why. The day ahead felt long. She glanced at the camera and inwardly groaned. Clicking her fingers, Suupiste scurried off into the bush. A lid was placed on top of the saucepan in case an eagle-eyed viewer spotted the illicit quinoa. She took a deep breath and turned the camera on.

'Hello. Day Nineteen here in Van Dieman's land. I know you haven't called it that for centuries.' She paused. 'It's inspiring being in the presence of old trees. It's an intriguing world. Time is measured differently here. It moves slowly. I met with the modern world today when the doctor came to visit. He was here for just a moment and then he was gone. It seems I am strong enough to continue.' She smiled, fidgeted and reached across for a cigarette before remembering she was on camera. 'Would you like to come with me to look at some old trees?'

Janelle

'Had my first visit from the doc. Been missing company and was excited when I saw the boat pull in. Bit anticlimactic. Aye it scunnered me. You'd think they might have been a bit cheery. But no. Not a touch of human warmth. I'm better off here with the birds and the bees for company.' She turned the camera off, picked up her journal and walked off into the bush.

Archie

Archie checked his fishing net. For the first time he'd caught a fish, a large flathead. For all the effort involved in threading the net he wondered if his time was better off spent hunting fish with a spear. And it'd be more fun. He brought the fish back to camp for skinning, being careful to avoid the poisonous spikes on the flathead's head. As the fish fried, he looked at the camera. It'd become an unwanted companion, always there, demanding his time.

ALONE DAY 22

Sebastian

There'd been no smoke signals or beating drum to signal that Galina would welcome another visit from him, however an early morning scouting mission had uncovered bush tomatoes, and with an eel and trout he'd hooked earlier, he'd a bountiful feast to share. He chipped another marker in his measuring stick, mentally noting that they were now in their fourth week of being *alone*. He'd taken the camera with him on the morning walk. It'd been an easy way to kill two of the five hours of compulsory filming. He threw his lines out again and then walked over to the raft.

C'mon Betty. It's time to visit your namesake.

. . .

Galina

Something had broken Galina's trap and she was perplexed. The vandalism had been well considered, with both traps set off. A design rethink and location move were needed as she pondered who the culprit might be. She scanned the ground for footprints and the nearby bush for clues. A kookaburra landed near her feet and looked at her.

'Was it you, *laughing one?*' The kookaburra ignored the question and scratched the earth, uncovering a bug before flying back up into the leafy canopy. The trap was reset in another location that appeared as a natural pathway for animals and Galina returned to camp. She was delighted to see Sebastian sitting by her fireplace cooking fish, Suupiste at his side. Seb looked up at her and smiled.

'Nothing in the trap?' She shook her head. 'Mine either. I could show you how to fish so you won't have to wait for the *Cross-River Uber Eats Delivery Service.*' Galina shook her head again.

'No. Trap will work next time.' Seb was a little surprised at her response and assumed that humour didn't translate across cultures or maybe he'd touched on something sensitive.

'It's just about cooked. Pull up a chair.' This time Galina smiled. Suupiste scurried off into the bush with the coveted fish's head. 'Now, partner?'

'*Jah?*'

'What will you spend the prize money on? You were

very non-specific on that first day.' Galina hesitated and looked down at her fingernails.

'Rebuilding a pier.'

'My word you're full of surprises Betty. I wasn't expecting that. What sort of pier?'

'A small one, near my home town.'

'And...?

'And what?'

'There has to be more to this story...' Galina lit a cigarette and stared down to the river through the trees.

'A boy drowned when part of the pier collapsed. The wood was rotten and the water freezing. He was there with his sister and...'

'And you couldn't save him because you couldn't swim?'

Galina closed her eyes. 'I tried. But I couldn't. I nearly drowned.'

'How old were you?'

'Eight.'

'My God Galina. So young. And your brother?'

'Five.'

'How horrible. Where were your parents?'

'My *isa* was away working on an oil platform and my *ema* was chatting with a friend. Not far away, but she didn't hear the screams, until it was too late.' Seb walked over and wrapped her in his arms as she gently sobbed into his chest.

.   .   .

Janelle

Nellie's days now followed a familiar pattern.

Wake at first light.

Shake head to chase away nightmares.

Boil water and make soothing mug of mint and honey tea.

Walk around perimeter of territory to calm nerves, and remind herself that she was safe.

Turn camera on. Remark on anything of interest from morning's walk.

Check fishing lines and place excess fish in corral.

Cook fish for breakfast.

Settle down for two hours of drawing followed by one hour of journalling.

Turn camera off.

Eat lunch, if food available. If not, drink another mug of mint and honey tea.

Check fishing lines.

Snooze.

Check fishing lines.

Listen to birdsong

Write in journal.

Doodle.

Cook dinner.

Go to bed.

Cross fingers for nightmare-free sleep.

· · ·

Archie

An aggressive shift in the behaviour of a local magpie was a sure sign that the chicks were out. Archie climbed a nearby tree and pulled his main camera up after him, using the paracord. The parents clearly recognized him as he wasn't dive bombed. He tied the camera firmly to the branch pointing the lens directly at the nest. Three tiny pink mouths could be seen reaching up to their parents for food. He figured viewers would forgive him for a few days of *Maggie Cam* instead of his usual limited bush chat. He shimmied down the tree, picked up his spear and ran off into the bush.

ALONE DAY 23

Sebastian

Seb had hated leaving Galina yesterday but she'd reassured him she was fine. Crossing the river, he felt was like crossing a line in their relationship. They'd moved from competitors to partners and now to friends. As he'd pushed into shore at Sailing Siesta, he could see there was another fish on one of the lines. He grabbed his tracker from the vine and then the camera from the shelter.

'Afternoon all. I've been out on my raft for a bit, hence the late start to filming today. Delighted to return and see something on the line. Let's go and see what I'll be having for supper.' He walked slowly backwards away from the water, gently reeling in the line. 'Ahh eel,' he said disappointedly as he pulled it onto the muddy shoreline. A quick knock to the head and another cricket was quickly threaded on the fishing hook. 'Gonna try again. I'm sick of eel.' He let the recording run, mentally counting down the minutes until he could shut it down. Sitting on his favourite fishing log was a pleasant enough way to while away the hours. From time to time, he glanced across the water wondering what Galina was doing.

He woke early the next day, planning to film for five hours before he pushed off for the other side.

'Morning all. Big day ahead. I'm full of optimism. Fish for breakfast perhaps? Let's see.' Seb set up the camera near his fishing lines. 'Oh well. Not this morning. Eel soup it is then, unless of course there's something in my trap. Let's have a look.' Seb hoisted the camera on his shoulder and headed off into the bush. 'Nothing here either, but something's been here,' Seb said pointing to a pile of uneven black balls. 'Wallabies or kangaroos, whereas this bigger ball over here, also belongs to a grass eater. You can tell a lot from a scat. I'd put my money on that being from a wombat. Yeah, a big wombat. Something with claws has been digging in the dirt and nibbling on the roots of this bush.' Seb carried the camera a few steps further. 'Aha. Detective Ward has spotted more animal poop. This one from a meat eater.' He poked the scat with a stick to break it up, revealing fur within its composition. 'I'd say we've had a devil through here and I'd guess he's been munching on a possum. May have to do that myself if the fish don't start biting.' He turned the camera off, noting he'd only filmed for two hours. He shook his head, turned the camera on again and walked slowly back to camp where he filmed the skinning, cooking and eating of the eel. After breakfast, he carried the camera down to the water's edge and discussed how he made the oar and punting pole in great detail, before pushing the raft off to the middle of the river. A bending fishing line had him rowing quickly back to shore where he pulled in a sizeable trout. He held the fish up for the people at home and did a quick time check. 'That's all for now folks. Until tomorrow.'

Galina

Suupiste heard his footsteps before she did.

'Bring anything for lunch?' she asked.

'Is trout OK?' Seb replied. Galina smiled and the quoll leant up against Seb's leg, nose pressed hard against the pocket with the fish. Seb watched Galina throw the fish-head into the bush, sending Suupiste on a race to retrieve the snack before another animal claimed it. Neither spoke for several minutes as Galina rotated the fish above the fire.

'No ciggie today?' Seb asked.

'Finished.'

'You mean, none left or you've given up?'

'Both. Now's a good time to stop. It's ready.' Seb sat down beside her and pulled a piece of trout from the stick she'd passed to him.

'Delicious.'

'I know. I'm a good cook.'

'And I'm a good fisherman. I also think I'd be a good swimming teacher. You should learn to swim before you come on my yacht.'

'Which yacht?'

'The one I'll buy. I'll need to win this competition first.' Galina's head bobbed. 'Betty, you've made the difficult decision to give up smoking. I think it's also the perfect time to learn to swim. C'mon. You should confront your demons; you know I'll keep you safe.' He stood up and held out his hands. She looked up into his eyes and then reached for his hands. He pulled her up to a standing position, pulling her close before leading her down to the water's edge, still holding her hand. They both stripped down to their underwear, with Seb entering the water first. He checked for floating debris then turned around and looked back at Galina. 'Give me ten minutes today. We just have to start.' Galina walked tentatively into the water. 'Excellent. Come out to me. OK. Lesson one is about *not panicking*. If you fall into deep water, come up to the surface, grab a mouthful of air and slow your breathing. Wanna try that first?' Galina nodded and Seb led her out into deeper water. She felt her panic level rising. 'I've got you Betty. You're safe. I'll do this with you.' Galina held tightly to his hands. 'On the count of three we're going to go under. OK? She nodded again and Seb counted to three. They both sank below the water line. Galina's heart thumped and she held tight to Seb's hands, resisting the urge to kick for the surface. A moment later he squeezed her hands and she swam up with him. 'Well done. You aced it. Ready for the next challenge before we call it a day?'

'Jah.'

'OK. Same thing again, but this time, you do it on your own. Again, I won't abandon you.' Galina looked about nervously. 'Let me show you how to tread water first. I'll need to let go of your hands. But I'll tell you when I'm about to do that.'

'Alright.'

'First you need to keep kicking, just as you're doing unconsciously now.' Galina smiled. 'And then you need to slowly circle your hands in front of you. OK. I'm about to let go of your hands now and I want you to do exactly what I'm doing with my arms. In one, two three.' Seb released her hands and started treading water. She followed his movements in moving her arms and circles and was delighted at her success. 'OK, I'm going to count down to ten now and then your first lesson will be over.' Galina watched him while she continued to tread water and he counted down *very slowly*. He stopped counting at two and she swam towards him and wrapped her arms around his neck.

'You are a devious teacher.'

'I kept my word and...' She kissed him, stopping him from finishing the sentence. His arms slid around her back and he returned her kiss. 'I've completed my five hours of filming for the day.'

'Me too.'

'I don't need to go back tonight.'

Janelle

Nellie was leaning against a fallen tree with her pencil at the ready and sketch pad in hand as she surveyed the bush. It had surprised her how much she looked forward to these daily drawing sessions. There was so much to see when you took the time to observe the smallest details. Drawing also calmed her anxiety and provided a way of capturing scenes that were important to her, that would always mark this moment in time.

Archie

The nimbus clouds were a sign that rain was coming. He climbed the tree where he'd left the camera filming overnight. The magpie chicks were now asleep. He wrapped the cord around the camera and gently lowered it to the ground. Returning to camp he wondered what he should film today. The tide was about to change so throwing out a few fishing lines now might mean he'd be eating a water-dwelling as opposed to land-based animal for lunch. He needed some variety.

ALONE DAY 38

Janelle

Nellie had not slept well. It was thundering outside and nightmares from the desert had returned. She felt miserable knowing she'd be confined again. How long would the rain set in this time? She reached for her journal and doodled an image of a skull, followed by lightning and streaks of rain. Tears welled up and she removed her glasses, pressing the palms of her hands into her eyes. Taking three deep breaths, she felt better. Looking out across the water, she could see one of her lines straining, and in danger of snapping. She ran out of the shelter into the rain and grabbed the line. Something big was putting up a fight, causing the line to jump and cut her fingers. Again, breathing slowly, she held firm and walked slowly backwards. A huge trout started flapping furiously in the shallows.

'I've got you baby!' Nellie cried. 'Woo hoo.' She momentarily lost her footing as the line slackened, and the fish splashed its way back out to the river's depths. 'No.' She was now angry and stomped her way back to the shelter, forgetting she'd left her glasses on the ground. Crunching glass underfoot was the final straw. She reached across for the handset. 'I'm tapping out.'

Sebastian

Seb was snoring gently, when he felt an elbow in his rib cage.

'Can you hear that?' Galina whispered

'What? The storm?' Seb said yawning.

'It's a motorboat. Too soon for another medical check. Someone must have tapped out.' Seb rolled over and attempted to go back to sleep. 'We might be the last two left?' she insisted.

'Come back and keep me warm, Betty, or I'll have to ask Suupiste to hop in the sack.'

'He's a very wriggly bed companion,' she said as she started tickling Seb's rib cage. Soon all thought of investigating the motorboat were washed away with the rain.

. . .

Archie

Archie could see from a distance that an animal had sprung, and then inadvertently moved, his trap. It must have struggled. He was delighted that the contraption had finally worked after a month of sitting dormant. He wondered which animal had been captured and was a little surprised to see an elderly possum stone-cold dead, with its neck broken. He knew it wouldn't be the tastiest food around but would provide calories and sustenance. It was enough for now.

ALONE DAY 39

Farnsworthy

'Three out and three to go. Shouldn't be much longer 'til we have a winner,' Farnsworthy announced. 'Ralph, when you take the doc out in a couple of days, ask a few casual questions of our campers to determine how they're *really doing*.'

'I reckon the cattle wrangler's a shoo-in, Nelson,' Ralph replied.

'Nah. I'd be putting my money on the sailor.'

'Not on the *Gothic One*? She's hard as steel.'

'Nope. I'm surprised she's not out already, given her smoking habit.'

Sebastian

Seb stroked his beard as he lay in bed listening to the rain. He figured he could measure time by the length of his facial hair growth, but then that was only easily done in the early days. As time stretched on, a beard curls and the days meld into each other. No. He needed to be disciplined in striking his measuring stick each day. Betty was itching to shave his beard off with her hunting knife. He smiled at the thought of her; at the thought of them. Their lives had taken a surprising turn. With this first task of the day completed he turned on the camera.

'Day two of downpour. Nothing new to report. Bored out of my brains.' He grimaced and poked his head out of his shelter, looking up at the charcoal-speckled sky. 'Rain clouds might be breaking up. I'm definitely breaking out. Wanna watch me check the fish lines?' The audience at home watched Seb collect and cook another trout. Disappointed that there was only one fish, he reported that the constant rain had upset fish feeding patterns. He let the camera film the rain for another four hours before turning it off, putting on his jacket and punting across to the other side of the river on the raft.

. . .

Galina

'Welcome first customer of the day. My barber's chair is waiting for you,' Galina said as he splashed his way into her camp.

'Can't I get changed out of these wet clothes first?' he asked.

'Well, yes. It's better that I cut your hair naked. You can then shower and change.'

'Yes please, I like the idea of you being naked while you're attending to my locks.'

'Not me sailor-boy. You!'

'Why not you too?'

'Because we'd be too distracted and...stop that. Keep your hands to your side.'

'Nope. Can't do it.' He nibbled her ear while staring at the intricate snake tattoo on her neck. The hunting knife fell to the ground and she pulled his face to hers, giving him a lingering kiss.

'You can do whatever you want to me now,' he whispered.

'Short back and sides then?

Archie

Archie watched the rain continue to fall while sitting cross-legged inside his humpy. There was a persistent drip at the back and he knew he'd need to repair it once the rain stopped. He was pleased he'd the foresight to collect more firewood before the rain had set in. His food stocks were low and he'd need to get out hunting soon. A strong wind suddenly pushed at the branches providing the structure to his home. They held firm, but his thoughts went to the magpies' nest, high up in the eucalyptus tree. He grabbed his jacket and went out into the tempest.

The wind was pushing through the bush, bending trees and sending leaves spiralling into the air. As he approached the tree housing the nursery, a powerful gust tore through the canopy and dislodged the nest from its perch. Two chicks were ejected and fell to the earth, their bodies broken by the fall. The magpie parents hovered around their motionless bodies, squawking furiously, in a futile attempt to rouse them. Archie had arrived in time to catch the falling nest with the one remaining chick inside. He placed the nest near the parents, so they were aware of the chick's survival, while he considered what to do next. The bird was too small to fly and with predators everywhere the nest could not be left on the forest floor. He scanned the surrounding area and spotted a hollow in a nearby tree. Scaling the tree, he noted possum fur stuck to the bark on the outside of the hole. Peering inside he confirmed it was free of inhabitants. His thoughts flickered to the possum he'd caught in his trap previously. Perhaps it'd been the original owner? The hollow was the safest solution for now, and if the original owner did return, ownership would need to be negotiated with the chick's feisty parents. He picked up the nest still holding the chick, as the parents noisily objected, and placed it inside the hollow. As he climbed down the tree, the parents flew in and the wind and rain began to ease.

ALONE DAY 44

Sebastian

Sebastian had spent the last three days at Sailing Siesta waiting in anticipation of a medical checkup. They'd come too far to risk him being caught at Galina's camp. He was buoyed by the thought that most contestants in similar competitions had *tapped out* by Day Forty. Maybe they were already the last two survivors? He was pulling in his second trout of the morning when he heard the motorboat approaching.

'Like your new look.' Ralph called out as he jumped off the boat. Seb was momentarily confused until he saw Ralph patting his cheeks. 'How'd you get such a close shave?'

'I took my time – which I have in spadefuls.'

'Good job. I see you continue with your fishing success,' Ralph said looking at the trout.

'I've had a lot of practice.'

'Evidently. Aren't you getting a bit bored with your limited diet?

'Some days yes. Other days I focus on the bigger prize.'

'I see.' Ralph didn't want to be drawn into a discussion about the competition, prize money or how close Seb might be to being declared the winner. His eyes scanned the foreshore and he spotted the raft.

'D'you use that for fishing?'

Seb was suddenly on guard.

'Nah. It's not very stable and difficult to steer. Would be better with a rudder and an anchor.' Ralph seemed satisfied with his response.

'So, a more thorough checkup required today.'

'Of course. Can you give me a moment to put this fish in the smokehouse. And can you ask your driver to keep an eye on it while I'm with the doctor. There's a wily possum in the vicinity.'

'This isn't a room service visit.'

'Listen, mate,' Seb replied with a generous dollop of attitude, 'there's not that much food around so everything edible needs to be carefully guarded. If I was able to call room service, I'd...'

'My apologies.' Ralph waved to the driver, signalling for him to follow Seb back to his camp and then watched with amusement from a distance while the fish was placed in the smokehouse and instructions issued on likely possum entry points. A few minutes later Seb joined the doctor near the shoreline where he underwent the now familiar battery of tests.

'Now Seb. How are you sleeping at night?'

'Very well, unless… there's a possum trying to steal my fish. Then I find it hard to get back to sleep.'

The doctor laughed. 'What about boredom?'

'Yes, it's a bit repetitive; throw out the line, pull in the line, put it in the smokehouse and repeat the next day. But I'm used to it.'

'What about being lonely? Do you miss having someone to talk to?'

'You mean apart from yelling at the possum?'

'Yes,' the doctor replied, laughing.

'Sometimes.'

'Do you have any concerns about the impact of having been so long out here, on your own?'

'Honestly?'

'Yes,' the doctor replied, leaning in.

'I wonder when this race is going to be called. I felt sure I'd be out of here by now. I'm meant to be back on the mainland preparing for the Sydney to Hobart. Really feel like I've let my mates down by being here so long.'

'I see. Any other comments?'

'Could you let them know I'm OK and still endlessly hopeful that I'll make it back in time.'

'Sorry Seb. No. You know the rules.'

'See you in two weeks then, Doc.'

Galina

'Where's your raft, Galina?' Ralph asked upon arrival at her camp.

'It came adrift during a storm last week. Disappointed to have lost it.'

'You're not the only person who's built a raft during the competition.'

'Really. Who else has one?'

'That would be telling.'

'So there's at least one other person left in the competition. Hmmm. Are they as good at hunting as I am?'

'You really are incorrigible, Galina.'

'I try.'

Ralph shook his head and looked across to the doctor. 'She's all yours.' The doctor took Galina to the side of her camp and performed the now familiar checks, rigorously scribbling on his clipboard.

'Firstly, are you sleeping at night?'

'I guess so.'

'What do you mean, *you guess so?*'

'As I don't remember being awake, then I must have been asleep.' The doctor added to his notes.

'How do you cope with boredom?'

'Who told you I was bored? I make traps, I build rafts. There's plenty of things to do.'

'Galina, tell me, how are you coping with the loneliness?'

'Who told you I was lonely. I've got a friend.'

'What? Who?'

'It's a large rat, that I'm not allowed to eat. There,' she said, pointing at Suupiste who was watching the activities from the sidelines of the camp.

'He hardly provides stimulating conversation.'

'Who said I needed *stimulating conversations*?'

'An assumption on my part.' Galina puffed out her cheeks and he again scribbled on his clipboard. 'Do you have any other questions or health concerns?'

'I'd expect you to tell me if you were concerned about anything, health or otherwise. You're the one with the clipboard.' The doctor was momentarily stumped; unsure how to respond.

'That's all for today. You have a remarkable constitution and mental disposition.'

'Let's hope it's enough for me to win the competition.'

Archie

Archie was high up in a tree, keeping his eye on the hollow in the tree where'd he placed the baby magpie, five days earlier. The parents had been coming and going but he'd yet to see the chick. Maybe it hadn't survived after all? The roar of the motorboat engine prompted him to scramble down the tree and head to the water's edge. He preferred to meet them there than in the sanctuary of his humpy.

'How are you, Archie?' Ralph called out cheerily.

'I'm good.'

'Bit of a longer consult with the doctor required today.'

'OK.'

'We'll stay here on the boat while the doctor comes ashore.' Archie held out his hand to help the doctor disembark into the shallow water.

'Shall we sit over there on the log?' the doctor suggested.

'OK.' Archie walked with him and then sat patiently while the doctor checked his heart, his weight and his blood pressure.

'Can you tell me how you're sleeping, Archie?'

'I usually get enough at night, but if something keeps me awake, I'll have a snooze in the arvo. The bush can be noisy at night.'

'Are you bored?'

'Most of the time.'

'Ahh,' the Doctor replied writing something down. 'How do you fill your day?'

'I hunt. I check my trap. I sleep. I think about my family.'

'I see. And do you get lonely?'

'Yes. Often.'

'Not surprising since you've been here six weeks. That's a long time to be on your own.' Archie didn't respond. 'You know Archie, you don't have to stay. I could write down here that I recommend that you leave the competition today. Nobody would blame you and you'd be on your way back to your family tonight.'

'Do you have any more questions?' The doctor tried to look at Archie's eyes, but he was staring at the ground.

'No. No more questions. That's it for today.'

'Then I'll be off to check my trap.'

ALONE DAY 50

Sebastian

Seb marked the fiftieth day in the bush on his measuring stick with mixed feelings. It was a milestone he'd hoped he wouldn't meet as he would've already won the competition and returned to prepare for the race. He wondered what Scott, Jason and the others would be doing today. *Bet they're at Bootcamp getting ready*. He dropped to the ground and attempted twenty push-ups, failing to rise at fifteen. Taking a moment to catch his breath, he then attempted twenty burpees, failing to rise at ten. *My fitness is shot*. Sitting on the ground and feeling despondent, Seb considered his options. He had the time to get fit, but probably not the calorific intake required to support a vigorous exercise program. But he could start, and adjust his activity each day based on food intake. His mood lifted and he turned the camera on.

'Hello world. I thought you'd have seen the last of me by now but here I am. Feeling a bit flat as my mates are getting ready for an important sea race. I wanna be with them, but I'm here and I'm outta shape. Sure, I've lost a few kilos, but my fitness has gone to the dogs. But I'm determined to do something about it, and you folks at home can be my accountability buddies. Well kinda. I know it's going to be a bit of a one-sided conversation.' He shook his head and chuckled. 'Each day I'll give you an update on what I've been doing to get my body buffed. Today's program will include ten jumping jacks, fifteen log presses and twenty sit-ups followed by a one-kilometre jog. I'm starting small as I've seven weeks until my stamina and sea legs will be tested.' The camera was readjusted and Seb threw himself enthusiastically into his new regime.

Galina

Galina was roasting wallaby when Seb arrived at her camp later than morning.

'You're late. Been enjoying a bit of beauty sleep, have we?'

'I've the glow of someone who's started a new exercise program. I'm feeling invigorated. And hungry. That smells fantastic. I'm ready for a protein fix.'

'It's not ready yet. You probably have time to build me a raft.'

'What? Why? I've already built *Betty's Boat*.'

'Which has come to the attention of the check-in crew. I was quizzed about its location on their last visit. If I've built one raft and lost it, they'd assume I'd make another one.'

'I don't think there's enough raw materials around to make anything viable.'

'Who said it had to be viable?'

Seb regarded her with awe. 'I'll get on it.'

Archie

Archie was checking his fishing net when a melodious warbling caught his attention. He turned to see the junior magpie being escorted around the campsite by its parents on a first foraging trip. The parent's black and white coats shimmered in the morning sunshine while the chick's light grey feathers ruffled in the breeze. They showed no fear of Archie as they chirped and gently nudged their offspring to mimic them in pecking at the ground. Archie enjoyed the parade. He was pleased the chick had survived and that its parents trusted him enough to let their infant wander so close. He returned his attention to the fishing net that had ensnared two flathead. It was going to be a good day.

ALONE DAY 54

Sebastian

'You've put on weight,' the doctor exclaimed on his fourth visit. 'How can that be?'

'Direct conversion of protein to muscle,' Seb replied. 'I've been eating a lot of wallaby of late and focussing on building muscle, which as you would know, is heavier than fat.'

'Why?'

'Cause it's hard to store food so you need to eat like a king when it's available in anticipation of lean times, and also cause I'm in training for the big yacht race. You're responsible for the change in my behaviour.'

'How's that?'

'Asking me all those questions last time about what I do to avoid boredom. Got me thinking about how I'm wasting my time here and more importantly, got me moving and focussing on improving my overall fitness. Thanks Doc.'

'Pleased to be of help,' the doctor replied, hoping Seb wouldn't notice his sarcastic tone.

Galina

'Cooeee Betty,' Ralph called out once the boat wedged firmly into the sand. 'We're on our way up.' Galina didn't bother to reply as she was sure they weren't expecting one. The three men entered her camp to discover her sitting on the ground threading vines through Huon pine branches.

'Don't s'pose you brought any snare wire with you?'

'Nah. Sorry,' Ralph replied

'Paracord will do.'

'None of that either Betty. C'mon. Stand up please. Time for your checkup. We've places to be and people to see.'

'Are there many places you need to be?'

'That would be telling. On the scales. Thank you.' The doctor completed his checks and note keeping then signalled to Ralph that they could go.'

'Good luck with the raft, Betty,' Ralph said as he turned to walk down the hill.

'I'll need it when I don't have any snare wire or para-cord,' she replied. 'Think about it.' Ralph waved a dismissive arm in the air without turning round. Galina followed them down the hill. Her interest lay not in waving goodbye but in noting the direction of their travel.

Archie

Archie pushed the baby magpie off his lap when he heard the motorboat approaching. He'd developed quite the relationship with the magpie family and was keen to keep it hidden from the medic and his minders as well as from the people at home. He waved as he walked out into the water to pull the boat onto the sandy shore.

'You're looking well, Archie,' Ralph said.

'I am. Do you need to check me out then?'

'Always. It's for your own good.'

Archie shrugged his shoulders and walked with the doctor to the same spot they'd used for the previous three medical checkups. This time the doctor did not make additional enquiries about his boredom or loneliness, which was a relief.

ALONE DAY 55

Farnsworthy

'You're joking? He's put on weight? How can that be?' Farnsworthy asked.

'It seems that if you eat a lot of wallaby and pump iron, or rocks as the case may be, you gain weight. He also seemed lighter and happier somehow. I guess that being alone suits him. The other two seem in good health and sound spirits as well.'

'My God, we're not running a flipping health resort. Ralph, can you check the weather forecast to see if any major storms, tornados or tsunamis are on the horizon? And I'm not kidding.' Nelson stormed out of the room leaving Ralph alone with the skipper.

'So who've you got your money on to win?' the skipper whispered.

'One hundred on the sailor. And you?' Ralph asked.

'Two hundred on Galina. That girl is gutsy. I reckon she's a sure thing.'

ALONE DAY 60

Sebastian

Seb was pleased that Galina had agreed to come fishing from the raft. It was another milestone in their relationship, reflecting their growing mutual trust. They'd undertaken two more swimming lessons, with Galina now able to tread water for ten minutes and swim breaststroke, freestyle and sidestroke. Her technique needed improvement but it was sufficient should she need to save herself. She seemed contented as she dangled her legs over the side of the raft with the fishing line held loosely in her hand. It was a cloudless sunny day with warmer spring temperatures making swimming a pleasurable experience. He looked at her with admiration and wondered if their relationship, would last beyond the competition.

· · ·

Galina

Galina was concerned she'd grown too attached to the sailor. Their arrangement regarding the competition's outcome had complicated her feelings for him. She'd been on her own for so long and maintained such strictly casual relationships that she worried she was about to be hurt. He'd probably leave her. Living this way in the bush wasn't real.

Archie

Archie's daily routine had been modified to incorporate a conversation with the young magpie, now called Rooster because of the bird's early morning wakeup call at the edge of his shelter. Magpies were known for their varied and delightful vocalisations and this one seemed to be rehearsing for an opera. The young bird then accompanied him when he checked the fishing net each day, always optimistic for a fishy morsel. He'd call out to report to his parents if there was anything in the net. He would also join Archie in the tree tops whenever he ventured up to survey his surroundings. Rooster wasn't sure what he was looking for but was pleased to provide visual and moral support.

ALONE DAY 80

Sebastian

Seb had finished three hours of filming fishing from the water's edge when he heard the motorboat approaching. He was feeling morose this morning and didn't welcome company. It was now three weeks until the starting cannon fired in Sydney and the *Blue Gazelle* raced to Hobart against an estimated eighty yachts. He needed to be back and by now was sure he'd been replaced.

'Ahoy Sebastian. It's the mail run today. We come with messages from home.' Ralph called out before the boat nudged into the sand.

'What? Really?'

'Well not so much in your case. Your sister hasn't returned any of our calls or emails.'

'She'd be out of range I reckon.'

'So we contacted your number two person, Scott Harmon.'

'Cap'n Scott? You're pulling my leg? What'd he say?'

'Pull that line in and come see for yourself.'

'The line's fine,' Seb replied as he quickly walked over to join them. He didn't notice that the skipper was holding a camera, recording their exchange.

'They've made a recording for you. Ready?'

Seb beamed.

'Hey Seb. Thought you'd have reported for duty by now. Guess you're having too good a time with all those wombats and devils.'

'And tigers,' Jase called out, forcing his face onto the screen. Scott elbowed him away.

'We're looking forward to hearing all your stories, not during the race of course as we'll be too damn busy, but after we pull into Constitution Dock, collect the cup and head to The Hope and Anchor for a celebration. We're still expecting you to join us in Sydney and have included you on the roster, but mate, we can only hold your space open for another two weeks.' Scott hesitated before continuing. 'In other news from home, it's three weeks until the twins are born and I become an uncle. The father-to-be has been bombarding me with requests for your contact details so he can interview you about your wilderness experience.' Seb heard a noise to his

left and looked up to see Ralph mouthing No way. 'My sister has inveigled my wife into going to London for the birth, so she probably won't make the party in Hobart.'

'Hi Seb,' Charlotte said, momentarily appearing on the small screen as she leaned in close to Scott. She waved before disappearing off screen as quickly as she'd arrived.

'Apparently, I'm not to expect a reply from you, so I'll understand that your absence will be your message. Here's my final one to you. Keep safe and keep doing whatever you're doing. From the crew of the Blue Gazelle. Bye Sebby.'

Ralph looked at Seb for a response. Seb didn't want to talk so walked back to his log and fishing line. He wanted to soak in the feelings of friendship and joking and mateship that the call had provoked. And to be alone.

'We'll be off then Sebastian. No medical check today,' Ralph called out as he climbed aboard the boat. Seb barely registered his message or their departure as he stared at the patterns on the water's surface.

Galina

Galina was already at the shoreline when the boat pulled in. It'd been over three weeks since her last medical checkup and she'd been listening carefully every morning for the distinctive sound of the motorboat, awaiting their arrival.

Curious. Only two today?

'Morning Galina. Are you well?'

'Jah.'

'That's lucky, 'cause we don't have the doc with us. We guessed you'd have called us if there was anything requiring medical attention.'

'So why are you here?'

'The morning mail run.'

'What?'

'We've a message from your mother.'

'No, you don't.'

'We do. You gave us her email cause she's your next of kin, and we've been in touch with her.'

'Why? I'm not dying.'

Ralph paused, astounded by her response. 'Because we thought you'd like to hear from family.'

Galina glared at them, suddenly aware their conversation was being filmed. Her outward appearance shifted.

'Thank you. I'd be pleased to receive it,' she said holding out her hand.

'It's a video message, Betty. Not an old-fashioned snail mail. Come stand beside me and we can watch it together.'

'I'd rather watch it on my own and suspect you've already watched it, so you don't need a second viewing.'

Ralph passed her the tablet and took a step back, checking that the skipper was still filming.

'So you are back in the forest Elizabeta. I know that is your happy place. I feel sad that it has been such a long time since we spoke. I hope you are doing well. I am back in Tallinn. On my own.' She paused. 'Like you. You were always better being on your own than I was. You are so independent, resourceful and strong. You don't need other people. I am so proud of you and know you will do well in this competition. I would love to talk to you when you come out. Perhaps you will even consider coming home to Estonia to see me?'

Galina's mother blew air kisses and waved goodbye. The recording ended and Galina continued to stare at the final image of her mother on the screen.

'Betty, can I ask you how you're...' Galina held up her hand and handed back the tablet. Everyone froze although the camera continued filming. She unconsciously shook her head, turned and walked up the hill back to her camp.

'Did you get that all Skipper?' He gave the thumbs up. 'Gold, and more importantly, I reckon she'll be tapping out by nightfall. Let's go. Only one more visit left.'

Archie

Archie was again about to spear a fish in the river when

the motorboat approached. He watched them cut the motor then grabbed the front of the boat, still holding the spear in his hand, much to the consternation and then amusement of Ralph and the skipper.

'We come in peace,' Ralph called out, which annoyed Archie. Actually, everything about Ralph annoyed him. He walked up onto solid ground and lay the spear down.

'Good news Archie. Come over here and join me on the log. We've a message from your mob up north.' Archie didn't believe him but walked across the pebbly shore and sat down, looking suspiciously at the tablet.

'Ngukurr. Hey Archie. How you goin' down there?' It was Anthony, his cousin and fellow jackaroo on Sheffield station. Archie's heart leapt and he was suddenly aware of his suppressed feelings of homesickness bubbling up. 'We missed you on the mustering today. You know Joey's no good at rounding up cattle, although he's a whizz with the branding iron. During the muster we found so many damaged fences. It's gonna take us weeks to fix 'em all, and that's gotta happen after we've repaired the water troughs. You must've taken all the rain 'cause there's none up here. Dry as a bone. We're worried about the fire season that'll surely come. Big worry. We need to get them firebreaks done.' Anthony stopped talking as someone off screen had told him to shut it. 'Sorry I've been dumping on you, mate. There's good things

happening too. It's just, we miss you Archie and wish you were here.'

The video ended and Archie's head sank into his hands. Ralph patted him on the back awkwardly.

'You OK mate? D'ya wanna hop on the boat with us now and head home?'

Rooster walked close to Archie's feet and emitted a short high-pitched begging call. Archie stood, picked up his spear and walked back into the bush, with the young magpie running behind him.

ALONE DAY 96

Sebastian

Seb woke up feeling despondent. Two weeks had passed since he'd listened to Scott's message and made the difficult decision to *not get on* the boat. As dawn broke, he knew it was now too late to make it back in time to be a member of the crew. He'd so wanted to sail from Sydney to Hobart, and not to let Scott down. Last night he'd seriously considered tapping out. He rolled over and turned on the camera as he lay in bed.

'Thought this game would be done by now. But still, I'm here. I miss my friends. They're my family. I'm sick of this place.' He turned off the camera and examined the roof of his shelter. After thirteen weeks of laying in this bed he knew every stick and spider intimately. As he lay there watching a beetle thread its way from side to side, and listening to the birds start their morning chorus, he could hear the beat of Galina's drum. Seb rolled out of bed, and turned on the camera.

'I'm off to check my trap again this morning. Would be grateful if you guys could keep an eye on my *smoking eel* while I'm away.' He turned the camera towards the smoke-house, picked up his oar and started whistling as he walked down to the raft.

Galina

Galina was roasting possum as he walked into her camp.

'Long time no see, sailor-boy.'

'I know. Been thinking about stuff. Did you miss me?

'Of course not.' They both smiled as he leant over and kissed her tenderly. He sat down beside her near the fireplace.

'I'm now officially off the crew.'

'Hasn't this race been going for a while and isn't there another one next year?'

'Yep. Started in 1945. It's just that we've had this most amazing year, me, Jase and Scott and we were all *so ready*. Winning this race was going to top it off.'

'On the assumption that you won.'

'We wouldn't have won on line honours, but we might

have placed on handicap. It was the thrill of being in this classic race. Been dreaming about it for years. Anyway, it's done now. If I'm lucky I'll make it out in time to cheer them off from Sydney Harbour, or if this game drags on, I should at least make it to Hobart to see them sail in. Thanks for listening, and sorry that I've been blabbering on about my own situation. How about you? Thought about going back to Estonia?' Galina turned the piece of possum over on the stick and Suupiste suddenly appeared at her side. 'I was wondering where he was.'

'He was sleeping. Think he had big night out.'

'He's not going to know what to do with himself once you've gone.'

'He'll be fine. We all learn to adjust when people we care about leave.' Seb looked at Galina who was looking at the fire. She didn't look towards him and his mind raced, wondering who she was referring to.

'Are you going to Estonia when we get out of here?'

'You mean, will I go and visit my mother?'

'Yes. That's what I mean.'

'I don't know.'

'What will you do then?'

'I don't know.'

Seb knew Galina well enough now, to know that she wasn't open to talking. He'd need to wait. She passed Seb a piece of meat that was nearly intercepted by Suupiste.

'I personally think he'll need counselling after you go.'

Galina smiled and slung a piece of meat far into the bush, sending the quoll scurrying.

ALONE DAY 103 – EARLY MORNING

Archie

Archie watched the forest raven scan the ground. Having collected several seeds it ran a few steps, launched and flew high up into a Huon pine. It settled and then regarded its surroundings like a king, inspiring Archie to also climb a nearby tree. From his vantage point, Archie could see across the water to the next mountain. There was a black yacht, sails down, moving slowly inland. *What's that? Someone's lost.*

He didn't know the depth of the river or the location of fallen logs and sandbanks, but he reckoned there were multiple opportunities for a yacht of that size to get stuck or snagged. Still, not his problem. His attention turned back to surveying the land, wanting to gather more knowledge on animal routes. Might be time to move his trap. The breeze suddenly intensified and the leaves rattled. An unfamiliar sound caught his attention. A dog barking? No. It was a branch creaking and the sound suddenly grew louder. It was too late for Archie to move. He fell to the earth with a thud then a crack and knew immediately from the pain surging through his body that he'd broken his left leg. If he'd been on a cattle muster, one of the other jackaroos would have come to get him. If he'd been out on his own with his horse, he would probably have made a sledge and got the horse to drag him home. He looked at his tracker and wondered how long it would take for the support team to realise he was no longer moving and needed assistance. His mind kept flitting to the first aid kit in his shelter that had bandages and more importantly, painkillers. If he took it slowly, he could make it back to camp within the hour. Maybe two. He removed his jacket and tied it tightly around his leg, gasping from the pain. A thick branch that had also fallen was within reaching distance and he used it to leverage himself from a seating to leaning position. His damaged leg was incapable of taking any weight, so he took a single hop and then used the branch as a crutch.

Two hours later, he lowered himself gently onto his bed and picked up the portable satellite phone. He hesitated, again considering possible ways he might still be able to avoid the three words that would end his stay. Nothing came to him.

ALONE DAY 103 – LATE AFTERNOON

Farnsworthy

'And then there were two,' Nelson crowed. 'However, the weather's getting warmer and those last two seem *all too comfortably settled* for my liking. We may never get 'em out. Maybe it's time the good doctor made a recommendation that one of then should be evacuated on medical grounds?'

Ralph raised his eyebrows. Which one do you reckon it should be?'

'They've both lost weight, but look healthy enough. Galina's the thinnest, and stating the obvious, *she's a girl* and her extraction would be the most believable.'

'You reckon, Nelson? She's tough as nails, a master trapper and well set up there on her hill. Even made a drum out of a wallaby skin. Like a trophy I reckon. I'd go with the sailor.'

'If only there wasn't so much video evidence that he'd been catching fish nearly every day.' Farnsworthy adjusted his tie then flicked his chin with his fingers. 'I'll get the doctor to do a *more thorough* health analysis on the next visit. That wouldn't be out of place. And maybe we'll discover something that'll enable us to send one of them on their way, and we can finally get this show done and out into the world.'

ALONE DAY 104 – EARLY MORNING

The blood-curdling squeal was both angry and unmistakable. Galina sat bolt upright in bed, and looked at Seb who was also wide-eyed and open-mouthed.

'I think you might've trapped a devil, darling.'

'I hope that's what it is. They're not that big,' Galina replied factually.

'Do not underestimate the beast. Can you not hear its roar? It's rather cranky this morning.'

'There are two of us. We'll find a way.'

'Cup of tea first?'

'Don't be ridiculous.' She smiled as she dropped a pair of trousers on his head.

Morning light was filtering through the gums as they walked the short distance to the trapped animal. They didn't speak as they cautiously approached the trap, the distressed animal glaring at them, teeth bared and growling.

'It'd be easier if we killed it,' Galina whispered.

'Nah. Not allowed and not right. Anyway, it's been captured on camera. They'd know if we did it in. Suddenly realising the risk in Seb's presence being filmed, they looked to the tree where the camera had been attached. It wasn't there. Their eyes scanned the grass and Seb pointed at the device, a short distance from the devil. It was in two pieces with a cracked lens. As Galina bent to pick it up, the devil charged and she jumped back quickly, but not before it had sunk its teeth into her left hand. She punched it hard on the nose and it released its grip. Seb yelled at the devil to distract it and it rushed at its second tormentor. Blood flowed down Galina's arm to her elbow and dripped in the dirt while she grimaced in pain. The cut was deep and ugly as its teeth had struck the bones in her hand. Seb picked up a rock and threw it with force at the devil's head. The animal fell to the ground, stunned by the blow, and Galina quickly stepped in to unleash it from the trap with her good hand. Seb looked on in wonderment. He stepped closer to the animal. It smelt like a wet dog, and it was diffi-cult to determine if it was still alive.

'Let's go,' she said calmly. 'He'll have a nasty headache when he wakes up.'

Back at camp, Seb washed her wound and applied anti-septic before gently wrapping a bandage around her hand.

She must have been in tremendous pain, but barely made a sound.

'An x-ray and stitches are needed, Betty. I know we had tetanus jabs before we started, but who knows what microbes were in that devil's mouth. You'll have to see a doctor.'

'We can call the medic. It's normal. But I don't need to leave.'

Seb raised his eyebrows. 'Betty, it doesn't matter. That won't be your call. Look. Remember. We're in this together. If I'm the last person out, I'll give you half the prize money. You have my word. If you ever need to find me, and I'm not returning calls, contact Scott. He'll know where I am. Or, you could always call into the Hope and Anchor Hotel in Hobart. I might be there having a drink.' He smirked and she wasn't sure if he was joking

'OK,' she said. 'You should go now.'

'Wait an hour or two before calling in?'

'Of course.'

'See you, Seb.'

'See you, Betty.'

ALONE DAY 104 – LATE MORNING

'What do you mean he isn't there,' Farnsworthy yelled into the radio.

'We can't find him. His tracker's swinging from a vine and his backpack's gone.'

'And the camera equipment?'

'It's still here.'

'Bloody hell.'

'Well, he's hardly topped himself if he's taken his things. And if he's left his tracker behind, he doesn't want to be found. Cor. When we eventually find him, I'm going to kill him.'

'Should we tell the police?'

'What? No.'

'Should we tell his next of kin?'

'No. Maybe. Not yet. Bring the cameras back and we'll

look at the footage. We might find a clue as to his mental state and where he might have gone.'

'Will do.'

One hour later

'Where the hell are you, Ralph? Why aren't you back here?'

'Can't find the second camera. We've looked everywhere.'

'Forget it. We've had another contestant request help. She's hurt herself. Take the doctor and go and collect her and don't forget to get some great footage.'

'Will do.'

'And Ralph.'

'Yeah?'

'She's the winner of the competition. Make sure you get footage of that moment when you share the good news.'

'Best bit of the competition.'

ALONE DAY 104 – EARLY AFTERNOON

Galina

It'd been difficult waiting two hours before picking up the satellite phone and asking for a visit from a medic.

'It's your lucky day, Betty. You were about to get a house call anyway. They're not too far away. What happened?'

'Bitten by an animal.'

'Not a snake I hope.'

'Nope. It was a...'

'Cooee,' someone called out

'They're here. I see them coming. I go now. Bye.' She put the phone back in its case. 'Can you hear that?' Galina said to Suupiste. The marsupial looked up at her. 'They're probably coming to get me. That's my collection boat. I won't be coming back. You'll need to find somewhere else to sleep.' The quoll scratched its belly, unmoved by the news. Its ears pricked at the sound of unfamiliar, footsteps approaching and it darted off into the bush.

'Cooee.' A voice cried out again.

'I'm over here,' Galina called out. Her eyes looked through the bush in the direction of the approaching footsteps. She was surprised that one of the men in the black shirts had a camera on his shoulder.

'It was only a bite,' she said defensively. They laughed.

'Well. I've news for you. You've won the competition,' Farnsworthy announced.

'What? No. Not possible,' Galina replied.

'We certainly weren't expecting that reaction, viewers. And at one hundred and four days, you've outlasted any other contestant, in any other game.'

Galina's eyes narrowed and she looked between the men.

'Who came second?'

'Archie,' Farnsworthy replied.

'And the sailor?'

'He was in the middle of the pack. Came out ten days ago,' Farnsworthy replied smoothly. Galina glared at them. *Why are you lying?*

'Excuse me,' the doctor asked. 'Can I look at her hand?' Farnsworthy stepped aside while the doctor unwound her bandage.

'What bit you?'

'A devil. Tasmanian. Caught in my trap.'

'My word. That's nasty and deep. Can you move your fingers?' Galina grimaced as she followed the doctor's instructions. 'Lucky it wasn't worse. You'll need to come to hospital to have that attended to.'

'Not before we've visited the site of the attack,' Farnsworthy said. 'Did your camera capture the action?' Galina reached down to pick up the broken camera and passed it to him.

'Perhaps. The camera also had an altercation with the devil.' Farnsworthy rolled his eyes and Ralph reached across to take the broken apparatus and examine it in greater detail.

'Might be able to retrieve something, Nelson. Don't panic.'

'But, just in case, come on, show us where it all happened,' Farnsworthy instructed as he clicked his fingers and pointed for the cameraman to follow.' Galina stood up with the assistance of the doctor and walked with a heavier step than usual, hoping that the noise would wake a possibly still-unconscious devil. She was relieved when they arrived at the trap to discover the animal was no longer there. *It's not dead. Thank God.*

'Elizabeta, talk us through what happened this morning,' Farnsworthy asked in his formal voice.

'I heard a noise from the trap when I woke this morning.'

'What sort of noise Elizabeta? I mean, was it loud?'

'Yes, it was loud. Quite loud. A screaming of sorts. I came to look. The devil had been caught in my trap for wallabies. I make good traps which is why it was stuck. It had thrown its body against the tree, breaking the little camera and winding itself in knots.'

'And what did you do next?'

Galina hesitated. 'I unwound the wire, which is when it bit me.'

'And then it ran away?'

'Jah. Yes. That's exactly how it happened.'

'There you have it, folks. Our winner, Galina-Elizabeta Ivanof, showing you just what you can achieve when you're alone, even against a formidable animal.' Galina smiled weakly. 'And cut. Good. Ralph, can you help Betty pack her things and dismantle the shelter. I'll meet you at the boat.' Galina watched the men file back to her camp. She waited a moment before following them casting her eyes around the remnants of her trap. The flattened grass and drag marks through the dirt had not been noticed by any of the crew. They had no reason to doubt her story. It was clear to her that the Tasmanian devil had not woken up. Something had dragged it away. Returning to camp, Galina swung her backpack over her shoulder with her good hand and walked carefully down to the boat.

'When do I get my money?' she asked Farnsworthy.

'Soon. We have the awards ceremony in Hobart in just over a week's time. You'll need to be there. It's a condition of the competition. We'll put you up in a hotel until then. And a reminder, Betty.' She looked into his eyes. 'I'll need you to be in a brighter frame of mind when we hand you the cheque. Our viewers will want to see a delighted winner. And don't forget, you can tell no one about your experience in the wilderness without our explicit written permission.'

Galina shrugged her shoulders. 'Of course.'

'There are bound to be reporters snooping around, particularly in Hobart, trying to get the inside scoop. You wouldn't want to do anything to jeopardise that cheque.'

'I'm good at following rules,' she said without a hint of irony.

PART 2

SYDNEY

DAY 70

Scott sighed as he reviewed the Sydney to Hobart race documents, including the *Crew Disclaimer* and the *Racing Rules of Sailing*. There was a lot to read and it all needed to be understood and complied with. The race rules had been tightened over the years to make the sport safer.

He looked down at the crew list that would need to be submitted.

Skye Le Roux (owner and navigator)

Scott Harmon (skipper and tactician)

Jason (Jase) Smith (trimmer)

Anika Svensson (chef and deckhand)

Archer (Archy) Middleton (bowman)

Rebecca (Becky) Bernard (bosun)

Alexis (Lexie) Ricci (chef and deckhand)

Nicholas (Nick) Bouras (deckhand)

Honey Demir (deckhand)

Oliver (Olly) Pellegrin (deckhand)

He'd had to replace Seb, but would welcome him aboard if he made it back at least a week before the starting cannon fired.

The crew had already spent two days obtaining their Sea Safety Survival Certificates. Scott was aware that this crew were less experienced than those on other yachts, with an average experience of five years in offshore racing. They'd also not previously sailed together. To be successful in such an arduous race, it was critical that the crew were familiar with the deck layout and rigging and had had practice working together in ever changing sea conditions. They also needed to be able to communicate without talking, a skill not easy for some.

It was a blustery day on the harbour, with winds up to twenty five knots, so perfect for a practice run. The rules had been tightened following the disastrous race of 1998, when six sailors died and five yachts were sunk in a mini cyclone.

Scott was adamant that every team member had to know what to do in the event of a wild storm and in case they needed to abandon the yacht. Everyone needed to be skilled in deploying the life raft, righting it when it had capsized and knowing what to do in the life raft if the yacht had been abandoned. Everyone was exhilarated as they practiced the different rescue scenarios. Hopefully it wouldn't come to this, but they needed to be prepared.

In the evening, he spent several hours with the owner of the *Blue Gazelle*, Skye Le Roux, discussing recent changes to the rigging and internal systems. She was originally from South Africa and now lived in Sydney. She'd made her money in mining, which funded her passion for offshore sailing.

DAY 92

Three weeks later, everyone was in good spirits as they attended the Race Sponsor's party. Multiple languages could be heard over the clinking of glasses. There was time to have longer conversations with other crews, in an atmosphere of camaraderie. The room was demarcated by status with those on the maxi yachts gathering together near the bar and engaged in competitive *war story* sharing, from previous races. Others examined the model yachts and beautifully mounted photos, a tribute to the race's long and colourful history.

There was a public roll call of each vessel and their registered location. Scott noted the six yachts he believed most likely to claim line honours. These included the 100-foot maxis such as the American *Eagle Express*, informally called *The Eagle*; the Monaco-registered French yacht

Sailing Nicoise; the Italian *Sopranos*; and the Australian *Fair Go Flyer*, which was also known as *The Flyer*. Of those yachts in the same 52-foot length category as *Blue Gazelle*, they saw the *Kiwi Kings* and the British owned *My Cup of Tea* as their peers. But in a race such as this, with so many weather variables at play, any of the eighty-odd yachts could be the ultimate winner on handicap.

A burly bloke from the *Kiwi Kings,* Brendan, asked Scott where Seb was.

'Honestly don't know mate. Somewhere in Tassie.'

'Thought he was a member of the crew this year?'

'So did we.'

DAY 98

Brisbane International airport was bustling in the run-up to the festive period with many choosing to fly to the northern hemisphere in search of a white Christmas. The terminal was alive with the rhythmic sound of luggage wheels rolling across tiles and excitable children screaming.

'I guess you didn't hear from Seb?' Charlotte asked Scott above the din.

'No. We've replaced him. He'd better win that competition or he'll have gained nothing from taking such a risk.'

'Who knows, he might have gained some skills, or met interesting people.'

'You do know he's alone down there and has been for nearly a hundred days?'

'There are wombats and wallabies,' she replied with a smile.

'And serpents and devils and maybe even some tigers,' he said with a twinkle in his eyes. Charlotte wobbled her head and her eyes rolled.

'Hope he's OK. That's not something I'd *ever* want to do.'

'He'll be fine,' Scott replied. 'Now, a few last-minute instructions. Could you give this to my sister, perhaps after she's given birth to our niece and nephew.' He hugged her tightly.

'Will do,' she replied. 'Anything else?'

'Thank you for supporting my sister in her hour of need.'

'She's also my best friend, remember.'

'But you're giving up Christmas with your folks. Miranda is grateful as are Mum and Dad. They'll be over for a shift-change in the new year.'

'You know it's not a hardship going to London. Even though it's going to be cold. I plan to take time out from supporting the new parents by checking out the costumes at the Victoria and Albert Museum and by attending a sustainable fashion exhibition. Hoping to get some inspiration.'

'Inspiration for what?' he asked.

'You know,' she said punching him gently in the arm, 'for when I'm attending the *Kaleidoscope on the Catwalk*. You promised me you'd be there as you're already going to be in Hobart.'

'Sorry. How could I forget. Perhaps Seb and Smithy could be models for you? They looked dapper in their kilts at the wedding.' It was only three months since Scott and Charlotte had married.

'No,' she replied laughing. 'And I seriously doubt they'll have *those outfits* with them. But I might ask Mason if he's interested in writing a piece about the event and in being a social media correspondent. He could do that remotely.'

'Remotely would be all Miranda would allow. But I need to express caution here. You know Mason can favour hyperbole over facts in anything he's writing.'

'Which is why he'd do it well. The whole point of the event is to provide an explosion of colour and to challenge our thinking around what we wear and when we wear it, and how we express our identity.'

'You've been warned. Which reminds me that I've committed to giving him a blow-by-blow account of the race, once it's over. Not sure how much I can say given the disclaimer I've signed. Covers everything media related. I'll have to check.' He leant over and kissed her tenderly on the lips. Breaking from his embrace she looked up at the flight information display. Scott was catching a flight, too.

'You'd better go,' she said. 'I hate goodbyes.'

He pulled her into another tender embrace. 'See you next year.'

'In Hobart,' Charlotte said as she blew him a kiss. She caught the elevator down to passport control and watched him stroll off to the railway station on his way to the domestic airport terminal to catch his flight to Sydney. She felt sad watching him walk away, but knew they'd have a wonderful reunion in two weeks' time.

DAY 100

Skye, Scott and Jason attended the compulsory Christmas Eve media conference organised by the Cruising Yacht Club of Australia. The event was principally focussed on reporting likely weather conditions for the race that would cover 630 nautical miles. This was important given the changeable nature of weather conditions on the route and previous experience of wild storms. Safety was of paramount importance in the race which was considered one of the most difficult in the world. While the mood was solemn during the official briefing, there was time to exchange playful jibes with other competitors when they picked up their information packs. The trio agreed that it was difficult to predict what the conditions would be like on Boxing Day, and even harder for the days that followed. Skye would be constantly monitoring weather channels and websites. As owner of the vessel and a highly experienced sailor, it was unusual for her not to be skippering the yacht. A car accident earlier in the year had resulted in extensive shoulder reconstruction surgery, from which she'd not yet fully recovered. As a result, she felt it best to leave command of the *Blue Gazelle* to Scott. They left the party just before midnight, leaving many swaying along to Rod Stewart's classic song, 'Sailing'.

As he snuggled down into his bed in Skye's basement at Mosman, Scott called Charlotte

'I wish you were here. I'd sleep a lot better if you were,' said Scott, using a soppy voice.

'Maybe. Maybe not,' Charlotte replied cheekily. 'You *do need* to get as much sleep as you can before your Boxing Day departure. You won't get much shut-eye for three days'

'I suppose.'

'Has Seb surfaced yet?'

'Not that I've heard.'

'Has anyone come out?'

'Again, not that I've heard. If the contractual rules for the game are anything like the ones we've had to sign up for, they'd need to keep quiet about their experience. I promise I'll let you know as soon as I hear anything.'

'OK. Good night.'

'Goodnight Charlie-Girl.'

'Bye.'

'Bye.'

Ten seconds later...

'Are you still there?'

'No.'

'Bye for real.'

'If I must.'

Two minutes later they both hung up.

DAY 101 – CHRISTMAS DAY

Scott checked his weather forecast app as soon as he woke. It looked like they'd enjoy clear skies and gentle breezes for the start of the race. He called Charlotte, who'd been sending photos of the dazzling Oxford Street Christmas lights and providing hourly text updates on the amusing conversations between Miranda and Mason about their soon-to-be-born twins' names. It felt like another world and he wished he could pop in for a chat, if only for an hour, before he set sail. He compromised on a family Zoom call that evening, which would be early morning in London.

His morning soon became occupied with overseeing the cleaning of the yacht, checking food stocks and reviewing rosters. Smithy had been organising the Christmas Day BBQ to be enjoyed by the half dozen crew members, already living on the yacht and away from home. It was good to get to know each other better before the stresses that would come from the estimated sixty-hour sail to Constitution Dock in Hobart.

Even though it was Christmas Day there were people everywhere who were a collective surfeit of nervous energy. Crew members were moving between their yachts and the amenities block to shower, and members of the press were roaming expectantly, seeking last minute opinions on sailing conditions and likely placings. Helicopters flew overhead and Santa Clauses were wearing board shorts and Hawaiian shirts, delivering packs of chocolate Tim Tams to each yacht. Depending on the time difference between Sydney and their home location, crew members called home to share Christmas greetings, to receive messages of love and also stern instructions on keeping safe, prompting a few tears.

DAY 102 – RACE DAY

An early morning mist over the harbour soon evaporated as the sun heated up. Seagulls were squawking and halyards were clanging against masts in the brisk morning breeze. Helicopters, owned by the television networks, dipped and soared overhead, providing stunning views to race enthusiasts watching the pre-race preparations from home. Online betting agencies were providing hourly updates of the odds and running advertisements throughout the pre-race breakfast television coverage. The harbour looked spectacular, sprinkled with colourful watercraft from one-man canoes to navy cruisers. Crew members on all eighty yachts were up early as they undertook final checks to the rigging and communication systems. They waited patiently for race officials to check the hoisting of storm sails and had furtive race-strategy conversations while they reviewed the latest weather fore-casts. At the same time, spectators and media people jock-eyed for preferred spots along the harbour's extensive shoreline.

Scott gathered the crew together for his final message before the race. They were jumpy, raring to go, looking resplendent in their new cobalt-blue t-shirts with lime green trim on the collar and sleeves. The dramatic white embroidered gazelle logo looked like it was flying.

'Well, mateys,' he announced to a collective cheer, 'we'll shortly be off on our grand adventure. While we've received notice that there are stormy waters ahead, be not alarmed. We've trained well for all weather scenarios and have a team that I know will be at its strongest when it is tested.' He paused as the crew laughed and several performed power poses. 'While our ultimate goal is to get to Constitution Dock as quickly as the *Gazelle* can take us, and hopefully not too far behind those *mighty maxis*, safety will always be our priority. Be on time for your watch. Always look out for each other, and enjoy the ride. TO YOUR STATIONS,' he cried out as if he was Captain Jack Aubrey on the HMS *Surprise*.

At 13:00, Australian Eastern Daylight Savings Time (AEDT), the starting cannon fired and eighty yachts unfurled their sails and raced toward Sydney Heads and out into the open ocean. The *Eagle Express* made its way out first through the heads and past the Sow and Pigs Reef, and then quickly tacked across to Hornby Lighthouse, with *Sopranos* one minute behind them. The *Blue Gazelle* battled with the *Kiwi Kings* for third place, with these artificial placement honours a symbolic psychological achievement rather than an actual one. Anything could happen now they were on the open water with a long way to go. The waves were already cresting at two metres and the wind was picking up, now at twenty knots. Crew members moved into well-practiced routines as they trimmed the sails, monitored the constantly shifting weather and waves and adjusted course in accordance with Scott's instructions. Several maxi yachts were choosing to sail further away from the coast, hoping to pick up on stronger winds, while the smaller entrants were keeping within sight of land.

There were 150 nautical miles to travel down to Eden at the bottom of the New South Wales south coast. Not straying far from the coast, the *Gazelle* had a faster than expected sail down past Bateman's Bay to Bega, filling the team with optimism. After eight hours they began the catnap roster, with one person leaving for a three-hour break, and then another, an hour later. They were soon on their own, with eyes always on the clouds, the waves and the barometer. The weather bureau was predicting that a confluence of low-pressure systems would create turbulent conditions as yachts approached the Bass Strait, which is colloquially referred to as The Paddock. The meeting of waves from the Indian Ocean on one side and the Pacific on the other can create wild winds and enormous waves in the sometimes-shallow waters.

Wind speeds picked up to thirty knots with a southerly swell as they approached Bega. They had already started reefing the sails at 25 knots and continued with this rolling of one edge of the canvas on itself, to ensure the vessel's stability. The sky darkened as a wall of black approached at speed. Within minutes it was as dark as midnight. Lightning began to strike around them and rain poured down like thick ropes. Those crew on their break became soaked in their bunks and wearily joined their colleagues again on deck. Skye was pouring over weather charts and discussing tactics with Scott and Jason when they heard the dreaded *Mayday Mayday* call over the radio. The *Kiwi Kings* were in trouble and had activated the *Man Overboard* (MOB) signal on the GPS system. Two minutes later, Seb's mate Brendan had been recovered. The Kiwi crew were rattled by the potential loss of a crew member and a short break near Mallacoota was agreed to, before the dangerous Tasman crossing. They needed rest and had their fingers crossed that sailing conditions would improve before they headed south again. Similar conversations were occurring on the *Blue Gazelle* as they examined the latest weather forecast.

WIND: 30/40 knots with strong gusts in a south to south easterly direction. Winds increasing and reaching to 40/45 knots.

*WAVES: 2 to 3 metres increasing to 4 to 5
metres*

*SWELL: 1 to 2 metres, increasing to 3 to 4 metres
south of Lennards Island.*

The crossing was going to be challenging.

'Whaddaya reckon, Skye,' Scott asked. 'Should we head out across The Paddock?'

'I'm a bit nervous. That low-pressure system is intensifying and the weather station at Wilson's Promontory is saying that wind gusts are picking up to forty-five knots. However, on the positive side, the yacht and the crew are doing great. I think we can do it.'

'Me too. But let's do it carefully.'

'Agreed.'

Moments later the radio buzzed with the second of the twice-daily *SKEDs*, the familiar name for the scheduled check-in from race organisers where they were required to report their longitude and latitude, crew capability status and sailing plans. Of interest to organisers was their intention to either proceed across the Bass Strait now, or to wait until conditions improved. They listened patiently as each of the eighty yachts in the race called out their location and status. Scott and Skye already knew that they were twenty nautical miles behind the *Fair Go* and *Eagle Express* maxis. It might be possible to reduce the gap if they enjoyed favourable conditions. The challenge was that favourable conditions for catching the race leaders were also very dangerous.

'Everybody ready to cross?' Scott called out to the crew.

'Bring it on,' Smithy replied.

There was a crew watch change to ensure that the freshest among them were at their best for the difficult hours they knew were in front of them. The spinnaker was lowered with only a storm jib remaining, to guide them over the ever-increasing waves in the storm. Extensive tacking was required and the pace slowed. For two hours the *Gazelle* inched forward, climbing waves sometimes reaching twenty feet in height. An hour later, winds reached fifty knots, waves were reaching thirty feet and the rain now felt like nails rather than ropes. Scott's very real concern for the survival of the yacht, was only overshadowed by his fears for the crew. Lightning was crackling and striking all around them, and Scott's cries to *hold tight* could barely be heard as the yacht dipped and tilted in the ever-growing maelstrom. The climb up always preceded a drop on the other side, with one particularly brutal descent tipping the yacht and flinging the crew across the yacht. Skye called out in pain as her damaged shoulder hit the wall at speed and her ribs cracked. She was helped into her bunk where she was roped in with lee-cloths for her safety and given painkillers. Other crew members were becoming incapacitated by sea sickness. Scott made the decision to lower the sail, throw out the sea anchor and to ride out the storm. As Jason and Scott were about to join the rest of the crew below, a blinding light caught their attention. It was coming from another yacht; one they didn't recognise and which was bewilderingly not showing on their computer screen as a participant in the race. It was approaching at speed and their immediate concern was a spectacular collision. They screamed and waved their arms to warn the yacht away, before collapsing on the deck with their hands pushed hard against their heads, as they unsuccessfully tried to stifle the ringing in their ears that was blocking out the sounds of the tempest.

Many hours later, Scott tried to open his eyes. Each time he did, nausea overwhelmed him. He'd lost all sense of place and time and water was washing over him. He tried to sit up and immediately threw up into the mixture of seawater, bilge and vomit that was sloshing across the floor of the galley. The automatic bilge pump had clearly broken. Wiping his mouth with the back of his hand, he pulled himself into a seated position against the wall and took three deep breaths. He opened his eyes slowly and his head started spinning again. There was nothing he could do to stop the dry retching that followed.

'Have some water Scott, or lemonade,' came a voice from a bunk overhead. It was Skye, looking down at him with concern. A deep groan caught his attention. Smithy was also lying amongst the swill on the floor. Scott crawled across to the fridge, pulled out two bottles of 7up, passing one to Jason, and then taking a long swig from the other. He placed his palm to his forehead willing the pounding to stop. Feeling slightly better, he stood up slowly and swept his eyes across the instrumentation panel. It was dark. *Power must be out.* A small battery powered clock was still ticking.

'What? Where did the last four hours go?' Scott asked, examining their coordinates. 'And where is everybody? Is everyone safe?'

'Yes. They're all on deck, and safe,' Skye said, 'and doing remarkably well everything considered.'

'One of the worst storms I've ever encountered. And did the *Gazelle* sustain any damage?' Scott asked, his rational brain kicking in.

'Yes, but we're still seaworthy according to Becky.' Skye replied.

'And did the other yacht hit us?'

'What?' Skye asked.

'The other yacht. The black and grey maxi,' Jason said groggily as he massaged his temple with his fingertips, trying to dull the pounding migraine.

'I don't know. I've been strapped in here throughout the storm. If you let me out and help me up, we can both go up deck and have a look.'

'Do you think you should get up? That was a nasty hit you took.'

'I'd like to try.'

Skye grimaced as Scott helped her first to sit up, and then to slide off the bed.

'Not a good idea for you to move around, Skye. I can tell that you're trying to disguise how much pain you're in. Even taking the companion way up on deck has its risks. If you're not going to stay in your bunk, it's best if you stay here in the navigator's chair, and not move.' She nodded and didn't refute his suggestion, recognising that he had her well-being and safety as his priority.

Scott and Jason held tightly to the guard rails as they went up on deck. They were both woozy, still experiencing what felt like seasickness on steroids. An audit of the damage to the *Gazelle* revealed a crack in the rudder, and that the jib sheets had nearly chaffed through. The communication and electrical systems had also failed. Smithy rebooted the system and they were once more online. Scott called for the sea anchor to be pulled in and for the main sail to once again be hoisted. He appreciated the feel of the evening breeze against his face. It helped him to think more clearly, although he still had a pounding headache. Looking up, he was pleased that he could once again see the stars. In some ways he was an old-fashioned sailor, preferring physical charts and star-gazing to modern maritime information systems. Still, these systems were important and revealed that they'd been caught in a mini cyclone within a larger storm front. Scott radioed a nearby oil platform to gain additional insights on local weather conditions. It was good to speak to someone who was literally in and out of the clouds, closely monitoring the lightning strikes, swell and wind speeds.

With favourable wind conditions returning, the *Blue Gazelle* charted a pathway on the inside of Flinders Island and then down between Clarke Island and Cape Portland, on the mainland of Tasmania. There was not a breath of wind when they finally arrived on the Tasman coast. The crew were soaked and fatigued. Everywhere, including the bunks, was wet and stinking, not providing suitable conditions for anyone to get rested. They were grateful when the sun came up. Those on breaks lay prostrate on the deck. As they approached Maria Island, they finally saw half a dozen of the other yachts in the race, including the maxi yacht *Sailing Nicoise*. They knew that *Eagle Express* and the *Fair Go Flyer* had already taken first and second place for line honours. Who would win on handicap was yet to be decided.

ALONE DAY 105

'Where the bloody hell is he then? If he's drowned or topped himself it'll be the end of the program. While they all signed an acknowledgement of risk and indemnification agreement, that won't stop the media storm or the family member insisting on compensation. Have you looked at his recordings and pulled any new insights?'

'His last post had him heading into the bush to check his trap, leaving us to watch a possum steal an eel from his smokehouse.'

'We know he wanted to be out of the competition in time to sail in the Sydney to Hobart.'

'But the race has already started. It's too late.'

'He was a bit flat after you showed him that message from the captain of the yacht. Maybe that pushed him over the edge,' Ralph said.

'What did the doctor say about his mental disposition?'

'Said he hadn't spent enough time with him to make a judgement either way. However, he did remark that you shouldn't underestimate the impact of isolation on anyone. We hadn't been to see him in over three weeks. If we'd kept to our regular two-week check in schedule, we'd have been in a better position to determine if was thinking of topping himself.'

Nelson ignored this last remark. 'What did the camp look like?'

'Camera and shelter still there, but we couldn't find his back pack. And most importantly, we found his tracker.'

'Aha. He took the tracker off as he didn't want to be found. Then the best working theory was that he left of his own free will thereby nullifying any insurance if he came to any harm after leaving the camp. I assume his raft was gone?'

'Don't know. I'll check when we go back.'

'Very important. Get a sniffer dog from your mate in the police service and see if they can find a path he might have taken. Look again for the second camera near a trap. There may be more than one trap. And leave the main footage with me. I'll go through it frame by frame and see what I can learn about his activities while he was alone.'

'Did his sister ever come back to you when you reached out to record that message for him?'

'No.'

'Can you put in a call to his friend Scott Harmon then. The number two emergency contact. All very low-key mind you. Just determine if Seb has been in touch.'

'Will do. The winner's already crossed the line, but his yacht's not yet come in. Should arrive in the next couple of days.'

'That's all the time I need to pull everything together. After that I'll have to tell the higher-ups we've got a problem and contact the police, and then all hell will break loose.'

'Extra strong,' Ralph said passing Nelson a large takeaway coffee the next morning. They were both back at the television studio's main office in Hobart. 'Guessing you did an all-nighter?'

'I didn't have a choice. The clock is ticking and my mind is spinning.' He sipped the steaming beverage, rubbed his eyes before signalling for Ralph to take a seat. 'I thought I'd get answers but all I have is questions. Like, why did he take the tracker off? Perhaps it was faulty, which it might have been as there are some bizarre movements around the camp that don't align with what the sailor said he was doing. Lots of time making and repairing the smokehouse.'

'We know he had trouble with a possum,' Ralph replied.

'And he was sometimes in the one place for hours. Just sitting there, or lying down, not moving. Depressed perhaps? The doctor said it was possible. From the footage and our visit, it was clear he had a couple of mood swings.'

'Then he's done a runner,' Ralph said.

'Could be. It's consistent with the missing backpack. Where would be go?'

'Who knows? Who cares? No longer our problem and we no longer need to go to the police if he's chosen to be missing in action.'

'How will we explain his disappearance to the other contestants?'

'Easy. He left without tapping-out, thereby disquali-fying himself from the competition. We can decide later on if we include his footage or not. If we do, it'd be a form of public shaming, and if we don't, it'd be as if he was never in the competition.' Nelson bowed his head, admiringly.

'Did you learn anything else from the footage?' Ralph asked.

'Sometimes a bit of repetitive banging in the back-ground. Could've been the raft battering against a log.' Nelson shrugged his shoulders. 'Anyway, we've gotta get on with planning the award ceremony. Can you check in on our two patients? Great if they could keep their bandages on for the final show, and let me know if you find out anything from Mr Ward's nearest and dearest.'

'Will do.'

DAY 106

It was approaching 5am on the thirtieth of December when the *Blue Gazelle* came into view of the three thousand spectators up early to welcome them and the other competitors to Hobart. The crew of the *Blue Gazelle* wearily returned their waves, recognising the good wishes. Two ambulance officers with a gurney were waiting on the dock to take Skye to hospital and another two officers checked each crew member over, to determine if they should also be admitted. Scott shakily stepped ashore and shook the hand of the race official.

'Well done, Scott. You made it.'

'Thank you, sir.'

'You caught a bit of bad weather.'

'That we did. One heck of a storm. Tested the crew, and

they shone, showing that they were more than worthy of being on the *Gazelle*.'

'We'll let you know the official results shortly. Anything you wish to report?'

Scott blinked. His brain was foggy, but he knew now was the time to flag the interference from the phantom yacht.

'We nearly crashed into another yacht.'

'Really? Which one?'

'Don't know. Our communications systems went down and I was violently ill.'

'That would have been the weather.'

'You'd think so, but nah. I've weathered bad storms before and rarely get sick at sea. This yacht, this maxi beast, had a laser that was pointed directly at me and Smithy. It created this instant and terrifying hum in my head, and I couldn't think or breathe and I pretty much passed out. So did Jase.' He paused, watching the official note down what he'd told him. 'Luckily, we were the only ones on deck as I'd ordered the rest below. They came back to get us and dragged us below. Look. We're all beat. Maybe I'll be able to give you more once I've had some sleep. I just wanted you to make a note in the race records. Is that enough for now?'

The race official regarded him sympathetically. 'Yes. We can talk later. Once you feel better. You ready to face the media pack?'

'No. Do I have to?' The look on the official's face

signalled that it was non-negotiable and Scott remembered that the pre-race briefing had emphasized this. It was a requirement from the sponsors. He gave the barest of nods.

'Give me three minutes.'

Scott turned to his crew, who were piling their belongings on the dock and had started cleaning the *Blue Gazelle*.

'Stop, stop, stop everyone. Cleaning can wait. It's time to rest and recover and tomorrow we'll celebrate. We may not have achieved our placement goals, but we achieved so much more. You should be proud. So proud. This is arguably the toughest offshore race in the world. It's certainly the hardest I've ever done and you did it. *We did it.* If I wasn't so damn tired with a monster migraine, I'd be shouting this through a megaphone. So.' He paused. 'Let's all stand proudly together for the media scrum that awaits us, and then go to our respective hotels and *sleep*, and tomorrow we'll properly toast our success at the Hope and Anchor. Agreed?'

'*Yes. You bet. Too right,*' came the joyful replies. Scott quickly texted Charlotte and his family, letting them know he'd safely arrived, before joining his crew at the end of the dock. He was in a daze as he walked towards the flashing lights of the media scrum. With his head pounding and his vision blurred, it felt like an out-of-body experience. Two minutes later someone had their arm around his shoulders shepherding him away from the noise and the lights. They accompanied him to his hotel, spoke with check-in and then guided him to his room. Scott muttered words of thanks as the door closed behind him and he was finally alone in the dark calm of a vanilla hotel room. He stripped and walked into the bathroom and was shaken by the mirror's reflection of gaunt eyes and sallow skin. Mechanically he turned on the taps and waited for the warm water to fall, before stepping into their soft embrace. The gentle rhythmic patter on his face was mesmerising, and moments later he nodded off, slipping to the floor and banging his head on the tiles. His hand reached blindly for the taps to stem the flow and then to the bump on his head. He groaned. Just another pain point in an increasingly aching world. He crawled out of the shower recess and pulled a towel from its rail. He dabbed himself dry and didn't notice the bright slash of blood steaked across the white bath sheet. Holding tightly to the bathroom door handle, he pulled himself to his feet, unsteadily walked to the bed, crawled inside the cocoon of sheets and drifted off into a black hole.

Scott was still lying unmoving in his bed, when a copy of the Hobart Mercury was slipped under his door the following morning. If he'd woken, he'd have been mildly annoyed to read how the *Blue Gazelle*'s journey had been reported.

DAY 107

At the Hope and Anchor, 31 December

'Skye's back in Sydney and having surgery today,' Jason announced to the crew gathered around a high table at the Hope and Anchor Hotel.

'Poor thing. Hope it goes OK. I wonder if she'll sell the *Gazelle*. Can't imagine she'll wanna go out again,' Lexie said.

'Maybe Scott knows,' Nick offered.

'Possibly. Where's Scotty? It's not like him to be late,' said Honey.

'Not responding to texts,' Lexie said looking at her phone. 'Did you see him at breakfast Jase?'

He shook his head. 'Has anyone seen or heard from him since the media meet yesterday? Everyone shook their heads, looking from one to the other.

'I'm worried,' Honey said.

'Me too,' Anika added. 'He wasn't great yesterday.'

Jason quickly scanned the face of each crew member. Their collective concern for Scott was clear. They all left, their half-consumed drinks abandoned on the table.

At the hotel

'My name's Jason Smith and I'd like access to the room of Scott Harmon. I'm a mate and I'm worried about him.'

'One moment please.' The receptionist typed a few keys and reviewed her screen. Her brow furrowed, she looked up at Jason and softly said, 'He's no longer here.'

'What?' Jason replied loudly, attracting a curious look from a woman checking in at the other end of the counter.

'The housekeeper found him unresponsive this morning. Looks like he fell and hit his head in the shower. An ambulance was called. He's been taken to the Hobart Royal Hospital.'

'Which is where, eh...?' Jason asked, feeling anxious for Scott and guilty that he hadn't checked in on his friend.

'It's a few blocks away. One of our team can escort you if you like...' she said. Jason didn't hear her offer as he was already out the door.

At the hospital

It took several frustrating minutes for Jason to establish his credentials as Scott's friend, and the nearest person to family, in Tasmania at this time. He explained to the nurse at reception, that Scott's wife and sister were in London, and that Scott's parents were on a plane somewhere, en route to London as they spoke, and out of contact. Jason identified himself by his driver's license, a joyful photo on his phone of Scott with the crew prior to race departure on Boxing Day and then, finally, by pointing to his crew shirt and the *Blue Gazelle* logo. The nurse put her hand softly on his arm.

'It's OK. I believe you, Jason. Come quietly with me. He's in intensive care.'

'For a concussion?'

'It's more serious than that.'

Jason frowned and followed her into the room with the scent of hospital-grade disinfectant and the constant beeping of monitors. They passed a row of beds containing patients with varying levels of obvious injury and distress. Scott was in the last bed, hooked up to two machines and with an oxygen mask covering his face. Jason was aghast at the physical state of his friend. The nurse signalled for him to follow her to a small room at the end of the ward, with a desk and two chairs. She pulled out a pen and paper.

'You clearly had a traumatic race, given his injuries.' Jason wasn't sure if this was a statement or a question.

'Yes, it was tough. Really tough,' Jason replied.

'We had one of your other crew members in yesterday. Also suffering from multiple injuries.'

'That would've been Skye.'

'Yes, Skye. She was flown back to Sydney for specialist surgery.'

'What do I tell his family about his condition?'

'It's best you get them to call me directly.'

'Of course,' he replied, understanding her need for discretion. He provided her with the names of Scott's immediate family. She checked her notes, looked back at him and hesitated.

'It's odd. Your friend is physically fit, but his underlying vital signs are of concern. Is there anything else that you can tell me which would he explain why he has slipped into a coma?'

'A coma?' Jason called out spontaneously, evoking a quick *shh* from the nurse.

'Does he take drugs?'

'Never.'

'Even something to keep him awake on the trip? Many yachties do.'

'No way. I would've seen it. You have no personal space on a racing yacht.' Jason put his hand to his temple aware that a thundering headache was building and his ears were ringing.

'OK. I didn't mean to offend. I've got to ask these questions. Are you OK, Mr Smith? Can I get you a glass of water?'

'Yes please,' he whispered. 'And a couple of paraceta-mols.' Jason threw back the offered painkillers and chased them down with a chug of water. He took two breaths, mentally steeled himself and stood up. He mentally wished away the nauseous feeling that was building.

'I think I should get one of my colleagues to give you a fuller checkup,' the nurse said, looking concerned.

'Not today thanks. I need to contact Scott's family. Then I'll have a snooze. I'm sure I'll feel better after I've slept.'

'OK. As you wish.' They stood and Jason walked over to Scott's bed. He leant close to Scott's ear.

'Mate. It's Jase. You're scaring me. Wake up if you can.' It seemed a stupid thing to say but was all that came to mind. He then leant over again. 'The team is rooting for you.' The nurse escorted him out of the ward and reminded him to look after his own health. He retraced his steps, and was soon outside in the bright sunshine, blinking furiously. He checked his pockets and realised his sunglasses were in his hotel room.

Jason was having difficulty thinking; processing what he needed to do next. He knew he needed to get the messages right, to avoid unnecessary panic. The team were waiting to hear from him, but he needed to speak with Charlotte first. *What time was it in London? Early morning? Would a text wake her? Would it matter?'* His hand flew to his temple. The painkillers hadn't kicked in yet. Like a homing pigeon, he focussed on his end destination, step by step. He needed to lie down. *Two minutes away. Nearly there. Press the number two button. Ten steps to go.* He opened the door to his hotel room and sank onto his bed. The pillow was so soft and he just wanted to... He shook his head, fighting the urge to slip away and sat up to text a message.

> Hey team. Pleased to see Scott
> getting great care. Passed on your
> wishes. Only family can visit.

He worried about what to say to Charlotte. His fuzzy brain had difficulty forming a coherent sentence.

> Scott fell and hit head at Hobart
> Royal. Call me.

PART 3

LONDON

DAY 103 – FOUR DAYS EARLIER

Christmas Day had been weird and wonderful; a day of contrasts with new traditions and old friends. *Pigs in blankets*, that is, sausages wrapped in streaky bacon, were served for breakfast together with savoury bread and butter pudding. Miranda ate most of the pudding, keen to feed-up, anticipating a long birthing process in the days to come. For lunch, Charlotte cooked a weighty turkey, with pork and cider stuffing, accompanied by roast potatoes and parsnips and served with Brussels sprouts on the side. Dessert was Christmas pudding with brandy butter. Back in Australia, Christmas Day lunch was still held in the front paddock at her grandparents' farm, just out of Bangalow. Charlotte reflected on how the Aussie Christmas would play out with prawns for starters, followed by baked lamb, crispy butter-roasted potatoes with thyme, served with crunchy Asian broccoli salad, which was doused with sesame ginger dressing. Dessert would be mango and passionfruit pavlova, with the mangos being pulled from her grandfather's trees. In Bangalow, they'd drive to the beach at Byron for an early morning dip, before the heat and the feasting that was to follow. Charlotte felt a little homesick but then reminded herself about the rarity of enjoying a Christmas in London.

The three of them donned woollen hats and strolled through nearby Wandsworth Park and then along the River Thames, enjoying the unusual overnight sprinkling of snow. Miranda and Charlotte then played five hundred while Mason washed up. They all went to bed by eight so they could rise early to watch the start of the Sydney to Hobart yacht race. It was exhilarating and colourful with the television reporters building up a sense of anticipation. As night fell in Australia, the race coverage stopped, so they switched on the television to watch the series *Death in Paradise*. With the tension building and just as Neville and Camille were about to uncover who had shot the concert pianist, Miranda's waters broke. Pandemonium ensued as Mason rushed to get her overnight bag and tried to book a taxi. This latter task proved difficult as it was a public holiday and few could be enticed to come out in the falling snow and increasingly icy driving conditions. Offer of a fifty-pound tip soon made the difference and the three were on their way to the birthing suites at St Christophers.

It was relatively quiet on the streets, with only a few out enjoying the novelty of snowflakes floating and falling.

Contractions were six minutes apart and lasting for thirty seconds when Miranda was finally settled in her suite. While it felt like birth was imminent, the midwife reassured them that there was still a way to go. Charlotte went off in search of a hot beverage vending machine while Mason checked the race status. His brow furrowed and he immediately started checking different racing websites.

'Everything OK?' Charlotte asked him when she returned with three coffees.

Miranda looked at him expectantly too. A reassuring smile blossomed across his face, masking his underlying nerves.

'While it's gently snowing here it's a bit stormy in southern New South Wales. It'll make for an interesting race and the placings could surprise everyone.'

'Scott has experience sailing in all types of weather,' Miranda said reassuringly, touching Charlotte's hand before spontaneously crying out following a faster-than-expected contraction.

'Room's a little crowded,' said the midwife, who had returned with a doctor. 'Can you give us a few minutes to check her over?'

In the corridor, Charlotte and Mason went into a

huddle looking at the latest race reporting on his phone. A yacht of similar size to the *Blue Gazelle* had tipped during the storm with a man overboard. The yachtie had been recovered. No other information was available at this time. The midwife returned.

'She's progressing well. Mason, if you'd like to come back in.'

Charlotte hugged him and watched him tentatively follow the midwife back into the delivery room where Miranda's moans were increasing in volume. Charlotte took a seat in the waiting room and googled '*incident during Sydney Hobart yacht race*'. Every website repeated the same information that Mason had already shared with her. She also learnt that the *Blue Gazelle* was not currently placed in the first five yachts. This mattered little to her. The yacht's safe arrival at Constitution Dock was the only news she was waiting on, apart from the safe arrival of Scott's niece and nephew.

DAY 104

Miranda's screams were peeling paint from the walls of the birthing suite at St Christophers, or so Mason thought. With each tightening sensation, the volume of her cries increased. Mason tried to comfort her, and was rewarded with a bone-breaking squeeze of the hand. The doctor popped in and out of the room, clearly attending to multiple mothers-to-be, while the midwife cooed reassuring messages to Miranda that she was doing *very well*. Meanwhile, Charlotte drifted in and out of sleep on the sofa in the waiting room. Her phone buzzed, waking her up a few hours later. It was five o'clock in the morning and save for the faint glow of light from a street lamp, still pitch dark outside. At first, she thought, that given the early hour, it must be a message from someone in Australia, possibly Scott but more likely her parents, as Scott was still racing.

She unconsciously flinched when she saw she'd received a message from Teal Dubois.

Teal's business card said that she supported international trade out of the Australian embassy in Paris, but her more substantive role was working as an operative for the Australian Security Intelligence Organisation (ASIO). Their paths had crossed when Charlotte had been looking for a missing friend in Italy the previous year. She'd met Teal at a party on a yacht in Rome, just before she was caught up in an international trafficking ring. Teal had provided surprising support and had then invited her to accept a more formal association with ASIO, resulting in an intelligence gathering trip to Myanmar, just as the generals staged a military coup. There'd been a disagreement about the way the assignment had been concluded, but Charlotte and Teal had remained on good terms, even though Charlotte had severed her relationship with the agency. Teal's message was a question.

> Can we chat at the Sustainable
> Fashion exhibition?

Teal hadn't checked to see if Charlotte was attending as she obviously knew she'd be there.

> Yes. Of course.

> Great

About...?

An opportunity

A reply with the usual lack of context.

'Why should I expect anything else?' Charlotte muttered to herself before switching her screen back to the main race websites. She could see that two maxis were soon to cross the finish line. The storm had slowed most yachts down, many still struggling to cross Bass Strait.

'Ahem.' Charlotte looked up to see Mason looking at her with tired eyes, wet cheeks and a huge smile. 'Our family has now officially doubled. Would you like to come and meet the newest members?' Relief and joy flooded Charlotte's emotions. She jumped up and hugged Mason, and then looped her arm through his as they walked to the birthing suite where two tiny, swaddled babies, were mewing in Miranda's arms.

Charlotte left the new parents and caught a taxi back to Putney where she tidied the house, and called her own parents with news of the twins' arrival, before crashing into bed. At midday she woke and cooked several batches of her friends' favourite comfort foods including lasagne, quiche lorraine and chicken tikka masala. She wanted a full freezer for when the family returned home. She also needed a distraction while she waited for news of the *Blue Gazelle's* safe arrival in Hobart. Checking her phone every two minutes, time passed slowly.

Back at the hospital later that afternoon, with a basket of raspberry and white chocolate muffins, Charlotte delighted in hearing stories of the twins' already superior powers of observation and intelligence, as reported by their father. More importantly, the babies had been named, Grace and Woodward, or Woody a nod to Mason's hopes that his son would share his interest in investigative journalism. Bob Woodward of Watergate fame was a hero for Mason.

'You know, Mason,' Charlotte remarked, 'maybe Grace'll be the one with the curious mind, tenacious spirit, and gift for words.'

'Of course. Yes. I like that idea. Maybe we could rename Grace...'

'No,' Miranda interjected firmly. 'Discussion over. Our children *have been named,* and will decide *their own life* direction. Now, darling. Why don't you focus your energies on investigating exactly where my brother is in the Tasman Sea.'

Mason leant over and kissed Miranda softly on the forehead, before turning his attention back to his phone. 'OK. Position update follows. He's sailing down the Tassie Coast, not far out from Ansons Bay,' Mason said.

'What a relief. So pleased they're in sight of land,' Charlotte replied, 'and if they can sail at ten knots, they should safely be moored at Constitution Dock by the time we wake tomorrow morning.' Looks of relief passed between them. 'It feels like Christmas Eve. I want to go to bed right now.'

'No way. I'm not so keen to repeat my most recent Christmas Eve. Memories are still fresh of heartburn, early contractions and the whole damn pushing out of these two little wriggly bundles,' Miranda said, before quickly adding, 'who are lovely. We're so lucky.' And then she started to weep. Mason lay down beside her on the bed, and Charlotte blew them both a kiss before leaving to get a bus back to Putney.

She was delighted to wake the following morning to see a text from Scott on her phone. She already knew from the race reporting that they'd experienced difficult conditions and that he was likely to be shattered. Scrunched together on the sofa, Mason and Charlotte watched a short piece on the BBC news about the race. Commentary touched on the winning yacht's celebrations, the tough sailing conditions, the incident of the sailor overboard off the coast of New South Wales and a registered dispute, between two yachts. There was a fleeting image of Scott and the crew of the *Blue Gazelle*, taken from a drone, looking exhausted as they stood together on the dock. She was disappointed that he hadn't called, but knew that as captain, he'd need to attend to the yacht, the crew and provide a report to race officials.

Still, there'd be plenty of time to talk about the events of the last week when they caught up again in person. It'd be like a second honeymoon.

She called her parents, and then Scott's parents to celebrate the yacht's safe arrival and to provide intricate details as to the twin's behaviour. Her description was less embellished than that provided by their father, but still joyfully received. Scott's parents were now excitedly packing their bags for their flight to London, to visit their daughter, son-in-law and first grandchildren. They'd been reluctant to pack until Scott had safely arrived in Hobart. Charlotte could now relax and enjoy visiting the sustainable fashion conference before packing her own bags to return to Australia, freeing up the guest room for Louis and Jenny Harmon. Their flights would cross, probably over India at thirty thousand feet.

DAY 106

Charlotte stepped out of her Uber at the exhibition centre at Canary Wharf, full of anticipation. The converted warehouse was imposing, with a wall of stained-glass windows, sparkling from the light of the winter sunshine, reflected off the snow. She unwrapped her scarf and removed her multi-coloured woollen hat and placed them in her tote bag.

At the registration desk, chaos reigned with phones ringing and voices talking excitedly in many different languages, as attendees waited patiently in an orderly queue to collect their conference lanyards. There was a band playing jazz in the main hall and the enticing smell of freshly baked croissants ensuring that the pop-up café would be a first stop for many. Charlotte moved slowly past the booths, taking as much inspiration from the fashion choices of others visiting, as from the showcase of sustainable products themselves. With their permission, she took photos of an asymmetrical, two-piece outfit designed by a Korean couple, which could serve as either medical scrubs or playful pyjamas. There were recycled woollen jumpers from Australia, transformed into tote bags and picnic blankets. She loved the simplicity of the linens and leather offerings from the Swedish contingent. And there were reimagined ballgowns from France, cut from outfits previously worn only once on the red carpet. Several stalls showcased casual-Friday jeans, recycled with clever applications of cotton, cartoon patches. As she walked by each stall, she overheard snippets of conversations about textile recycling and ethical production practices, with a tech-savvy designer demonstrating an app to track the carbon footprint of each piece of clothing. To her left, there were garments in colours of caramel, peach and hunter green made from organic cotton and hemp, and to her right clothing made from recycled marine debris, including stylish swimsuits crafted from discarded fishing nets. At the Indian stall, she admired linen garments coloured using dye from natural pigments like turmeric and cinnamon with the nearby scent of lavender from craftswomen in Provence, creating a titillating olfactory experience. As she was admiring the display of fabrics made from Sea Island cotton in the Caribbean a familiar voice from behind her said,

'C'est charmant, n'est-ce pas?'

'Hi Teal. Indeed it is a lovely piece. Are you looking for any particular type of fabric or garment today?' Charlotte asked, enjoying being a part of the façade.

'Maybe. More importantly, I have an opportunity for you to get even closer to beautiful fabrics and enchanting designs while you're participating in the Kaleidoscope on the Catwalk in Tasmania.'

'Tell me more. I've learnt by now that a simple proposal from you is rarely that.'

'Let's take a coffee and a croissant.'

Steaming beverages and pains au chocolat were ordered and the two women sat at a tiny table in the far corner of the hall, where they could have both privacy and a prime position from which to survey the bustling activity all around them.

'I have a contact at the Museum of Old and New Art who would value your assistance with the organisation of the event.'

'Go on,' Charlotte said.

'A liaison point with the other dozen designers show-casing their collection, discussing their specific needs for the evening.'

'And is there anything *or anyone* you'd like me to partic-ularly focus on?' Charlotte asked.

'Well, yes. Anya Orlov is one of Russia's most avant-garde designers. I'd like you to go out of your way to get to know her, and if possible, to meet her husband, Yuri. I hesitate to suggest that you ingratiate yourself with them as they are both smart and would pick up on any insincerity. If you can get them to trust you, and to disclose a little about their life, that would be helpful...'

'And can you tell me more about her husband Yuri?'

Teal regarded her thoughtfully. 'He's from Belarus. Was a scientist at a government-run organisation, not dissimilar to the Commonwealth Scientific and Industrial Research Organisation in Australia.'

'And which area of science does he, or did he, specialise in?'

'The energy sector.'

'That's a bit non-specific.'

'There's not that much publicly available information.'

'We both know *that's* not your primary source of information. If you want me to help you, I need more. Why are you resisting telling me more?'

'I'm trying to protect you. The less you know the better.'

Charlotte's eyebrows flickered involuntarily. 'That's concerning,' she dryly remarked. 'How dangerous is this person of interest?'

'The man himself? I don't think he's dangerous at all. He's a highly skilled researcher who loves the arts. It's how he met his wife.' Teal paused, looking at her thoughtfully, evaluating how much more she would share. 'However, there are dangerous people within his circle. You need to avoid them.'

'That's a contradictory request. You want me to get close to this couple, but not too close. Where's the line?'

'I don't know,' Teal replied. 'It's ambiguous.'

'I think you should ask someone else.'

'We have others working on this, but no one with such an easy pathway to forming a relationship with the couple, that would not arouse suspicion.'

'Can I let you know?'

'Take the liaison role with the Museum. You're already exhibiting at the event. You can decide once you are there, if you feel comfortable doing more.'

'I'll let you know,' Charlotte replied firmly, refusing to be coerced into something she knew too little about.

'Of course. You know where to reach me.'

Charlotte ran the conversation with Teal over in her mind as she waited to catch the Jubilee tube to Waterloo where she'd change onto the South Western Railway line to Putney. She had reason to be cynical about any request from an ASIO operative that on the surface appeared straightforward. At least Teal was being honest about not sharing everything with her about the request, and that there was danger involved. This had not been the case when she had ventured into Myanmar on a *simple* information gathering exercise, before the military launched a coup d'etat. She remembered the danger she'd been in, but also that she'd been supported. Taking a bigger role at the fashion show was not a commitment to do anything else. As long as it didn't take time away from her catch-up with Scott. Which reminded her that he'd not sent another text or tried to call. Looking at her watch she knew he'd be asleep now. She'd call first thing in the morning. Outside Putney station she was pleased to bump into Mason carrying a small overnight bag.

'How's Miranda, Woody and Grace?' Charlotte asked

'Miranda's milk is in and the twins are feeding well. A bit of a bumpy start there, but now they're gaining weight. Their mother is feeling *more herself* after a refreshing blood transfusion. Might be home tomorrow, or the day after. I hopefully have the last change of clothes with me to drop off. Speaking about dropping off, have you heard from Scott?'

'Only the text message that he sent when he arrived.'

'Miranda's miffed that he hasn't asked what his niece and nephew are called. But maybe Jenny's told them. I'm personally feeling a little neglected as he promised to give me the *real story* around what it's like to captain a vessel during an offshore race in difficult weather conditions.'

'You know he's limited around what he can say 'cause of

the terms and conditions of signing up for the race. Sponsors are precious about their brand and media commentary is tightly controlled.'

'I know, I know. I could work with that. It's just... anyway, let him know that his next call should be to me, when you hear from him. Well, after he's called my wife of course.'

Charlotte smiled. 'I will.'

Charlotte packed her bags and spent the evening tidying the flat in preparation for the arrival of the two newest members of the Murray family, as well as Miranda and Scott's parents. Snuggled under the blankets she kept checking her texts, emails and racing updates, ever hopeful she'd hear from Scott. Now that the results had been communicated and the winners celebrated, media interest had moved on to the upcoming Australian Open tennis match, due to start in Melbourne in two weeks' time. She was restless and heard Mason returning to the flat just after midnight. He was then on the phone to his parents for an hour. It took another hour to fall asleep, with her phone held tightly under the covers.

The following morning at 6am, Charlotte read Jason's text.

Scott fell and hit head at Hobart
Royal. Call me.

Confused, she tried to call Jason. *Why had he fallen at a hospital? Why was he there?*

It went through to voicemail after three rings. She left a message and walked out to the kitchen to make a cup of tea, hoping it'd provide mental clarity. Mason was also awake, sitting at the dining table intently reading something on his tablet. He looked up as she walked out, concern etched across his face.

'You'll want to read this. Something potentially dangerous happened during the race between the *Blue Gazelle* and another yacht. There's an investigation underway.'

Charlotte leant across to read the article when her phone rang. It was Jason. She answered immediately.

'Jase. It's Charlotte. What happened to Scott?' she blurted out, forgoing any friendly informal banter. Jason cleared his throat before responding.

'He fell in the shower and hit his head. A housemaid found him and called an ambulance.'

'So he didn't fall at the hospital? Why did he fall? Did he slip on something?'

'Um. I don't know,' Jason replied slowly. Charlotte paused and looked at Mason.

'Are you OK Jase? You don't sound yourself.'

'It was a brutal race. Several crew were injured and we only narrowly avoided crashing into another yacht, using dirty tricks.'

'What do you mean, *dirty tricks*?'

'They had these lights shining on us, me and Scotty, when we were desperately trying to secure the boat and keep everyone safe during the storm.'

'Did they do that to anyone else? The light shining thing?'

'No, not that we've heard. No one's seen them. In fact, it seems like they weren't even in the race. So go figure. Why would you bother doing that if there was no sailing advantage to be gained?'

'What have the officials said?' Charlotte asked.

'Not much. Scott lodged an official compliant and they're investigating. But they're sceptical. I'd be making my own investigations except my thinking's stuffed and my head hurts. Scott made the same complaint last time I spoke to him.'

'Which was when?'

'At the media conference when we arrived.'

'And nothing since then?'

'Nope.'

'But you've been to visit him in hospital?'

'Yep, I did, but he was in a deep sleep.' He paused. 'Like a coma.'

'What!' Charlotte said incredulously.

'You should call the hospital,' Jason said, giving her the number.

'Get some rest Jase. Sounds like you need it in spades.'

'I will.'

'And thanks for calling, and for looking out for Scott. I've got this now. As long as my flight isn't delayed, I'll be there in a little over thirty hours. I'll call you once I'm back.'

'OK. Talk then. Safe travels.'

Charlotte hung up and immediately called the Royal Hobart Hospital. The nurse in Intensive Care reassured her that Scott was stable and that they were carefully monitoring his vital signs. She said that the body was an unusual self-managing organism and that it was difficult to know when Scott would wake up.

Charlotte put her phone down and looked at Mason as he took a long sip of tea from his Star Wars themed mug.

'Did you hear any of that?'

'I did, and like you, I'm considering how much we should tell everyone.'

'Do you agree we hold off on telling any members of the Harmon family about Scott being unconscious until we know more?' Charlotte asked. Mason tapped his index finger on the table, considering her request and then glanced at his watch.

'Yes. Louis and Jenny will shortly be airborne and impossible to contact. Let's save them any unnecessary worry during the long flight.'

'Agreed.'

'And Miranda's still in recovery mode herself. Can't afford for her milk to dry up given the challenge she's had in getting it going.'

'Good. We're on the same page. Now, I just need to manage my final call to her before I leave.'

Fortunately for Charlotte, Miranda was feeding the twins and unable to talk. She sent her virtual hugs via the nurse, along with a promise to call once she was back in Australia.

It was noisy waiting at the departure gate for the flight to open for boarding. Scattered among the business folk were holidaymakers, easily distinguishable by their playful demeanour and straw hats. A family of four sat near Charlotte, the parents looking tired. The father, in a paisley shirt, tried to entertain his young son with a game of cards, while the mother, rummaged through a backpack in search of snacks. Their teenage daughter, sporting ripped jeans and wearing white branded headphones that nearly swallowed her head, scrolled continuously through her phone, occasionally glancing up at the electronic departure board.

In the far corner, a football team occupied several rows; the players dressed in matching maroon tracksuits bearing their club's logo. Some engaged in animated conversations, while a few took the opportunity to rest, eyes closed and slouched back uncomfortably in the metal seats.

Charlotte felt her phone vibrate. It was Teal, the last person she wanted to speak to. She momentarily considered not taking the call, but this was a perfect opportunity to respond to her request.

'Hello Teal. I'm in a noisy departure lounge and about to return to Australia.'

'I know.'

'Of course you do,' Charlotte said softly. She wasn't sure if Teal had heard her.

'I have additional information for you which will…'

'Let me stop you there, Teal. I can't help you in Hobart. I'm thinking about pulling out of the fashion show altogether. I have a family emergency…'

'I know you do. That's why I'm calling. We have reason to believe that Yuri Orlov was connected to the attack on the *Blue Gazelle*.'

'Attack?'

'Yes. An attack. A weapon was deployed.'

'A weapon? This makes no sense. Why the *Blue Gazelle*? They're not a naval craft.'

'I know. I'll have more information by the time you arrive in Australia. We'll talk again then.'

The pre-boarding announcement for the flight to Sydney via Singapore echoed throughout the lounge, creating a ripple of movement, and making it impossible to continue the conversation. Charlotte rang off and watched the business folk pack away their devices, the holiday-makers gather their belongings and children, and the football team stand up, almost in unison, and noisily stretch. All of them had a back story and were in transition to the next chapter. She wondered what more would be revealed in the *Blue Gazelle's* story when she finally arrived in Tasmania.

DAY 107

'You are very lucky. That's healing nicely,' the doctor said, examining her hand. Galina was only half listening. It'd been three days since she'd been transported to the Royal Hobart Hospital by helicopter, but it'd felt like two months. In that time, she'd examined every scenario that would explain Seb's disappearance. The possibility that he'd drowned on his swim back across the river, felt like the most plausible outcome. If this was the case, his body might soon emerge as the breakdown of his flesh would produce gases that would inflate his corpse, much like a balloon. Her heart sank. 'Yoo hoo, Galina,' the doctor said, breaking into her spiralling negativity. She looked up and gave him her full attention. 'Make an appointment with my assistant to see me again and be careful to keep your hand in sterile environments.'

Galina picked her bag up off the floor and walked out of his office.

'Oh hello. Didn't expect to meet a jackaroo from Dagoman land here,' she said as she walked into the waiting room. Archie smiled, touched she'd remembered which mob he was from. 'What happened to you?'

'Fell out of a tree. And you?'

'Encounter with a devil.'

'Goodness. You weren't trying to kill it, I hope?'

'Nope. Quite the opposite. I was trying to set it free from my trap and it bit me.'

'Nasty. You OK?'

'Jah. A few broken bones.' She held up her bandaged hand.

'Me too.' He pointed at his thigh-length plaster.

'Guess you're hanging around in Hobart until the big announcement and final filming?' she asked. Archie dipped his head.

'Do you know anyone in town?'

'Nah.'

'Wanna catch up for a drink at the Hope and Anchor Hotel? It's not far.'

'Yeah. Sure. Thanks. I'll be free once I'm finished here. Meet you there in thirty?'

'Done.' Galina made another appointment and waved at Archie as she left.

The Hope and Anchor Hotel remained the oldest licensed pub in Australia. It was a beautiful building with antiques and artefacts adorning the walls and sailors overflowing onto the pavement. It would be difficult to have much of a conversation, but that suited Galina. She took a stool at the bar and ordered a coke. When the barman returned, she signalled for him to lean in close.

'Have you seen Sebastian Ward lately?'

'Sebby? No. Not yet. His yacht arrived yesterday so he should be around. Mind you, they had a bit of trouble on the way down and maybe he's caught up in that.'

'What do you mean?'

'Complaints of interference. Look at today's paper.'

She gave him the thumbs up and started googling on her phone.

'Thanks for saving me a space,' Archie said as he leant his crutches against the bar and hopped on the stool beside her. She smiled at him and turned her phone upside down on the counter.

'Who d'ya reckon won?' he asked.

'The yacht race?'

'Nah, silly. Our competition.'

'Oh. I don't think they know yet.'

'What do you want to drink?'

'Ginger beer.' Galina waved at the barman and ordered

his drink. Archie scanned the room, enjoying watching the lively banter.

'Not surprising that there are so many people in here given the number of yachts out there. I actually spotted one of them that day I fell out of the tree and broke my leg and ended my dream of collecting the cash.'

'What? You're kidding me. You couldn't see the yachts here, no matter how tall your tree was. We were on the other side of Tassie.'

'Course not. I think it might've got lost. Must have had some crappy navigation to be so far off course.'

'What'd it look like?' Galina asked.

'I don't know much about boats. Big, black, grey and shiny,' Archie said thoughtfully.

'And where was it exactly?'

'In the river of course, not too far from my camp. Maybe it couldn't get a spot at the dock,' he said, chuckling.

'Or it was hiding?' Galina suggested.

'Huh. Why would it do that?'

'We both know that the west side of this island is the perfect place to get away from it all.' Galina flipped over a beer mat and passed it to Archie with a pen.'

'Could you draw it for me?'

'What? The yacht. Why?'

'Cause I'm curious, and if I bump into the crew while I'm here, I'm gonna ask them what they were doing.'

Archie thought this an odd request, but then the

serpent tattooed lady was a little odd herself. He sketched the yacht as best he could remember, without making further comment.

'Here you go,' he said a few minutes later, passing her his beer mat with yacht doodle. 'I've gotta go. Got a bit of a pain here. Need to get my leg up.'

'Of course. Sorry. I should have got us better chairs. Thanks for the drawing.'

'You're welcome.'

'See you at the *Big Reveal*.' Archie stood up and the yachting crews, previously huddled together, cleared a path for him to walk out, leaning on his crutches. Galina turned her phone over and read the news item the barman had referred to.

Hobart Mercury 31 December
The Blue Gazelle Cries Interference

Limping into Constitution Dock yesterday was the Blue Gazelle, captained by Scott Harmon. It was a disappointing finish for a yacht which so many thought would secure an early place in this year's Sydney to Hobart yacht race. Like other competitors, the yacht struggled through the storm. Upon arrival they made an official complaint about an unidentified yacht shining 'lasers' during the tempest. No other yachts witnessed this event, with the yacht's behaviour being described as 'like a *tiger' attacking in the night. Officials are trying to identify the phantom yacht. The Blue Gazelle has been placed 25th on line honours and 23rd on handicap.*

Galina looked up and scanned the room. Sailors, gathered in tight clans, were sharing dramatic stories from the race and frequently toasting each other's success. Most were noisy and joyful, with the exception of a small team gathered around a tall table in the corner. They looked serious as they spoke in hushed tones. In their huddle it was impossible to see if there was an identifying logo on the front of their blue shirts. Galina's deliberations as to her next actions were interrupted by a voice behind her.

'Hello gorgeous. Which yacht did you sail in on?' Galina swivelled around in her chair and looked at the inebriated sailor wearing a shirt identifying him as crew of the *Eagle Express*. It was obvious from the tone of his question, and the glassy look in his eyes that he was hoping to leverage his team's recent race success, to success in other areas.

'I'm not a sailor,' she replied.

'Then a model, perhaps?' he asked. Galina sighed and regarded the man carefully.

'No. I work at an abattoir. My speciality is disembowelling pigs.' The man froze, suddenly lost for words.

'Sorry to disturb you, ma'am,' he said before pivoting and returning to a table of men seated on the far side of the hotel. They raised their glasses to her and boisterously exchanged fifty-dollar bills, having clearly made bets on their colleague's ability to *score*. Galina turned around and looked for the crew in the cobalt blue shirts. They'd gone.

DAY 108

Charlotte felt shattered as she handed over her passport to the reception staff at the hotel where Scott had been staying. She'd hardly slept on the flight. The receptionist looked at her sympathetically.

'How's your husband?'

'He's resting.'

'Please give him our best.'

'I will.'

'And there's a letter for you,' she said, looking at her monitor. 'One moment please.' A letter was retrieved and pushed across the desk. Charlotte slipped it into her bag and caught the elevator to Scott's hotel room. She was struck by how perfectly tidy and sterile it was. No sign that someone had fallen and left a bloody mess in the shower. She threw her bag on the rack and opened the letter.

.   .   .

CONFIDENTIAL

Western governments believe that a military force has been deploying a high-powered, microwave style weapon against drones and other intelligence gathering devices. The weapon emits directed-energy, disabling the device and causing a wide range of symptoms for persons nearby including nausea, vertigo, headaches, cognitive difficulties and in some cases, brain damage. The illness that results from the impact of the weapon has been dubbed Havana Syndrome. For some, the negative impacts are short-term while others acquire a long-term disability. The definitive source of the weapon is unknown, with suggestions that the Cuban, Chinese and/or Russian military are involved. To date, those persons mainly impacted have been diplomats, intelligence officers and military personnel, who have been caught in the line of fire.

The envelope also contained several pages of background information and explanatory notes. Charlotte sat on the bed and read them with increasing alarm. Then she placed the synopsis and notes in the room's safe and walked briskly to the Royal Hobart Hospital.

Charlotte was disturbed by the way Scott looked. Pale

and fragile, two words that had never been used before to describe her husband. She brushed aside a long strand of hair on his forehead and looked at the machines beeping quietly beside the bed. The nurse had been unable to provide any more detail than what Jason had told her before she left London. Charlotte felt conflicted, knowing that his head injury had resulted from both a fall and from exposure to an unknown energised weapon. *Would this knowledge, shared with the medical team, impact on the treatment being provided?*

'Excuse me Mrs Harmon. There's someone here to see you.'

Charlotte walked out of the ward where a woman of short height and strong stature was waiting.

'I'm Dr Deidre Duell. I've flown down from Melbourne at the request of Ms Dubois. Do I have your permission to examine your husband and undertake a few scans?'

'You do.' Charlotte introduced the doctor and nurse to each other. They spoke briefly and customer records were printed before Dr Duell went over to examine Scott.

'She's not your only visitor,' the nurse said. 'There's been a man coming for the last two days, hoping to speak with Scott.'

'His name?'

'Ralph something. Didn't catch the last name. Had the impression he didn't know Scott that well.'

'Was he a race official? Or a reporter?'

'Possibly. He was certainly persistent. I've seen him hanging around in the reception café. He might be there now.' Charlotte looked back to Scott and Dr Duell. Preparations were clearly underway to take him somewhere else.

'He'll probably be gone for an hour or so,' the nurse said.

'I'll go and get myself a coffee then,' Charlotte said to the nurse, who nodded before returning her gaze to the monitor.

The café was crowded, but quiet given the number of people there. Tired eyes and whispered conversations among family members, who like Charlotte, were killing time. She checked her phone again as she waited in a queue for her macchiato. Jason had texted asking when would be a good time to meet.

'Coffee for Charlie,' the barista called out. Charlotte thanked the server, collected her drink and walked across to a small table, where she put down her paper cup and picked up her phone. She was about to respond to Jason's text when an unfamiliar voice caught her attention.

'Excuse me. Are you Charlotte Wyatt-Harmon?' Charlotte looked up and regarded the man wearing a Channel-13 branded t-shirt and jeans.

'Yes I am,' she replied cautiously, waiting to hear his question.

'I need to speak with Scott Harmon, as a matter of urgency.'

'I'm sorry. Who are you and why do you need to speak with my husband?'

'It's about a friend of his. Sebastian Ward.'

'Seb isn't here,' Charlotte replied. 'I can't help you, and I need to go back to my husband now.'

'I just need to know if he has heard from his friend. Perhaps you could read his messages?'

'What! No!' Charlotte replied disbelievingly, attracting the attention of the elderly couple at the next table who were now staring at them.

As Galina walked into the hospital reception, she was surprised to see Ralph engaged in a heated conversation with a woman.

'I will not read his mails or messages without his permission and I am aghast that you are even asking me. Tell me again why you think I should be doing this?'

Ralph was clearly unsure of himself.

'My apologies,' he stuttered, 'your husband was given as the second emergency contact, and not that there is an emergency, it's just that we've lost contact with Mr Ward and need to organise a few things for an upcoming event.'

'This behaviour isn't like the Seb I know. If he hasn't been in contact with you then there would be a very good reason.'

'But...'

'No.'

'If you hear from him, can you call me,' he said

thrusting a card towards her. She reluctantly took it and shoved it in her top shirt pocket.

'I'll tell him to contact you, if I hear from him,' she replied. Galina stood behind an oversized plant box as Ralph walked outside into the January sunshine. She watched the woman walk over to the elevators, her arms crossed tightly over her chest, and her brow furrowed in concentration. The doors of the elevator opened and Galina quickened her pace and followed her in. The elevator doors slid shut, enveloping them in a moment of quiet, before the lift began its ascent, Galina seized their moment alone.

'You must be Charlotte Harmon.' The woman looked startled. 'I beg of you to give me one minute of your time, because I am also looking for Seb Ward, who I know is a close friend of your husband's, and who desperately wanted to sail with him in the yacht race, and who has inexplicably gone missing.'

'Who are you and who are you to Seb?' Charlotte replied feistily.

'I was a fellow contestant left alone in the wild... and his friend. We...' The elevator doors opened and an orderly joined them in the lift. The conversation stopped and an awkward silence filled the small space. Neither spoke and they both stepped out of the lift at the next stop, three seconds later.

'You have every reason not to trust Ralph, who you

were just speaking with,' Galina continued. Chalotte now look bewildered. 'I don't know what I can tell you that will enable you to trust me.'

'Tell me about his family,' Charlotte replied.

'His sister is currently sailing around the world on a yacht with her partner. Last communication from her was that she was near Guatemala. His parents died in an accident when he was a kid. He grew up and learnt to swim at Opoutama Beach in New Zealand and...'

'OK. Enough. You definitely couldn't have pulled that from the internet. What do you want from me?'

'Seb told me that if I ever wanted to find him, I should speak with Scott.'

'But Scott hasn't spoken to him since September.'

'Maybe he might know where he'd go. Can I speak with him? I'll only be five minutes.'

'No. That's not possible. Even if I wanted to say yes, I couldn't. Because he's in a coma.' Galina's hand flew to her mouth.

'How awful.' Without asking permission she leant across and hugged Charlotte then quickly let go and stepped back. 'I'm so sorry. Inappropriate on my part. I'll go.' Galina turned, walked back to the elevator and pressed the call button.

'What's your name?' Charlotte asked.

'Galina-Elizabeta Ivanof.'

'And where are you staying?'

'At the Ibis, but you'll mostly find me at the Hope and Anchor Hotel, hanging out with the yachties.'

'Alright then.' The elevator doors opened and Galina stepped inside without another word from Charlotte, who stared after the woman with the serpent tattoos.

Galina was surprised when Charlotte Harmon pulled up a chair at her table when she was eating breakfast the following morning.

'The Hope and Anchor doesn't open until midday and I can't wait that long. I have too many questions.'

'Yes,' Galina replied. 'That does not surprise me.'

'How could you get to know Seb during the competition when you were meant to be alone in the bush?'

Galina raised her eyebrows and cheekily winked. 'We may have broken the rules.'

'That does not surprise me either. Go on,' Charlotte replied, warming to this intriguing woman.

'We collaborated to share food. We agreed to work together so that one of us could win the competition.'

'That's just not enough. How did you meet each other? How did you communicate?' Galina tapped her fork on her glass, startling the people at a nearby table and catching the attention of the waitress.

'Can I order a coffee for my friend please, and I'll have

another as well?' The waitress nodded. 'I'm a drummer. We communicated by drumming.'

'What?'

'And by smoke signals.'

'You're kidding me.'

Galina looked directly at Charlotte; her face expressionless. 'We also had a few words on the first day. I'd assessed we were unlikely to be far apart. Later, he saw and heard my invitation to cross the river, and that's when we got to know each other better.'

Charlotte didn't reply, taking in the strange story that had been shared by an even stranger woman. 'There is a lot more to tell, but all you need to know is that Seb and my collaboration went beyond sharing food.'

'I'd guessed that,' Charlotte replied with the hint of a smile. 'And when was the last time you saw him?'

'A week ago. He'd just bandaged my hand after I'd been bitten by a devil.' She held up her hand as if she needed to prove this part of the story. 'And he was heading to the river to go back to his camp. When the evacuation team came to collect me two hours later, they said that Seb was no longer there and that I was the winner. It made no sense. We'd made plans. I couldn't ask questions without revealing what I knew.'

'What do you think happened to him?' Charlotte asked.

'Drowned. Bitten by a poisonous snake. Taken by a tiger...I just don't know. But I do know that I don't trust the organisers. They're hiding something. They're pretending he has just *left* the competition. I cannot ask them more without raising suspicion.'

'But I possibly could. I have an open invitation to go back to this Ralph.' Charlotte placed his business card on the table and Galina's eyes lit up. She was about to respond when a BREAKING NEWS message flashed across the ticker on the television screen.

Male body washes up on Binalong Bay. Police investigating. No missing persons have been reported.

'My God,' Galina gasped. 'Seb.'

Charlotte reached across and put her hand on Galina's arm.

'That's a long way from when you last saw him. Don't jump to conclusions. We'll go and see the police. Do you have a photo of Seb?'

'No.'

'Wait a second.' Charlotte scrolled through the photos on her phone. 'I do.' She passed Galina the phone, displaying a photo of Seb wearing a kilt and playing a drum. 'Taken at our wedding in September. He provided quite the performance.' Galina stared at the photo and the corner of her mouth crinkled.

'Can you send this to me?'

Charlotte transferred the photo, and the two women left the hotel together for the police station, a fifteen-minute walk away.

'So when was the last time you saw your boyfriend?' the burly policeman asked.

'My ex-boyfriend,' Galina corrected. 'A week ago.'

'And you think this person who washed up on Binalong Bay might be him.'

'He's a sailor so it's possible.'

'Have you tried calling him?'

'Of course. But we've broken up so he might just be avoiding me.'

'And where was it that you last saw him?'

'I'm not sure exactly. We were having a picnic in the bush. He took me there as a surprise.'

'And then he broke up with you?'

'Yes. That was the surprise.' The detective looked from Galina across to Charlotte and then back to Galina clearly doubting what he was hearing.

'Ma'am?'

'Yes?'

'Did he hit you?'

'Don't be stupid. Of course not.'

'And you didn't hit him?' he asked staring at her tattoos.

'That is ridiculous. Why would I be here reporting him missing if I had done him in?'

'Stranger things have happened. Give me more information. His age?' Galina hesitated and looked at Charlotte.

'Thirty-two,' Charlotte replied quickly. Galina's pause was noted by the detective.

'Do you have a photo?'

'Yes,' Galina quickly replied holding up the image on her phone.

'A drummer, eh.'

'Yes, from New Zealand. He's very good,' Galina added unprompted, hoping to recover her credibility.

'Send the photo to this address and I'll send it to the detectives managing the investigation. I've got your number in case there's anything to report.'

'There's nothing more you can tell me now?'

'I'm sorry.' Disappointment was etched on Galina's face. 'You won't be leaving the area in the next couple of days, will you?'

'No, I'll be here, waiting for your call.

The women didn't speak as they left instead throwing each other a sympathetic glance. Once outside the station Charlotte checked her phone.

'Any messages from the hospital?' Galina asked. Charlotte shook her head. 'I'm sorry. I was so wrapped up in my own search for Seb, I didn't think to...'

'It's OK. There's nothing new to report. He's in the best place for now.' Charlotte's clipped response gave Galina the impression that she didn't want to talk about Scott, which was frustrating as Galina had wanted to ask questions about the incident during the race.

'I have things to do,' continued Charlotte. 'Work related things. I'll ask Ralph to meet me at the Hope and Anchor at midday. I'll have a better chance of getting more information from him if we meet in person and he has a drink or two.'

'Where are you going now?' Galina asked. Charlotte hesitated before responding.

'Back to the hospital to check on Scott. Gotta respond to a few emails and then meet a contact in the fashion industry who's participating in an event I'm attending at the Museum of Old and New Art next week.'

'I'll be at the MONA next week too, but at a distinctly non-fashion focussed event. It's run by the network that organised the game. We'll be wearing ex-military gear or mountain climbing kit. Definitely not high fashion. They're interviewing us and announcing the winner followed by a little party. Ralph'll be there, along with his boss, Nelson Farnsworthy.'

'Hmmm,' Charlotte said, taking in this information.

'What you thinking, Charlie-Girl?' Galina asked. Charlotte was taken aback by her use of Scott's pet name for her.

'Different things,' she replied, refusing to reveal her thinking.

'Can I come along with you to visit this fashionista? I've nothing else to do. What's their name?' Galina asked.

Charlotte stared at her. 'Do you always ask someone you've only just met this many questions?' Galina shrugged. 'Anya, her name is Anya Orlov.'

'Probably Russian. You could do with an interpreter.'

'We'll be speaking English, and she won't be expecting me to bring along a translator or a friend for that matter.'

'But maybe an assistant assigned by the MONA? I could take notes.'

'Dressed like that,' Charlotte said waving her hand from Galina's spiked hair, velvet pencil skirt, and silver studded black leather jacket to her thigh-length purple boots. 'She's unlikely to believe that you work in couture.'

'But she'll know I love fashion. It'll be a conversation starter.'

'I don't know.' Charlotte paused and looked across at Galina, her finger unconsciously tapping on her lip. 'It might be a useful distraction. Alright. I'm meeting her at the Crowne Plaza. I'll see you there in an hour.'

'Excellent.'

'And Galina...'

'Yes?'

'Follow my lead and don't talk.'

Galina took in the plush furnishings of the Crowne Plaza reception as they waited for Mrs Orlov to collect them. It was easy to see why this hotel rated several stars above where she was staying. Moments later a woman with long, blonde wavy hair wearing a pink Chanel jacket over a straight navy skirt, arrived. She was petite, with a purposeful stride. The reception area was suddenly infused with a delightful floral fragrance. A beautiful smile blossomed across her face as she approached them.

'I was going to take you to our suite, but Yuri is there, and he's in a bad mood. Better we go to the bar on top of the hotel instead. I'm Anya, by the way,' she blurted out.

'Hello Anya,' Charlotte replied holding out her hand, 'I'm Charlotte and this is ...'

'Betty,' Galina said. 'I'm here from the MONA extended support team to ensure that you have everything you need.'

'Thank you, Betty,' Charlotte replied with a hint of formality, while glaring at Galina. 'Lead the way, Anya.'

Comfortably seated at a table on the rooftop bar, the women opened their folders, ordered a round of drinks and then discussed each matter listed on the agenda Anya had prepared.

'You know that the word *kaleidoscope* has several meanings,' Anya began. 'Most people know it as a toy where you can observe constantly shifting colourful patterns. Others know that the etymology of the word is Greek and means *observer of beautiful things*. It is the perfect thematic frame for this event. This will be a small and intimate affair. A dozen different models gracing the catwalk, watched by the editors of the fashion press, journalists from the major mastheads, sponsors of course, designers like yourself, Charlotte, a sprinkling of carefully selected fashion influencers and the obligatory local politicians. While the event itself is of tremendous value, more important are the reels and images we capture and create for distribution to the world. They'll have a life online and on billboards for probably the next four months, *if we do this right*.' She sipped her drink and thought about what she'd just said before continuing. 'As you know Betty, the MONA will be closed to the general public except for our event and another, much smaller function being held outdoors at the Moorilla Estate.'

'Yes, I'm involved with both events,' Galina replied, not looking up from her notebook. The conversation then moved to details of the lighting, music selection, filming locations, dressing and transition areas and welcoming and management of guests. Galina was a model of administrative efficiency as she scribbled furiously while Charlotte and Anya described every phase of the fashion spectacular over the next hour.

'Ah here comes Yuri. Yuri, these are my collaborators, Charlotte and Betty.'

They said hello.

'You have an accent Betty. You are from...?'

'Bavaria. I'm Betty from Bavaria, although I left Germany a long time ago.'

'My ear for accents is off then. I thought you might have come from Belarus, my home country, or maybe a northern European country.'

'Nein. Dresden is the farthest north I've travelled in Europe.'

He wobbled his head and turned his attention to Charlotte.

'And you Charlotte, where do you hail from?'

'Queensland on the Gold Coast, at a place enticingly called Runaway Bay.'

'Sounds lovely. I'd love to have my own *Runaway Bay*,' he replied without explaining his response. 'I won't interrupt your meeting any longer. Can I organise a refreshment of your drinks?'

'Thank you darling,' Anya said, waving him away.

Their meeting finished thirty minutes later, with mutual cheek-kissing and an invitation to catch up the following day.

'Betty from Bavaria? What was that all about?' Charlotte asked Galina as they walked out onto Liverpool Street.

'If they knew I was from Estonia, they would guess I spoke Russian. Many Estonians do. As I wasn't being used as a translator, I thought it might be helpful to keep this skill unknown. I also speak German. Now back at you, Miss Mysterious.'

'Yes?' Charlotte replied cautiously.

'The questions you asked Anya, made me think you had an agenda beyond the fashion show.'

Charlotte regarded Galina carefully. 'I can't answer that question. Do you want to come with me when I interview Ralph?'

'I'll come, but I think it's best you talk with him on your own. I don't want him to know we're friends.'

'We're friends, are we?' Charlotte asked, barely disguising a smile.

HOPE AND ANCHOR HOTEL

There were only a handful of other patrons when Ralph arrived at the Hope and Anchor at midday. He spotted Charlotte at the bar and pulled a stool closer to her, which she found unnerving.

'I was pleased and a little surprised to receive your call,' he said.

'You had cornered me after a particularly difficult day. I realise I may have appeared rude.' He waved his hand, dismissing her concern. 'I'm sure you can appreciate that your request was,' she hesitated, 'well, it was bizarre. And I'm a little confused and need more information.'

'What do you need to know?'

'Why did Seb leave the competition before it had finished?'

'I don't know the answer. All I know is that his backpack is no longer at his camp, that he removed his tracker watch, and that he didn't try to call us to arrange an extraction. He must have made it out of the bush on his own, and we just wanted to check that he's OK.'

'Are you sure he hasn't fallen over somewhere or been bitten by a snake?'

'We've had a tracker dog move over every inch of his territory. Of course, if he had travelled beyond his allocated area, he could be somewhere else entirely. But the dog didn't pick up a trail indicating this. He'd built a raft, so it's possible he left by water, but the raft was left behind.' Charlotte said nothing, as she reflected on what he'd said. 'So back to my original question. Did he try to call your husband?'

'No. I've checked Scott's phone. There are no messages.'

'Can you think of anyone else who had a close relationship with him who might know where he is?'

'Jason Smith was a friend and also a crew member. I'll check with Jase and let you know.'

'Thank you,' Ralph said placing his hand on Charlotte's arm. 'And if there's anything I can do to help, call me.' Charlotte swivelled off her chair and picked up her bag as though she was about to leave.

'I will,' she replied, knowing that she'd only do this if absolutely necessary.

.   .   .

Galina watched the door close behind Ralph. She'd been hiding in one of the hotel's other bars and with the coast clear, re-joined Charlotte.

'What did you learn?' she asked.

'His backpack wasn't there. Seb, or someone else, must have taken it.'

'At least it confirms he made it safely back across the river,' Galina said, feeling relieved.

'They used a tracker dog which didn't find a trail beyond Seb's perimeter. He must've left by water.'

Galina looked away, deep in thought. She steepled her fingers a few times before turning to Charlotte.

'Archie said he saw a yacht the day he was evacuated. Perhaps that's how Seb left?'

'But why?'

'I don't know.'

'Charlotte,' came a voice from the bar. They turned to see an unshaven man approaching, wearing an oversized t-shirt, cotton trousers and boating shoes.

'Jase,' Charlotte replied, reaching out to hug him. 'Great to see you. How you feeling?'

'I'm OK,' he replied flatly

'What does OK mean, Jason?' Charlotte said looking at him closely.

'I'm still getting these damn migraines.'

'I'll go get some drinks,' Galina said. She noted their preferences and left for the bar, leaving the friends to talk.

The bar was busier than when they'd first arrived. While waiting to get the barman's attention she overheard Russian voices in the corner and moved closer to listen in. Two men were upset, blaming each other for an incident on board their yacht during a recent storm. They were speaking in hushed tones and she was only able to hear, every second word amongst the din of customer chatter.

'What can I get you, love,' the barman called out. Galina placed her order and stood perfectly still, straining to hear the conversation. The two men finished their drinks and stood up. Galina grabbed her order and walked quickly to their table, plonking the three ciders down, with her eyes on the departing sailors.

'You're not much of a bar attendant,' Jason offered with a smile.

'I've gotta go,' she replied as she grabbed her satchel.

'I'm sorry. Just a stupid joke,' Jason called out as she ran for the door. She frantically looked both ways and could see the two men about to turn left onto Collins Street. She sprinted up the road and had closed the distance between them by the time they'd turned right onto Argyle and left onto Liverpool Street where they entered a Woolworths supermarket.

Galina scooped up a shopping basket at the store's entrance. One of the men glanced at her as she entered their aisle and she feigned interest in a product description, before placing a loaf of bread in her basket. They entered the next aisle and loaded their cart with formulated dehydrated meals, flavoured rice, dried fruit and long-life milk before heading to the checkout.

'Would you like a bag for that?' the woman at the checkout asked. Galina nodded with her focus on the men getting ready to carry their shopping bags outside.

'Do you have a loyalty card?' Galina shook her head, irritated.

'Card or cash?' Galina pulled twenty dollars from her pocket as she watched the men hail a taxi.

'Your change,' the checkout operator called out as Galina rushed to the door. It was too late. The men were gone.

Charlotte and Jason were engaged in an intense conversation when Galina returned to the Hope and Anchor fifteen minutes later. She stood away from the table, not wanting to interrupt and waiting for them to notice her before approaching. Charlotte waved her over and Galina sat down and picked up her drink.

'And the authorities say they have no idea which yacht it was?' Charlotte asked. Jason shook his head.

'Not one registered for the race. And if it was a pleasure yacht, why on earth would you go out in a storm. It was a sophisticated beast and would have had excellent technology for tracking the storm. Who knows what that red beam was, shining on our vessel.'

'And what did *the beast* look like?' Galina asked,

injecting herself into the conversation.

'Big, dark and shiny,' he replied thoughtfully, with two seconds hovering between each word. Galina put her drink down and reached into her pocket, pulling out the beer mat Archie had scribbled on.

'Did it look like this?' she asked. Jason stared at the drawing wide-eyed then looked at Galina.

'You've seen the boat?'

'No. No I haven't. But someone I met in the competition, did.'

'Where was it?' he asked.

'Near his camp, where the competition took place. We were really in the wilderness and it struck me, when Archie mentioned seeing it, that a boat of that size had probably come to get away from it all, or to hide.'

Jason took out his phone and took a photo of the drawing. 'OK if I share this with the yachting community?' he asked.

Galina hesitated. 'Not yet, please.'

'What's your concern?' Charlotte asked.

'We might scare them away and never be able to find out what happened to Seb.'

'Who are they and why do you think this has anything to do with Sebby?' Charlotte asked.

'There were two Russians sitting over there when I was at the bar. I overhead snippets of conversation. They were talking about a storm and an incident with a crew member in rough seas. One was blaming the other for not having checked the harness. And there was concern over what they'd tell his family.'

'That still doesn't implicate Seb.' Charlotte replied.

'I know. I'm as you say, clutching at straws. But Seb is inexplicably missing, he's a sailor and a body's been found on a beach.' Charlotte and Jason's phones pinged simultaneously.

'It's not him,' Jason said looking at his phone. 'Police have released a description of the person with an identikit image. The description reads: Caucasian. Male. Medium build. Bald. Aged around fifty.'

Galina clapped her hands and reached for his phone.

'Do you know him?' Charlotte asked.

'No,' she replied, 'but I think we could ask Yuri?'

'Yuri Orlov? Why?'

'Because one of the Russian sailors said that *Dr Orlov was furious.*'

'Who's that?' Jason asked.

'Friend of a business contact,' Charlotte replied dismissively.

'I know this will sound like a James Bond plot, but do you think the Russians are involved in attacking our yacht?' Jason asked.

'That's a bit stereotypical Jase, and Yuri Orlov is from Belarus, not Russia,' Charlotte replied.

'Sorry. You're right. Sorry. My head's done in and I think

I've another migraine coming on so I'm going back to the hotel for a lie down.'

'Do you want us to come with you?' Charlotte asked.

'Nah. I'm good. It's just around the corner. Catch up later, eh?'

'Of course, and if Sebby calls you, tell him he's in big trouble,' Charlotte replied. Smiling faintly, Jason gave a thumbs up and ambled out of the hotel. Galina finished off her drink all the while watching Charlotte take a photo of the image on the beer mat and sending it somewhere. She didn't offer an explanation to Galina.

'Who are you? I mean...you say you're a fashion designer, but I think you're more than that. You're smart and you ask good questions. I know you're not telling me stuff, and if I was to guess, I'd say you were a spy.'

'I'm not a spy,' Charlotte replied, sipping her cider. She looked back at Galina. 'However, as a result of things I've done in the past, I do have connections in helpful places. It suits my personal and professional interests to be here, now, gathering information. You know my husband, and others have been injured by something we don't quite understand, by a technology whose source and purpose are unclear. I'm aware that Yuri Orlov is an internationally respected scientist married to a high-profile Russian designer. Now what I'm about to tell you must not be shared with anyone. Understood?' Galina nodded. 'It's been suggested that Dr Orlov's connected to the development of a powerful laser beam, which causes a side effect that's been dubbed Havana Syndrome. It has impacted those working in the intelligence community, for a number of years. As I said, I'm gathering information. That's all. For reasons I can't elaborate on, the agency doesn't want to create an international incident.'

'Are you able to use your contacts to help me find Seb?' Galina asked.

'I've already done that. Here's the text I received at the same time Jase received his news alert.'

IT'S A RUSSIAN SAILOR – NOT SEBASTIAN WARD

Galina stared at Charlotte's screen trying unsuccessfully to identify the man. She then looked directly into Charlotte's eyes.

'I think it's time we looked into these Russkies a bit more. Don't you think?' Charlotte titled her head and gave the barest of smiles. 'Where was the last place you saw them?'

Galina provided the location of the supermarket and Charlotte entered the details into her phone.

'Now we wait. Do you want another drink?'

'I'd rather be doing something to find Seb. But OK.

Same again?' Charlotte nodded and Galina returned to the bar to order another round. She returned to their table five minutes later as Charlotte's phone pinged again.

'OK. I have the coordinates where they were dropped off by taxi. It's near Seven Mile Beach, about half an hour from here. They then boarded a dinghy to take them out to a vessel, which could be the yacht that attacked the *Blue Gazelle*.'

'That's not information you get from a surveillance camera. It's from a drone or a satellite,' Galina said.

'I don't know. Probably,' Charlotte replied.

'Let's go,' Galina said standing up, and slinging her satchel over her shoulder.

'Sit down and take a breath, Betty. I admire your bias for action, but we need to be careful. There are broader objectives to be achieved here and we don't want to blow an opportunity to realize a bigger goal by going for a smaller one. There are eyes on the yacht now so it can't disappear. Before we do anything, I want to have a conversation with Mr Orlov about the *scientific projects* he's working on.'

'But what about Seb?'

'We're just speculating he's on that yacht. He could be anywhere.'

'I want to eliminate that option so I can look elsewhere.'

'Give me a little time to get help from my contact. We should know more soon. Are there any other avenues of inquiry you can pursue while we wait?'

Galina flicked each finger on her left hand. 'Maybe the other contestants saw something. I don't know when they left and where they were located. Maybe Nelson Farnsworthy, the TV producer responsible for the game knows more than he's letting on? What about the race organisers? They say that all yachts in the race were tracked and have been accounted for. Maybe they caught sight of the phantom yacht through a tracking system that they're not sharing with us? A bit like your mysterious friend who has access to footage from satellites. Indeed, can you ask them to find footage from the area where we were in the bush?'

'I thought you didn't know where you were?'

'I can give you the coordinates for where we were dropped off before we were transported in mini vans to the assessment site. Together with the date and time, I'm sure that's more than enough for your contact to find our previous locations in the bush.'

'Send the information through and I'll see what can be uncovered. I want to get back to the hospital now.'

'Of course. Can we meet back here again in a couple of hours?' Galina asked.

'Why here?'

'We might meet other sailors who have useful information. And more importantly, Seb told me that if I was ever looking for him, this was the place to be.' Charlotte smiled and placed her hand over Galina's.

'I'm sure we're getting closer.'

HOBART ROYAL HOSPITAL

Charlotte's phone rang as she held Scott's hand. He was pale and lying motionless in his hospital bed. Glancing at the caller's name she quickly moved out to the corridor.

'Hey Mason?'

'How is he?'

'The same. Still in a coma. The doctor says this is the best way for him to recover.'

'My word. What do I tell Miranda?'

'That his vitals are good and we remain optimistic.'

'What about you? How you holding up?' Mason asked. Charlotte exhaled.

'Still jet-lagged, but fine. Really, I'm fine.'

'Do you know anything more about what happened out there in the race?'

'Jase didn't reveal more than what we know already.

There was an intense storm. They were alone and battling to keep the yacht stable against huge waves, when this other yacht suddenly appeared and then disappeared just as quickly. They didn't recognise it and it doesn't appear to have been part of the fleet heading for Constitution Dock. I'm still making enquires and have an appointment to see the race organisers later.'

'Hopefully you'll have more luck than I did. I sensed a distinct hesitancy about sharing any negative information when I made enquiries. Guessing that's because of the race's reputation. They just don't want a bad news story.'

'Everyone seems to be hiding something here,' Charlotte said.

'Whatdya mean?'

'Sorry. Just sounding off. A bit tired.'

'Understandable. D'ya know if Seb has come out of *that* competition yet?'

'No. I don't know where he is?' Charlotte said softly, unconsciously shaking her head.

'He's missing all the action and excitement.'

'Wherever he is, he's probably pleased he was safe and sound in the bush and not on the *Blue Gazelle*. How are Jenny and Louis settling in? Hope they're not spoiling the twins.'

'Wrong. It's helpful they have jet lag too, as they're helping Miranda throughout the night, while I'm sleeping. Anyway, they're actually standing behind me and are anxious to speak with you. I'll talk to you tomorrow.' The phone was passed across and Charlotte spent the next twenty minutes repeating the information she'd just given Mason and providing as much reassurance as she was able to about Scott's condition, given the limited information she had. She looked at Scott as she spoke to them, hoping that all her reassurances were true.

TWO HOURS LATER

Galina was sitting at the same table in the Hope and Anchor when Charlotte returned two hours later. She immediately guessed where Galina had been and shook her head.

'I asked you to wait until we had more information,' Charlotte whispered.

'Got your spies following me now?' Galina replied accusingly.

'No. You've got sand in your hair and you're sunburnt.'

'Oops,' Galina said as she bent over and ran her fingers through her tousled hair, dislodging the evidence of her visit to Seven Mile Beach.

'A logical deduction. Did you learn anything?' Charlotte asked.

'Not much. They're hardly hiding there. It's the only

yacht anchored for miles. Impossible to approach without being spotted. Spent my time hiding in the dunes, taking photos. Didn't see Seb.'

'But he's there,' Charlotte said.

'What?' Galina spat out. 'Why didn't you call me?'

'Because we were worried you'd tried to board without backup. A clearly justified concern.'

Galina stood up, pushed her knuckles against her waist and started circumnavigating the table.

'We've a number of options and possible approaches,' Charlotte said.

'You tell me yours and then I'll tell you mine.'

'I will. But first, let me outline our objectives. We want to gather as much information as we can about this weapon. If we assault the vessel, they may destroy it.'

'We?' Galina said incredulously. 'Who's we? It's not me. And you sound like you're reading from a military handbook.'

'OK. I may have been sent terms of reference, for the next stage of this operation.'

'Operation? Does it have a name?' Galina said cheekily.

'It does. It's called Operation Silent Night.'

'Because...?'

'I think that's a bit obvious, don't you?'

Galina shrugged and patted her pockets, looking for a cigarette, before remembering she'd stopped smoking.

'You want to get the bad guys and the weapon without

attracting attention.'

'Pretty much,' Charlotte replied. 'There are many people and organisations that will benefit from the information we collect. Five Eyes are particularly interested.'

'Who?' Galina asked.

'Five Eyes are an intelligence alliance formed between Australia, Canada, New Zealand, the United Kingdom and the United States. They want to know the names of anyone else involved in the weapons development and to take Yuri Orlov, and the weapon, into custody.'

'And *we* want to rescue Seb.'

'Of course. As I've said, we want to avoid media attention. Our longer-term objectives are best served if ...'

'OK. I've listened. This is what I'm doing.' Galina outlined her plan.

'We suspected you might say that.'

'*We did, did we?*'

Charlotte let a smile wash across her face. 'If you are successful in boarding the vessel, we want you to plant a listening device.'

'Can't you hack into their communication systems?'

'They have encryption systems we've not been able to penetrate, for the moment.'

'So I'm on the payroll then. We'll need to discuss my remuneration.'

'You'll need to discuss that with Teal.'

'I'm looking forward to meeting her.'

ALONE DAY 104 – ONE WEEK EARLIER

Seb made it to the water's edge in ten minutes. He'd have preferred to cross the water again on the raft, but it'd been made with snare wire that he didn't enter the competition with. *Too risky,* even though he'd been recorded as saying he'd found the wire. It was simply too *new* looking. Might raise questions when he eventually left, which might be soon. He looked up and down the river to check for the presence of boats, before pushing off to swim to the other side. Fifteen minutes later he had traversed the river and was running along the water's edge, back to Sailing Siesta. He smiled as he passed the second raft Galina had asked him to make. They wouldn't need it now they were on their way out.

He was changing his clothes when he heard the distinctive sound of a motorboat. Waving his hands high he walked down to the water's edge and called out.

'Have you come to collect me?'

'Only if you're a sailor.'

'That'd be me. Brilliant. Let me get my things.' Seb raced back to stuff his clothes into his backpack, not noticing the puzzled looks on the men's faces. Seb passed his backpack to the man who looked like a bouncer from a nightclub and noticed the camera equipment near the shoreline had not been taken aboard. It was also a different motorboat to the one used previously to carry the doctor. This was a dinghy, not dissimilar to those used by yachts.

'You guys new?'

'Yep,' the one closest to him said.

'Aren't you gonna get that equipment?'

'We'll pick it up later.' Seb's eyes shifted suspiciously between the two men. The boat's engine was fired and they were reversing out into the river.

'I thought you'd want to do some filming, to capture these moments for the show.' Seb knew something was amiss when neither responded. He readied himself to jump overboard when a heavy hand grabbed his shoulder.

'*Istu maha*. Sit down and shut up, sailor.'

DAY 112 – SEVEN MILE BEACH

The sailors watched the dark-haired woman in the dinghy push off from the beach and head for their yacht, a noisy bell clanging, announcing her arrival. She pulled up close to the front of the boat and the two men leaned over the railing.

'What do you want?' one of the men called out.

'Ice creams. Do you want to buy an ice cream?' Galina replied. The two sailors regarded her suspiciously.

'How much?'

'Ten dollars each.'

'That is robbery.'

'OK. I give you two for eighteen dollars or four for thirty dollars. Do you think that Uber Eats would deliver out here?'

'Highway robbery.'

'Perhaps. I've also got booze.'

'What?'

'Wine, gin and vodka.'

'That's more interesting. How much?'

'Very nice drinks. Two bottles each. Six in total. Four hundred dollars for the lot.' Galina stood up and pointed at the bottles behind her, revealing a white macrame dress barely covering her string bikini. The men's mood shifted and they smirked as they glanced at each other.

'Will you come aboard and be our waitress if we say yes?' the taller of the two said. Galina hesitated and looked between them, feigning interest in their request.

'You'll have to help me to bring them aboard and be patient with me. I have a damaged hand,' she said giving them a seductive royal wave, with a part of the bandage blowing in the wind. The men disappeared inside and emerged at the back of the vessel, throwing a small metal ladder over the side.

'Paying cash or do I need to bring my electronic payment device with me?'

'Cash,' they called out in unison.

Galina passed up the bottles one by one and then took the hand of the sailor with a gold front tooth, that sparkled in the morning sunshine. She followed the men down the stairs and into the galley, where a collection of beer cans was quickly swept aside. A tea towel was theatrically used to dust the table and bench seat where Galina was invited to sit, while the tall one pulled three tumblers from an overhead cupboard.

'Can I have a glass of water?' Galina asked. 'It's thirsty work being a travelling saleswoman.'

'Also lonely I would think,' the gold-toothed one said.

'Agree. It can be lonely, particularly as I had a fight with my boyfriend,' Galina said, holding up her hand again. The tall sailor reached into the cupboard and pulled out another tumbler which he filled with water. He passed it to Galina and asked,

'Are you OK?'

'I am fine. My boyfriend, I mean my ex-boyfriend, not so much. In hospital with head injury. He slipped and fell.' The men momentarily froze, and then laughed. Galina poured them both a generous serve of vodka, ever smiling.

'You must join us in a toast,' the tall one insisted.

'Why of course,' Galina replied. 'What are we celebrating?'

'To the end of bad relationships and to the beginning of new ones,' the gold-toothed one proposed.

'Agreed,' Galina said, pushing her glass across the table to the bottle, while sticking the listening device underneath the bench seat.

'Now I must insist on payment before the first toast. I get tipsy far too quickly. Let's get the business transaction completed then we can enjoy the next phase of my visit.'

The tall one pointed to his colleague with his head,

indicating he had to leave and get the cash. When *Goldy* was gone, he observed Galina very closely. Aware she was being scrutinised, she fiddled with the drawstring tie on her macrame dress which came undone at the neckline, revealing peach-like breasts. He lost his focus.

'And what is your name, ice-cream lady?'

'I'm Betty. Betty from Bavaria.'

'You don't sound German,' he replied.

'I ran away when I was fifteen. My accent changed as I moved countries. You need to do that to blend in.'

'Australia is a long way from Germany.'

'It is. My father was Australian. I can stay here as long as I want.'

'Here it is,' Goldy announced, returning to the galley. He peeled off eight crisp, fifty-dollar notes from a roll. Galina took them and tucked them into a zipped compartment on her belt.

'Business completed. First toast of the day to our first business transaction.' Galina raised her glass, clinked it against the others, and took a generous swig. The men mimicked her. She reached across for the vodka bottle and refilled their glasses.

'To the end of bad relationships and the beginning of new ones,' Galina said. They again clinked glasses and downed the vodka.

'Tis good, but very strong,' Goldy said eyes blinking

slowly. He sat down unsteadily. The tall one also began to sway and then fell over.

'Can I get you anything?' Galina said while she continued to sip from her glass of water. The gold-toothed one looked at her then placed his head on the table.

'What did you put in our drink, Witch?' he whispered before shutting his eyes.

With both men unconscious, Galina stood up and called out for Seb. Nothing. She raced from cabin to cabin, opening every door and cupboard, finally finding him in a bathroom with his hands tied behind his back. She was surprised at how much joy she felt in seeing him and the delighted look on his face indicated that the feeling was mutual.

'Come on, sailor boy. Let's get you out of here.'

Seb climbed down the ladder first and then reached up for Galina and lifted her into the dinghy, enjoying their moment of intimacy.

'How's the hand, Betty?'

'Getting better.'

'Good.'

The dinghy bounced across the waves and soon hit the sand on Seven Mile Beach where a man and a woman were waiting for them.

'Who are they?'

'Spooks.'

'Really?' Seb laughed. 'What's going on?'

'We're taking you to the airport.'

'Why?'

'Cause you need to go back to Sailing Siesta and *tap out*. You have four hours to come up with a plausible story as to where you've been and what you've been doing.'

'What! Why? Can't you come with me?'

'Nope. Because I've already tapped out.'

'Like I thought I was doing when that vessel arrived eight days ago. I thought there was going to be a party to celebrate, me, and when I say me, *I mean us*, winning the competition. Instead, I was the prisoner of two mad Russians, on an unwieldy vessel, that clearly needed at least three crew to operate. Tell me again, why do I need to go back to the bush and lie about where I've been?'

'Your actions will contribute to world peace.'

'Since when did you care about world peace?' Seb asked. Galina grinned.

'It's in my new job description,' she replied cheekily.

'Again. What?'

'By the way, I've met some of your friends. Charlotte, Jason...'

'And Scotty? How is he? How did the race go?'

'Not Scotty. He's had a fall and is in hospital. Race not so great for them. We think your Russian captors were involved in mischief-making on the high seas.'

Seb looked at her, bewildered.

'You have a lot of explaining to do, Ms Ivanof. When will I see you again?'

'Soon. At the filming of the final episode of the *Alone* game at the MONA. By then, I should be able to answer all your questions.'

'And spend some alone time, just with me?'

'We'll see. You could get lucky.'

ALONE DAY 112

It felt odd being dropped back in the wilderness. It was like he'd moved through a wormhole, in and out of different universes. From the shores of Sailing Siesta, onto the Russian vessel, and back again thanks to the daring of his mad Estonian friend. *Is that what she was? Just a friend?* He had so many questions as he watched the speed boat depart. But the questions would need to wait. He needed to finish this game and then life could return to normal.

His shelter was still in place, but it was clear that someone had searched through the things he'd left behind. On the flight to Smithton, during the drive to the western coast, and then on the journey by speed boat to camp, he'd had a lot of time to conjure up a story to explain his absence over the last eight days. He took in the calm of the bush setting, breathing in the smell of the eucalyptus leaves and enjoying the chatter of the birds. He picked up the handset and pressed the call button. It rang five times before being answered.

'Hello?' Ralph said tentatively.

'It's Seb. I'm tapping out.'

'What!' he screamed into the phone. 'Where the hell have you been?'

'Bit of a long story. I went hunting and got lost.'

'You took off your tracker.'

'I did. I knew that I wasn't meant to be leaving my territory.'

'Too bloody right you weren't. You've disqualified yourself from the race.'

'I thought as much.'

'What were you hunting?'

'I thought I saw a Tasmanian tiger.'

'What! My word. Did you really see it?'

'Not sure. Didn't get close enough.'

'Did you film it? Ralph said excitedly.

'Sorry.'

'Film anything? A tail. A rustling bush. The sound of a bark.'

'No. Again sorry.'

'You idiot. You're meant to film for five hours a day. Even a glimpse of the tiger, would've been ratings gold. You know the last one died in captivity in 1936, although there have been sightings reported since then.'

'I know,' Seb replied, feigning despondency.

'And there's nothing from the camera tied to the tree?'

'Haven't checked it. I'll take a look.'

'Do that. We'll be there in an hour to collect you, and to film the dismantling of your shelter and to record you telling us your reasons for tapping out. They'd better be good.'

'Righteo.'

Seb put the handset on his bed and headed back into the bush to the tree where he'd tied the motion-activated camera. It was gone. He was sure it was the right tree as there was a piece of cable tie on the ground. Rain had washed away any footprints and he recognised his limited skills in connecting any of the nearby animal scats to specific animals. They could be from kangaroos, wallabies, wombats, quolls, or devils; anything apart from the apparently extinct Tasmanian tiger. *Mind you. Only something with strong teeth could have chewed it off. That'd eliminate wallabies and kangaroos. Or maybe a human had hacked it off?*

Seb shrugged his shoulders, returned to camp and walked down to the water's edge. His three fishing lines had become tangled around rocks and logs while he'd been away. He was cutting them free when the television network's speed boat arrived. He waved and watched the boat drive firmly into the sandy bank. Ralph jumped ashore with a camera man close behind.

'Hey Seb. How are you?'

'Fine Ralph, but I'm ready to go home.'

'Really? Tell us why? You seem to be a master fisherman and you've made it past a hundred days.' Seb's heart raced as he replied.

'I promised to crew for a friend in the Sydney to Hobart and missed it and now, I'm missing a girl I didn't realise meant so much to me.'

'You didn't mention her at the beginning.'

'I didn't know at the beginning.'

'Lovesick, eh? Well, let's get your camp deconstructed, and we can get you back to civilisation.'

'Looking forward to that,' Seb replied with a twinkle in his eye. Ralph signalled to the cameraman to stop filming.

'That's a wrap. Well done Seb. I'm guessing you don't have any footage to share of the tiger?'

'Fraid not. Suspect a devil didn't like his reflection in the lens and took it down.'

'Now that'd have been a bonza piece of footage,' the cameraman said and Ralph sighed.

For the next hour, the cameraman filmed Seb pulling down his shelter, packing his remaining things, and finally, the boat pulling away from Sailing Siesta as they headed up river.

DAY 112 – CROWNE PLAZA HOTEL

Anya Orlov was a little startled to see Teal Dubois standing in the hotel foyer with Charlotte.

She looked between the two women before addressing Charlotte.

'Where's Betty?'

'Catching up with a friend,' Charlotte replied. 'This is Madame Dubois. She'd like to speak with Yuri.'

'I'm afraid he's way too busy. He has a difficult work situation he needs to manage.'

'I'm here from the Australian government and have a few questions for your husband. Depending on his responses, I may be able to offer help in managing his *difficult situation*.' Anya stared at the well-coiffed woman with a French accent, and said nothing. 'This is a time limited offer of help, Mrs Orlov. In thirty minutes, I will have no alternatives.'

Anya closed her eyes, said nothing and walked to the elevator with Teal and Charlotte close behind her.

'Yuri, darling. Can you come out here please,' Anya called out as she entered their apartment. A clearly sleep-deprived Yuri Orlov walked out of their bedroom.

'Mr Orlov. There is a vessel moored near Seven Mile Beach that will shortly be impounded by Australian Border Force. It did not register with Customs upon arrival into Australian territorial waters and there are questions to be asked of the captain in relation to a body found, presumed to be a sailor from that vessel, that washed up on Binalong Bay. They will be wanting to view the crew manifest as a result. Additionally, there has been a report made of a person being contained against their will on the vessel. These are however minor matters in relation to a more serious charge of espionage. It is believed that there is a weapon aboard that interferes with communication and military systems and which has a devastating health effect on those nearby when it is deployed.'

Yuri stared blankly at Teal and then across to Anya and smiled faintly.

'This has nothing to do with my wife.'

'We have no evidence of her involvement, although she clearly has knowledge of your expertise and activities.'

'She knows nothing about my activities. Partners of

employees of the Russian government understand that they are safer the less they know.'

'So you are an employee of the Russian government?' Teal asked.

'Yes. But not by choice. I have been *co-opted*. I have very few choices in my life. However, where I can, I act in accordance with my values.'

'What does that mean?' Teal asked.

'Deployment of the weapon has side effects on those nearby. I have done everything in my power to limit the impact.'

'And for those who are impacted, who are hurt by the machine, what remedies have your developed?' Charlotte demanded, injecting herself into the conversation. Yuri regarded her carefully.

'I can offer no pills or treatments. However, it appears that deep rest has a positive impact on all symptoms.'

Yuri's phone rang, interrupting the conversation. He looked at the number and then at Teal, who nodded, providing permission for him to answer. A conversation ensued in Russian, and Charlotte was sorry that Galina was not with them for translation. The call was short.

'I have to go now,' Yuri stated.

'No,' said Anya. 'You hate boats. You're not a sailor. You'll fall overboard.'

'Darling. You know I have no choice. The vessel needs three people to operate it.'

'Defect now,' Teal said firmly. 'We can offer you protection.'

'But not protection for our family in Russia who will immediately be sent to an internment camp, probably in Siberia. And you cannot offer me protection here. The Russian government has a long reach. At some time in the future, I will be hit by a car or fall out of a window at a hotel. Not today or even tomorrow, but in that moment when I finally feel safe. I'm doing all I can to limit the impact of the weapon. Let me continue in this role.'

Teal's phone rang and she answered it immediately.

'Hold off for now and await instructions,' she said briskly before ending the call. 'Go. We will be in touch again, next time via Anya.'

Yuri hugged his wife, kissed her head, and grabbed a small bag from their bedroom before racing out the door as Charlotte's phone buzzed. It was the hospital, ringing to let her know that Scott had woken up.

Thirty minutes later, the taxi dropped Yuri at Seven Mile Beach. A flat cap covered his bald head, and a polar fleece his body. He was shivering, from fear as well as from the feisty mid-summer breeze. Squinting into the fading light he could see a lone figure standing beside a small, rocking speed boat, waiting at the shoreline. Even at this distance, he recognised Ivan from the deep scowl across his weather-beaten face. With the loss of Victor during the storm, Ivan had become the most senior member of crew. He had neither the technical or interpersonal skills required to assume this leadership position. Answers were being demanded from central control as to what had happened and he knew they would all be vigorously grilled when they returned to Russia.

Yuri had not been on board when the incident happened. He was not a sailor and indeed, hated being on the water, but with the loss of a crew member and a need for three able bodies to manage the super yacht and the weapon, he had no choice. Ivan's decision to 'recruit' Seb had been one of his most stupid decisions. Did he not realise the attention that a missing person might attract? His decision to anchor at Seven Mile Beach, in full view of locals, was equally short-sighted. They were now openly in Australian territorial waters and were required to register on arrival and have the vessel inspected. It was only a matter of time until they were approached by Customs officials.

Yuri was regretting so many decisions he'd made in his life. Most recently, he shouldn't have come with Anya to Hobart, having offered to oversee the testing of a modified weapon in adverse sea conditions. The rare opportunity to leave Moscow had been too inviting to ignore.

'You're late, Yuri,' Ivan barked in Russian, his irritation palpable.

'Traffic,' Yuri replied curtly, his tone dripping with sarcasm. 'Tasmania is full of it.'

Ivan snorted and gestured for Yuri to get into the boat. The engine roared to life and they sped out to the super yacht, the tension between them thick in the air. They reached the yacht and clambered aboard. Immediately the engines were fired, and they headed out to sea. Yuri picked up a pair of binoculars and scanned the horizon, spotting a motor craft approaching slowly from the direction of Hobart. He hesitated, then called out 'Australian Border Force approaching,' feigning panic.

The boat's engine revved louder as it increased its speed. Ivan rushed to the mounted weapon, preparing to fire at the approaching vessel.

'Are you insane?' Yuri shouted, grabbing Ivan's arm.

'We can't let them catch us!' Ivan roared back, shoving Yuri to the ground as he again focussed the weapon on the approaching vessel. Yuri climbed to his feet and threw his full weight at Ivan, resulting in them both tumbling down the stairs into the galley where things went flying and a map caught fire on an open flame.

Gleb, the gold-toothed one, who was steering the yacht, shouted from the bridge for them to stop as fists continued flying across the deck. Yuri was knocked to the ground again, dazed and bruised. Ivan, scampered up to the deck, and again aimed the weapon at the approaching Border Force boat, his finger pressing on the trigger. Summoning his last reserves of strength, Yuri pushed himself up and lunged at Ivan, who swivelled the weapon at him and fired, hitting Yuri and the yacht's instrumentation. The super yacht's motor stopped and Yuri collapsed to his knees, a pained gasp escaping from his lips before he fell unconscious, fire raging around him.

'We have to abandon ship!' Ivan shouted to Gleb over the crackling flames. Seeing the fire spreading and the naval vessel approaching more quickly, Ivan and Gleb abandoned the yacht for the speed boat, and took off. Several minutes later the naval vessel approached the burning yacht and focussed their energies on extinguishing the fire and rescuing Yuri, who lay unconscious and badly burnt on the deck.

From their command station, the officers tracked the fleeing motorboat as it raced out to sea and then stopped. Moments later a Russian submarine surfaced and the two men climbed abord. The submarine submerged as quickly as it had appeared. This was not the concern of the officers of Border Force as they towed the burnt super yacht back to their maritime compound and ensured the speedy transportation of Yuri to the Garrison Health Centre at Anglesea Barracks.

HOBART ROYAL HOSPITAL

Charlotte could not contain her delight in seeing Scott sitting up in bed, eating pasta and watching television. He'd been moved out of intensive care and into a public ward, a clear sign of the doctor's optimism for a full recovery.

'Hello sleepy head,' Charlotte said, 'Or should I call you Uncle Scott?'

'Absolutely. Oh my goodness. Where's my phone?'

Charlotte pulled his mobile out of her handbag and held it in her hand.

'I know you're keen to talk to your sister, and your parents and to meet your niece and nephew, Woody and Grace...'

'I love those names.'

'But I need you to be a bit measured with what you

share with them,' she whispered, aware that she was in a public space.

'I'm listening,' he replied, mirroring her softly spoken voice, grinning all the while.

'What do you remember about the race?'

'It was damn difficult. Huge waves, strong winds, Skye being thrown against the wall of the galley, breaking her ribs, and a poorly-mannered competitor with a blinding light.'

'Alright. For the moment, are you OK with saying that everything about the race remains foggy? You can barely remember sailing out of Sydney Heads. In the fullness of time, you'll possibly have the opportunity to talk about your sailing experience. You can be sure that Mason will be dogging you for details from your first call with him.'

'So many questions, but as you wish. And only because I love you and I've missed you, and of course I trust you. How long until you're able to tell me the *why*?'

Charlotte was about to reply when she noticed a BREAKING NEWS announcement on the television. She reached across for the remote control and unmuted the sound.

'Several watercraft from Border Force have attended a fire on a vessel not far from Seven Mile beach. The fire has been brought

under control, and one person taken to hospital. No further details are available at this time.'

They both looked at the footage of the sinister black and grey yacht.

'That's the yacht that attacked us,' Scott said angrily.

'I know.'

'What's been going on while I've been asleep, Charlie-Girl?'

Charlotte exhaled and was about to respond when her phone beeped.

'It's your sister. You ready for the onslaught of questions and messages of concern about to follow?'

'Give it to me,' he said, waving his fingers.

'And remember, you don't remember *anything* about the race.'

Scott gave his wife the thumbs up sign, adjusted his pillow and pressed the green telephone symbol on his phone.

'Hey Sis.'

'Eeeeek! Scott,' Miranda shrieked. 'Mum, Dad, he's awake.' The phone was passed to his parents whose faces moved from disbelief to delight.

'Now son,' his father said in a stern voice, 'What the heck were you doing in the shower?' They all laughed.

'You look thin,' his mother said frowning.

'Didn't get too much time to eat when we were in the race, Mum. I'll be eating properly now I'm up and about.' The phone was then commandeered by Mason.

'Speaking of races, I've been more than patient waiting for you to wake up from your little nap, Scotty. You know you promised me the inside story on your sailing experience.'

'Did I?' Scott said half-jokingly. 'Mate, you'll have to give me a bit of time. My memories a little wobbly on some of the details. The doctor has told me to be patient and not to overdo it.'

'Leave him alone about the story, Mason,' Miranda said, grabbing the phone from her husband. 'Now shhhh. Come look at the twins. They're blissfully asleep.' Miranda carried the phone into their bedroom where twin bassinets were lined up next to their bed. Scott and Charlotte cooed at the babies, swaddled in orange and purple onesies, barely moving in their cribs.

'They're gorgeous, Sis,' Scott whispered. Miranda and Mason beamed with pride.

'I'm so looking forward to cuddling them again,' Charlotte added. The parents tiptoed out of the bedroom and closed the door.

'Well, what's next for you, Captain Scott?' Mason asked. Scott limited his reply to attending to the repairs on the *Blue Gazelle*.

'Don't you have to follow through on your lodgement of interference in the race?' Mason asked.

'I can't remember much,' Scott replied vaguely.

Mason looked at his friend thoughtfully. 'I'm sorry mate.' He was about to make further comment when the doctor arrived.

'The doctor's here, Mason. I'll call you tomorrow.' Scott waved and hit the red disconnect button.

He looked up at the doctor and smiled. 'This is my wife, Charlotte, and we were hoping you'd give the OK for me to check out today.'

'I did not say that, you sneaky sailor,' Charlotte said with mock offence.

'The turnaround in your condition is nothing short of amazing and I can understand your desire to get out of here. However, you have a nasty head injury and an unusual *exposure*, and you've also been asleep for some time. I think it's best you remain here for one more night. If your vital signs are within normal parameters tomorrow, then you should be good to go,' Dr Duell said.

'There's someone here to see you,' the nurse said. Scott and Charlotte looked up to see Jason waiting in the corridor with a race official. They glanced at each other a little nervously, a gesture observed by the doctor.

'The patient is still recovering, so let them know to keep the conversation brief, very brief,' the doctor said to the nurse.

Jason was all smiles as he walked across the room and fist bumped Scott.

'The Commodore has been waiting to speak with you about your complaint of race interference.'

'My short-term memory is shot after my fall in the shower. I'm embarrassed that most of the race is just a foggy mess, sir. Could I call you tomorrow, after I'm discharged?'

'Today is the last day we can take any action. As it is, most yachts have departed for their home bases and we've not identified any vessels that were within five miles of the *Blue Gazelle* at the time of the incident. There were many lighting strikes in your area at the time of the incident which could have appeared to come from a phantom vessel. When you are exhausted, your mind plays tricks on you; you see things that aren't there.'

Scott could tell that the Commodore was giving him an easy out, a simple way to resolve the complaint. He looked at Charlotte who gave him the slightest of nods.

'I agree sir and officially withdraw the complaint.'

'I think that's best. Can you sign here to confirm your decision?' The form was notarized and the race official exited the ward moments later.

'Now the next official business is to sort out the party,' Jason said.

'Party?' Scott asked.

'A little bird has told me that Seb is officially out of that damn competition.'

'About time,' Scott replied.

'I'm going to leave you two to sort out the arrangements. I have things to organise for tomorrow's catwalk.' Charlotte leant across and kissed Scott lightly on the lips. 'Get a good night's sleep and don't forget to wake up tomorrow morning.'

Charlotte accompanied Dr Duell to the nearby Anglesea Barracks at the Garrison Health Centre, in a vehicle arranged by Teal. Neither spoke on the journey. Yuri was still unconscious when they arrived, with Anya sitting beside the bed in a distressed state, holding tightly to his hand. The rhythmic beeping of his heart monitor provided a sombre soundtrack in an otherwise silent room. The doctor checked in with the local medical team and reviewed his records, while Charlotte went over to the bed and placed a reassuring hand on Anya's shoulder.

Several minutes later, Dr Duell asked Anya and Charlotte to leave the room while she examined Yuri. She smiled reassuringly at Anya and told her not to worry as she left. Charlotte and Anya ordered drinks from a vending machine and walked outside into the sunshine.

'I always feared this day would come,' Anya said. 'They

will be watching and listening. And they will want him silenced.'

'I'm sure Teal can arrange for you both to disappear,' Charlotte replied.

'What sort of life would that be? Our children. I cannot bear the thought of never speaking to our children again. Perhaps it would have been better if Yuri had died.'

'Don't say that,' Charlotte replied softly.

'It's true.' A cough behind them, interrupted the conversation. It was Teal.

'Can you both come back inside again.'

Anya involuntarily shrieked when she walked into the ward and saw Yuri sitting up in bed, drinking a cup of tea.

'Bozhe moy. Ser'yozno. My god. Seriously.' She rushed to his bed and hugged her husband, all thought of him being better off dead, vanishing. 'What happened to you when we left the room?'

'We have a new treatment which appears to be working...well,' the doctor said. 'Both Scott and Yuri have reacted positively and I am hopeful that the improvement is permanent. Time will tell.'

'I am so grateful. *We are* so grateful,' Anya said before kissing her husband's forehead and squeezing him.

'The burns to his arms are minor and he reports no other ill effects.' Yuri grinned, supporting the statement. 'But I'll keep him here overnight for observation. This is also a secure facility. It will keep him safe for now, and give you time to decide what to do with him to keep him out of harm's way going forward,' Dr Duell said.

'I've an idea I'd like to discuss with the Orlovs,' Teal said.

'I'll leave you to it.' Dr Duell picked up her clipboard and left the room.

Charlotte and the Orlovs looked towards Teal with curiosity. Their eyes widened as she described what she had in mind. Charlotte's phone rang, breaking the reverie. It was Mason.

'Excuse me. I'm taking this call.'

Teal nodded and began answering the Orlov's questions, while Charlotte walked outside.

'Hey Mason. What's up?'

'Just checking in on the arrangements for the catwalk, you know so I can do my best with the images and social media coverage.'

'You don't sound too excited, Mason?'

'Fashion's not really my thing, but I'm a professional. This is a job and I'll give it my full attention, particularly as I haven't managed to get any back story out of Scott from the yacht race.'

'Give him time. He's only just woken up and his memory is not what it was.' She paused. 'Look, leave it with me.' They said goodbye and hung up. As Charlotte turned around, she saw the doctor departing. She sprinted across the road and had a quick conversation, resulting in receipt of the doctor's telephone number and a promise for a consult with Jason, before she returned to Melbourne.

The following day, two short pieces appeared in the main stream press, authored by journalist Mason Murray.

A report of interference in the recent Sydney to Hobart yacht race has been withdrawn by the skipper of the Blue Gazelle. *No evidence was found to substantiate the claim. It is noted that the skipper of the yacht, Scott Harmon, suffered head injuries during the race and has subsequently lost his short-term memory. No further commentary is available.*

A fire on a super yacht was brought under control by the Tasmanian Fire Service. The captain of the vessel, Yuri Orlov, experienced major head trauma and sustained burns to twenty percent of his body. He was transported to a burns facility where he is receiving specialist care. It had been expected that he would support his wife, Anya Orlov, at the Kaleidoscope on the Catwalk event being held at the Museum of Old and New Art. When asked for comment, Mrs Orlov said that her husband was a fighter and a passionate supporter of the arts, and that if he could possibly be there tomorrow, he would be.

ALONE DAY 113

Standing on the deck at the Moorilla Estate, Nelson Farnsworthy soaked in the natural beauty of the surroundings as he looked out across the perfectly mown grassed bank where the ceremony would be filmed, and down to the Derwent River. The water was shimmering in the late afternoon sunlight, reflecting the azure blue sky and the lush greenery along the river's banks. His eyes glanced over the rows of grapevines to the distant rolling hills. He finally felt calm. The ten-month journey to arrive at this destination had been fraught with challenges, but they'd done it. The six competitors had made it out and each had a unique story to share. He could see that Ralph was busy issuing last minute instructions to the cameramen and arranging the placement of the wooden benches where contestants would take their seats around a fireplace, and share their stories of being alone.

A barking dog broke his reverie and he scanned the area to spot the source.

'Come here Kevin,' Nellie called to the Alsatian.

Farnsworthy shrugged his shoulders, feeling irritated. He'd not given permission to the military veteran for the animal to attend. *It'd better be quiet during filming.* Nellie took her seat at the end of the bench with Kevin seated obediently beside her. Moments later she was joined by Raj, Valda, Archie and Galina.

'Where's the sailor?' Ralph called out.

'Here I am,' Seb said, panting as he ran across the grass. 'Car park was full so the taxi dropped me miles away.'

'We need makeup,' Ralph barked, prompting a young woman to sprint across the lawn and dab Seb's face with foundation and powder, seconds after he'd taken the last seat beside Galina. He glanced at her. She'd already had her makeup done and positively glowed. He couldn't quite reconcile the change. Farnsworthy stared at them and observed the slightest of movements as Galina's left leg swung left and touched Seb's leg. *Maybe it was involuntary?* Seb didn't appear to notice as the makeup artist made the final touches. Galina looked across at Farnsworthy and met his gaze. Her eyes sparkled and she winked at him. Nelsen sucked in his cheeks, cleared his throat and looked away.

'Attention ladies and gentlemen. We're about to start recording. I need silence on the set.' A wave of shushes settled any remaining noise and Kevin's ears pricked up on high alert.

'Three two one and action,' the cameraman said.

'Good evening viewers and welcome to the Moorilla Estate here, beside the Museum of Old and New Art in Hobart. My name is Nelson Farnsworthy and I am the producer of Alone. This evening, we are not here to drink wine, as delicious as it is, or to view modern masterpieces. Instead, we are here to share stories from deep inside the Tasmanian bush, where six contestants competed to take home the coveted cheque for $250,000 for having lasted alone, the longest.' He paused and the camera panned across each competitor. 'Today we will be announcing the winner, but not before we have revisited the journey that they have each been on. What did they see? What did they experience? What moment was the catalyst for tapping out and coming home?' He waited again while ominous music was played. 'Let's start first with environmental officer Valda. Valda?'

'Yes, Nelson.'

'Why did you enter this competition?'

'I was trying to escape a bad personal situation and was confident that my bush skills would ensure I didn't go hungry. I was also hoping to have time to reflect and to reclaim my sense of self. And maybe to find happiness again.'

'And what did you learn about yourself?

'That I'm rubbish on my own. I get bored. Really bored. That my friends mean a lot to me and that I like being around other people. Oh. And I also hate camping in the wet.'

'Hear, hear,' Nellie added and all the competitors laughed.

'Nellie,' Farnsworthy said, 'tell us why you entered the competition and what you learnt about yourself?'

'I entered the competition because I had the time and skills to live alone in a remote location. But like Valda, I hated the rain and I hated being alone. I also missed Kevin.' The dog barked once on hearing his name and she patted his head and looked affectionately into his eyes. 'And I know he missed me.' Kevin put his head on her lap.

'Galina. What about you? How did you find being alone?'

'I wasn't alone,' she replied.

'What?' Farnsworthy said. Several contestants gasped and leaned closer, awaiting her reply.

'I made friends with a white-spotted rat,' Galina replied.

'I think you'll find that was an Eastern quoll,' Valda chipped in while Archie snorted and slapped her on the knee. Seb grinned and laughed along with the others.

'And was it this rat, I mean this Eastern quoll, that bit you? Perhaps not such great company after all?' Galina looked at her bandaged hand and then held it up while the camera zoomed in'

'No it was a devil. I didn't mean to catch it, and I had some difficulty letting it go.'

'It was unharmed?' Nelson asked.

'I believe so. It ran away.' The other contestants looked at her with wonder. Except for Seb, whose face brimmed with admiration.'

'And did you get bored?'

'Never. I made a drum.'

'Or hungry?'

'No. I had plenty of food.' Nelson was irritated by her short answers so turned his attention to another competitor.

'Raj?'

'Yes Nelson?'

'How did you go being alone? Were you hungry?'

'All the time. Drove me crazy. My tummy did not stop rumbling. Yoga helps me to overcome many things, but not hunger. It was a beautiful setting and a precious experience, but one which I am keen to *never repeat*. My wife is a wonderful cook and I missed her.' He blew a kiss to the camera and waved.

'Archie?'

'Yes Mr Farnsworthy.'

'Tell us about your experience. Were you lonely?'

'Sometimes. I thought about my mob a lot but most

days I was OK. Like Galina I made a few, well not friends exactly, but there was an understanding with the animals I shared the space with.'

'I think we have some footage of that.' Nelson said. A short video of the magpie parents feeding their offspring high in the eucalyptus tree was shown on the screen. 'Great footage Archie. Thank you for capturing that for us. You climbed a tree to film that?' Archie nodded.

'You climbed a number of trees, didn't you?'

'I did.'

'And unfortunately, that was your undoing, wasn't it?' Archie smiled and tapped his cast.

'Yes, it was difficult, well impossible to be in in the bush, on your own with a broken leg.'

'Indeed.' Nelson said with emphasis before taking a step closer to Seb.

'Finally, we come to our sailor, Sebastian Ward. A contestant who proved to have superior fishing skills.'

'Yes, my fishing experience came in handy. But it's also a numbers game. Key to success was always having several baited lines out in the water and trying different casting out points. It increases your chance of success.'

'And you made a raft to help with fishing too?' Nelson asked. Seb hesitated, wondering where this question might be leading.

'Yes. I sometimes fished from my raft,' he said.

'And were you ever *alone*?' Seb glared at Farnsworthy and gulped.

'No. I wasn't.'

'Really, do tell.'

'There was something in the bush. An animal. Moving around. About the size of a dog. It would circle my camp at night.'

'And...' Nelson prompted.

'It had stripes.'

'What?' Nelson said turning directly to the camera before pivoting back to Seb. 'Was it a thylacine? That elusive marsupial believed to have been extinct for nearly one hundred years?'

'Maybe,' Seb replied. 'I looked for it but couldn't find it. If it was the Tasmanian tiger, it was impossible to find.' The contestants looked between each other, asking if they'd seen any evidence of the fabled animal. Farnsworthy let them chatter for a moment, imagining the same conversations happening on settees around the world. A few minutes later, he called for silence.

'Unfortunately, in his desire to find this animal, Sebastian inadvertently breached the rules of the competition. He boarded his raft and set off looking for clues, travelling way beyond his assigned space. Missing for days, causing us no end of grief. When he finally tapped out, we had to let him know he'd been disqualified.' Seb dropped his head remorsefully. 'His dream of winning the competition was over, leaving room for another winner to be declared.' The song by the band U2's song 'A Beautiful Day' suddenly burst forth from the speakers. 'For many in this competition, the day they tapped out was a beautiful day.' Seb glanced at Galina who returned a cheeky smile. 'For one person, today will be very special as they take home a cheque for $250,000. Drum roll please.'

Seb and Galina patted their legs in unison, complementing the sounds from the speakers.

'It's my pleasure to announce that, having spent more than one hundred days alone in the Tasmanian wilderness, Archie is the winner.' There was a moment of stunned silence, followed by a round of applause, initiated by Galina. She stood up clapping, and the rest of the contestants followed. 'Can someone please pass the man his crutches so he can come over here to receive his cheque.' Archie's eyes filled with tears as he took the crutches from Ralph and hobbled over to stand with Nelson. Archie turned first to the camera and then to Nelson.

'This is so unexpected I don't know what to say. Um. Thank you.' The music was turned up, confetti guns exploded spraying the contestants with colourful pieces of paper. Kevin started barking and jumping up to catch the tiny pieces of paper floating in the evening breeze.

'And that's a cut,' Farnsworthy cried out. 'Well done everyone.' The contestants gathered around Archie to shake his hand and pat his back. Galina had been first up to say congratulations, before melting back into the crowd which now included the production team.

Seb felt a hand on his shoulder. It was Nelson Farnsworthy.

'The cheque could've been yours Seb. You were this close,' he said holding his thumb and index finger up to his face.

'Wasn't to be.' He looked around at the other competitors talking amiably in a circle. Galina wasn't with them 'Is that it? Can I go now?'

'If you like, but there's an open bar on the terrace and a few nibbles.'

'Oh. Alright. Nice. I'll see you up there.'

Seb scanned the crowds looking for Galina. He walked to the edge of the grassed area thinking she may have snuck off for a cigarette. *But she's given up, hasn't she?* Lights were reflected on the Derwent River. It had a glistening beauty, but he was enjoying it on his own. He could hear music being sound-tested from the nearby gallery at the MONA and wondered what event was running. He pulled out his phone and called Galina but it went through to voicemail.

'Are you joining us, Seb?' Raj called out. 'C'mon over. I've heard that the nibbles on the grazing board are fantastic.' Seb jogged across the grass to join them, still scanning the area for signs of Galina. Seb took a beer from the tray offered by the waiter as he followed the others onto the deck. There were dozens of cheeses, dips, sliced meats, fruit, crackers and bread sticks laid creatively across an enormous piece of timber.

'I bet you wished you'd had that in the bush,' Nelson remarked to no one in particular. Seb's phone vibrated in his pocket. He didn't recognise the number but hoped that it was Galina ringing on someone else's phone.

'Hello,' he said cautiously.

'Hi Sebastian. It's Mason Murray calling. Scott's friend.'

'Oh,' Seb replied struggling to contain his disappointment. 'Hello. You were at Scott and Charlotte's wedding, wearing all those hats.'

'Yep. That was me on the big screen. Thank goodness for Zoom. And you were wearing a kilt and playing a drum.'

'Guilty as charged. What can I do for you Mason? I'm in a bit of a rush.'

'Um. I've heard that you may have seen the Tasmanian tiger when you were in the bush.'

'What? How did you hear that so quickly?'

'I'm a journalist. I have sources, and I'm fortunate enough to know someone who was in ear shot of your interview during the filming of the finale tonight.'

'Who?'

'I'd rather not say as they work there, and weren't meant to be listening in.'

'OK. Again. What do you want Mason?'

'An exclusive. I want to hear the story of your encounter with the tiger.'

'It wasn't really an encounter.'

'These are just details in a story that will excite thousands. Could I interview you as a first step?'

'I've signed a non-disclosure agreement. I don't think I could help you.'

'I am certain that the producers would love to have the release of the final episode of *Alone* coincide with a major breaking story.'

'Perhaps. Again. I'm not the person to speak to.'

'Who is?'

'Hold on?' Seb looked up from his phone. Farnsworthy was cutting a piece of brie from a cheese wheel while chatting with Valda. Seb tapped him on the shoulder and he turned around. 'I've got a journalist on the line who has already heard about the Tasmanian tiger sighting.' Farnsworthy beamed, clearly delighted at the news. 'He wants to run a big story and I've told him he needs to talk to you.' Seb passed him the phone and watched him turn and walk to the end of the terrace.

'Have you seen Galina?' Seb asked Valda who had just popped several grapes into her mouth.

'I have, although she was barely recognisable. Dressed up to the nines. Must have a serious date with someone.'

'Oh,' was all Seb could think to say. 'Bit disappointed I didn't get to say goodbye.'

'You staying around in Hobart long?' Valda asked.

'Not sure. Probably not. I need to get on with my life.'

'I get that,' she replied.

'Sebastian,' Farnsworthy called out. His hand was waving, for him to come over.

'Excuse me,' Seb said to Valda. He joined Farnsworthy and was curious at the huge grin on his face.

Nelson gave him back his phone, and said, 'I have a wonderful opportunity for you. I'm going to let your journalist buddy interview you and then we're going to send you back to the bush and film you looking for the Tasmanian tiger.'

'I don't think so,' Seb replied without hesitation, having anticipated the request on the short walk across the deck. 'My obligation to this production is now officially over.'

'We'll pay you. I know how disappointed you were to not be taking that big cheque home with you.'

'How much exactly?'

'We can discuss that.' Seb hesitated again, looking at his feet and suddenly keen to leave Tasmania behind him. 'And you can take your girlfriend with you.' Seb's head snapped up in surprise. Nelson's face was inscrutable but the flicker of his eyebrows revealed that he knew about their relationship.

'I'd need to speak with her.'

'Of course. We can finalise the details tomorrow. Why don't the two of you meet me at our offices at ten.' He thrust his business card into Seb's hand and left to join the other contestants without waiting to hear his reply. Seb's phone vibrated and this time he recognised Mason's number.

'Hello Mason.'

'I'm so excited. When do you think you'd be free to talk to me?'

'Don't know. I need to talk to my girlfriend first.'

'Well, she won't be free until tomorrow morning.'

'How do you know that?'

'Cause she's helping Charlotte with the *Kaleidoscope on the Catwalk* event happening one hundred metres away from you at the MONA.' Seb looked up and could see lights on next door. 'Thanks for letting me know, Mason. I'm on my way over.'

'Stop. Stop. You won't be allowed in. It's by invitation only.'

'Oh. OK. I'll call you tomorrow after we've confirmed arrangements with the production company.'

'Great news. Thanks.' Seb hung up and was about to put his phone back in his pocket when a ping announced the arrival of a message. It was from Galina.

> Sorry I didn't say goodbye Sebby. I have a job tonight. Will be late. Lots to discuss. Talk tomorrow?

Indeed, they had a lot to talk about. Seb replied with a

smiley face emoji and rejoined the others at the grazing table. Nellie's dog nuzzled his hand.

'He likes you. Are you a dog person?'

'Not particularly, but I'd make an exception for Kevin.'

A band started playing and the contestants started swaying.

'Join me?' Valda asked. Seb smiled at her, and walked out onto the dance floor, welcoming the distraction.

KALEIDOSCOPE ON THE CATWALK

The light filtering through the stained-glass cubes created a wonderful kaleidoscope of colour in the room that had been set up for the fashion parade. An elegant catwalk runway snaked around the centre with curved sofas and small palm trees providing a sitting-beside-the-river feel. Guests began to arrive, each greeted by a waitress offering a glass of champagne before they were shown to their seat. Soothing music played in the background, a seamless blend of classical and modern tunes. Chatter was interspersed by the gentle clinking of glasses. Many took the opportunity to admire the avant-garde art. The guests themselves were dressed to make a statement, aware that photos would be taken and shared across the organisation's social media channels.

Behind the scenes, models were in the final stages of

preparation, with last minute adjustments being made to their outfits, hair and makeup as each was transformed into a living work of art, perfectly complementing the gallery's aesthetic. Anya was busy making last minute adjustments to her opening remarks and liaising with museum staff about the placement of cameras, all the while watched by Yuri, seated in a wheelchair near the entrance, with both arms dramatically wrapped in bandages, blending perfectly with his all-white suit and shoes.

Anya nodded to the technician and the music was turned down. She sauntered out onto the middle of the runway and smiled.

'Welcome guests. Welcome friends. It's wonderful to have you here today in this magnificent building with so many inspiring artworks, for the Kaleidoscope on the Catwalk.'

A spontaneous ripple of polite applause echoed around the room.

'This evening, we will be showcasing sixteen remarkable outfits from designers who have embraced our remit for creating colourful, inspiring and distinctive clothing.

'I'm delighted to have my husband with me today. He has supported me and my passion for fashion for the last twenty years. As you can see, he's recently had an accident that has damaged his arms and impacted his memory, so this is my last event for a while. We're going to a sanitarium where he can get the rest he needs. I hope that you will support each of the wonderful designers displaying this evening. I can assure you this will be a memorable event.'

She waved to the technician and the lights were lowered and the music volume increased. The audience hushed in anticipation.

At the same time, the technical room was a hive of activity as internal and external cameras were actively monitored, with Galina's eyes fixed firmly on Yuri. A lone drum started beating and the first model emerged wearing an oversized floor-length scarlet dress, with vintage bustle, ruffles and long chiffon sleeves. Cascades of tight auburn curls fell down her back from the crown of her head. Moments later she was followed by a model wearing a classic strapless a-line dress, billowing with multiple petticoats and sprinkled throughout with diamantes. She sparkled as she twirled under the lights. They exited to polite applause as a couple dressed in yellow suits walked out arm in arm. Her suit had a satin shirt with enormous bow, straight legged pants and traditional jacket. His outfit came with a boater hat and feather and on his feet were black patent shoes, that constantly caught the overhead lights.

In the technical room, all eyes remained fixed on the monitors. Each security member was reporting in to Teal at three minute intervals. Apart from an occasional burst of laughter and barking of a dog from the nearby Moorilla estate, there was nothing exceptional to note. Another couple emerged onto the catwalk and with a change in music, danced through their promenade. The female model wore a fuchsia pink pant suit with vest and flared trousers and he wore a soft pink suit with white shirt and coordinating pink satin tie and handkerchief. The male model dipped his companion just before they exited off stage. Anya observed the expressions on the faces of the guests. Some were whispering furtively to the person sitting beside them, but most were taking photos which she hoped they were sharing with their online communities.

A couple in green emerged next. His suit was dark green satin trimmed with black velvet over an unbuttoned crisp white shirt. The female model wore a cactus green suit with long gold chains over a short bustier with matching straight-leg trousers and a matador's jacket on top, engraved with gold writing. Two children aged around eight walked out next, holding hands. He wore a dark purple suit with white shirt with large black dots and a green tie, and the girl wore a green suit with orange shirt and purple cravat. While they stood at the end of the runway, they were joined by another couple wearing matching orange and green outfits, styled as play clothes, which delighted the audience with the allusion to changes in roles.

In the technical room, the arrival of a small boat with an outboard engine at the public pier was noted. All staff moved to high alert as the nautical themed couple walked out on to the stage. The male model wore a navy jacket with a gold crest logo over a white collared shirt and trousers, while the female model wore a halter neck navy pantsuit accompanied by a sailor's cap. There were over-sized hooped earrings in her ears and around her neck on a silver chain hung a small set of binoculars. The security camera zoomed in on two black figures emerging from the boat. The song 'Sing a Rainbow' by Peggy Lee burst from the speakers and all the models came back for another tour on to the stage making obvious the nod to the song's lyrics of red and yellow and pink and green, purple and orange and blue. A mirrored disco ball was struck my multiple lights making the walls of the room a kaleidoscope of colours. All the models did a turn on the catwalk before exiting, leaving the catwalk empty. The lights dimmed and the audience fell silent again wondering what was coming next. When the lights came on, a couple wearing masks were on the catwalk performing a mime, pretending they were separated by a large invisible wall. The audience were transfixed as the couple tried to find a way to be together.

Seb was talking to Nellie when Kevin suddenly barked twice. In the darkness, his attention was focussed on the building next door. Seb walked over to the railing and squinted, trying to see what had caught his attention. Kevin barked again. There were shadows moving slowly near the bushes. Seb could just make out two figures hunched low, wearing black and now stealthily creeping along the wall of the building.

'OK if I take Kevin for a walk?' Seb asked Nellie. She passed him the lead, and turned back to her conversation with Archie. Kevin strained at the leash, keen to go outdoors.

'I need you to be quiet Kevin. Shhh. Don't bark unless I say so.' The dog let out a low growl. They moved quickly down the internal stairs and out into the night. Once on the grass, Kevin strained on the leash. Seb let himself be pulled along by the dog and they covered ground quickly as they raced to the fire exit door at the MONA, which had been jammed open. They slipped inside and moved towards the music and laughter.

Two models wearing masks were performing a mime as they modelled outfits featuring piano keys and dominoes, the black and white images a stark contrast to the colourful outfits that had preceded them. None of the guests noticed the two black figures slinking along the back wall to where Yuri Orlov was now alone and asleep in a wheelchair. The tall one grabbed the handles and pushed the chair towards the exit while the shorter one dramatically held up a Glock pistol, threatening anyone who dared approach. Kevin barked and the audience turned their attention from the catwalk to the mini theatre playing out in the corner. An audience member laughed and held up his champagne flute to celebrate the performance. Others started clinking their glasses or chatted to the guest sitting beside them, about the cleverness of this theatrical addition. The two men quickly left, with Kevin and Seb in close pursuit.

The shorter man in black walked backwards with his pistol now pointed directly at Kevin while the taller man raced ahead with Yuri. Seb held the lead tight to stop the dog from charging and wondered where the security team was. Surely, they would appear any moment. A single glint of gold from his assailant's front tooth confirmed Seb's suspicions that this was one of the Russian sailors.

'Stop. Stop!' Galina's voice called from behind him. He turned to see her teetering along in high heels and a turquoise ball gown. Seb was horrified, watching her as she ran towards the sailor brandishing the gun. A shot exploded from the Glock hitting her directly in the chest, and she crumpled to the floor.

'Nooo,' Seb screamed as he dropped to her side, releasing Kevin in the process. Galina moaned and the Russians ran out the door.

'Galina, where have you been hit?' Seb was distraught as Galina attempted to respond. He cradled her in his arms and tears pricked his eyes as he searched for the point of impact on her gown. Galina attempted to speak again. He leant closer as she whispered,

'Call Kevin back.'

Moments later they were surrounded by medics and Seb was pushed aside. Galina's bullet-proof vest was removed and she was lifted onto a stretcher and transported to a waiting ambulance.

'She's just been winded, Seb,' Charlotte said reassuringly, 'although that might not be what is reported in the papers tomorrow.' Not for the first time Seb felt confused.

'Kevin,' he suddenly shouted, before racing out the door. He could hear the dog barking and was relieved to see that the Alsatian was now back at Nellie's side. He scanned the area and saw no sign of the men in black. However, the man in white in the wheelchair was speaking softly in what he presumed was Russian, with a woman in a scarlet gown.

'What just happened?' he asked Charlotte. She smiled.

'We've played a part in a ruse and hopefully in disabling an awful weapon.'

'I'm still not any clearer and, I don't particularly care. I want to see Galina.'

'You can see her now. She's standing behind you.' Seb slowly turned to see the smiling face of the person he cared for, far more than he imagined. He walked over to her and threw his arms around her, holding her tight.

'Careful, sailor-boy. I've just been shot.'

DAY 114

Galina was startled to open her eyes and see Seb frowning at her.

'What's wrong Sebby?'

'Look at that bruise on your chest. You could've been killed last night.' Galina glanced at the red and purple circle in the centre of a distinct swelling between her right shoulder and breast. The stitching from the bullet-proof vest had also made an imprint around the point of impact. Her hand reached up and she gingerly touched the injury, wincing in pain.

'See. You're in agony.'

'Agony might be overstating it,' she replied.

'But the fact that you could have died is not. Tell me again how you came to be running after Yuri and the Russians at that fashion show.'

'I'll admit that things didn't go according to plan, but everything worked out well in the end.'

'Yuri Orlov was nearly kidnapped,' he replied a little louder than he intended.

'No, he wasn't. He was going to be retrieved by the time they'd reached the river. We hadn't reckoned on you and Kevin joining in the pursuit.'

'Who's "we"?'

'The security company I've taken a job with.' Seb looked at her suspiciously.

'Is this a government run organisation?'

'Kind of. We've achieved a great more than you're aware of that I can't share with you. I've had to sign an oath that I won't disclose secrets.'

'Well then, can you share with me the reason why you let Nelson know about our collaboration in the bush?'

'My new employer demanded a lower public profile. They thought it best I didn't win the competition and receive fame and glory.' Seb's mouth gaped open and he reached across and playfully swatted her leg. 'And did you meet Archie?' she continued. 'He's delightful and we both know that he's the real winner.'

'Sometimes I think I don't know you at all.' Seb rolled on his back and looked up at the ceiling of the hotel's room. 'I have a new job, too.'

'Really? And you're only telling me now. Look who's keeping secrets.'

'If you hadn't abandoned me last night you'd have been there when Farnsworthy offered to pay me to tell *my story* of *tracking the Tasmanian tiger* deep into the bush.'

'Oooh. My word. So you're also commencing a career in subterfuge?'

'With such a perfect partner for this task, how could I say no.'

'I'm your partner, then?'

'Do you want to be.'

'What do you think, sailor-boy?'

Seb's phone pinged. He looked at the message and sat upright.

'It's from Evelyn.'

'Your sister?'

'Yep. She's in Tangier on her way to Europe. A bit concerned as she's received a couple of messages from someone called Nelson Farnsworthy.' They both hooted with laughter. Seb pressed her number and the phone rang five times before it was answered.

'Hey Seb.'

'Hey Sis.'

'Good to hear from you, bro. Where are you?'

'In bed, in Hobart.'

'Of course.' She laughed. 'I understand you've been missing in the wilderness. Anything I should worry about?'

'Nah.'

'Good oh. And you've told Nelson you're safe and sound.'

'Of course.'

'So what's been happening?'

'I've got a girlfriend.' Galina grinned and tickled Seb.

'A girlfriend eh. So these two things are related? Having a girlfriend and being missing?'

'I could never get anything by you, Evie.'

'And your plans?'

'Having a few beers with some friends.'

'And after that?'

'Not yet defined.'

'Why don't you come over here for a bit. Meet us in Marseille and we can go for a bit of a sail around the Med.'

'Can I bring my girlfriend?'

'Of course. What's her name?'

'Galina. Galina-Elizabeta Ivanof. She mostly responds to Betty.'

'Nice. Can she sail?'

'Of course. Betty's a very competent sailor.' Galina's hand flew to her mouth to suppress a giggle.

'OK then. *On se verra à Marseille.*'

'Yes. We'll see you in France, Evie.' Seb hung up and took in the huge grin on Galina's face. She was clearly feeling joyful.

'And maybe, after we've finished sailing around the sea, we can go up to Estonia to meet my mother.'

Charlotte was startled to open her eyes and see Scott smiling at her.

'What's up, Captain? Why you in such a good mood?'

'Because I'd forgotten how much I love waking up beside you.' Charlotte reached up and touched his face and he delicately kissed her fingertips. 'Everything went off without a hitch last night?' he asked.

'Pretty much. The audience enjoyed a few extra theatrical interludes. I have a wrap-up meeting this morning and I'll need to chat with Mason this evening about the social media plan going forward. He did a stellar job last night. What about you? What d'ya need to finish off so we can officially start our holiday?'

'More repair checks and I've gotta chat to Skye about transportation of the *Gazelle* but I think we're nearly there.'

'Wonderful. And if you're free by midday you can join us at The Hope and Anchor where we'll be celebrating Seb's return from the wilderness.'

'Nothing would keep me away from that.'

Charlotte, Teal and Galina met at the roof top bar in the Crowne Plaza Hotel. They were the only patrons, which was not surprising at ten o'clock in the morning.

'It seems that our ruse has worked,' Teal reported. 'Online chatter in Russian military circles is that Yuri Orlov has lost his memory and is physically disabled. We are hopeful that they believe he is no longer worth pursuing. The significance of this acquisition cannot be overstated. Yuri will be able to help us to develop a device to counteract the weapon.'

'Where are they now?' Galina asked. 'I thought they'd be here today.'

'They're already out of the country in a secure location. We think it's best they lay low for a while. Gives us time to work with Yuri.'

'Will Anya be ever able to travel again on the fashion circuit?' Charlotte asked.

'Maybe. Not for a while, but time will tell. It's good that you're able to wrap everything up with the fashion show for her.' Teal's phone beeped and she glanced at her screen. 'My driver's here. I need to go.' She kissed them both on the cheek and was gone a minute later.

'She didn't say when she'd next be in touch?' Galina remarked.

'Probably doesn't know, and it doesn't matter. We're now free to get back to our normal lives.'

'Whatever they are,' Galina said as she picked up her cup of tea.

HOPE AND ANCHOR HOTEL

The Hope and Anchor was nearly empty when Jason arrived shortly before midday, a far cry from the wall-to-wall sailors squeezed in the previous week. He placed the cake box on the table, ordered a beer and asked for a tab to be set up. He checked his watch. His flight back to Brisbane was leaving in three hours. There'd be enough time to hear Seb's, *possibly exaggerated*, stories of survival in the bush and Scott's recounting of sailing through the storm. He sipped his drink and scrolled through the morning's local news, stopping at an article written by Mason Murray.

Theatrical Chase provides Wonderful Finale to Fashion Parade in Hobart

A small and elite group of fashionistas met at the MONA last night to watch a pageant of colourful ensembles from several of the world's leading designers. The theme of the event was Kaleidoscope on the Catwalk and the stained-glass room at the MONA was the perfect setting for this mesmerising experience. There were dramatic robes and two-tone suits worn by stunning women, handsome men and delightful children. The climax of the show was a black and white collection modelled by actors, miming a breakout scene, that would have been at home in any James Bond film. This was the last event in the fashion calendar to be hosted by Anya Orlov. Links to stockists below.

Jason started scrolling through the photos.

'Hey Jase.' Charlotte pulled up a chair. He turned his phone to show an image of Charlotte standing with her arm around Anya Orlov on the catwalk.

'You look gorgeous,' Jason said.

'Thanks Jase.'

'Can I see that?' Scott asked. Jason passed him the phone.

'Wow,' he said. 'Spectacular shots and not too much exaggeration from Mason.'

'Yes, he did exercise restraint with the commentary, and he's been a powerhouse with the sharing of images on social media. Anya will be chuffed with the number of likes and comments his posts have been receiving,' Charlotte replied.

'Ahoy mateys,' Seb said as he and Galina pulled up chairs. Scott came around the table and gave Seb a tight bear hug.

'Good to see you.'

'You too,' Seb replied. No further words were needed.

Jason asked them what they were drinking and went to the bar to place orders, returning moments later with a large knife and half a dozen small plates. He opened the box and placed the cake in the centre of the table, prompting squeals of delight from Galina. The colourful cake featured a lone fisherman sitting on a log beside a river, with a kangaroo on his left and a possum on his right. Behind the trees watching him suspiciously, was a dog with stripes on its back.

'Where am I?' Galina blurted out before laughing at her question.

'What d'ya mean?' Jason asked. 'You two weren't together in the bush. Or were you?'

'We will be today,' Seb replied, surreptitiously avoiding his friend's question.' We both have to go back to film a new story about the competition.

'When are you leaving?' Charlotte asked.

'In an hour,' Seb replied.

'So soon. And after that, what are you doing?'

'Giving my girlfriend sailing lessons.'

'Oooh,' Jason replied teasingly. 'Because...?'

'Because we're going to fly to France to join my sister sailing around the Mediterranean.'

'Sounds like a perfect warm up for the Sydney to Hobart race,' Scott said. 'We've two berths available for next year's race.'

'What d'ya reckon, Betty?' Seb asked. Galina looked at each of Seb's friends, then turned to look at him.

'I'm in.'

ALONE DAY 115

It felt weird returning to Sailing Siesta for the third time. Seb now knew the route well and looked out for familiar markers on the journey up the river. They pulled into the sandy shore and Seb helped Ralph to unload the camera equipment. Together they'd mapped out a story that they hoped had the right balance of evidence and intrigue.

'How long do you think you'll be?' Galina asked Ralph.

'Not sure. One hour, maybe two.'

'Good. I'll take the raft and visit my old camp. You can pick me up on the way back.' Ralph agreed arranging to meet her at the landing point near her old camp.

'And if you're not there when we pull in, we're leaving without you.'

'Of course,' Galina replied. 'I wouldn't want to be left alone.'

Ralph still didn't know what to make of this woman. He watched her push off using the long pole for navigation, and called out,

'Don't fall in.'

'Doesn't matter. I can swim,' she replied defiantly.

Twenty minutes later she pulled the raft up onto the bank and sprinted up the hill, over the uneven ground and back to her old camp. Her shelter was still in place as they'd had no time to dismantle it when she'd tapped out. The wind had blown the dirt around the camp revealing the hole where she'd buried her spent cigarette butts. She rarely missed the habit and was pleased it was now something she *used to do*. She sat down on the rock near her fireplace and listened to the wind blowing gustily through the undergrowth. The wallaby skin was still stretched tightly between two trees and she felt around for her drumsticks. They were inside her shelter and she scooped them up with delight, and started banging out 'In the Air Tonight'. Several minutes later a familiar noise behind her made her temporarily stop and pivot. Suupiste was sitting on a log, watching her.

Meanwhile, back at Sailing Siesta, Seb was lying on his stomach examining animal scats when he heard the familiar drumming from the other side of the river. He smiled. Ralph was momentarily confused and then his eyebrows flickered when he guessed the source of the sound.

'Cut,' he called out. 'Five-minute break.'

Seb stood up and dusted himself off.

'I'm taking a comfort break,' he said. Ralph gave the thumbs-up and walked back to the water's edge.

As Seb was relieving himself, he noticed something in the long grass catching the sunlight. He zipped up his fly, took two steps towards the object and squatted down. In a small hole amongst the grass lay the motion-activated camera. He looked back to Sailing Siesta and could see Ralph and the cameraman drinking from a thermos. They paid him no heed. Remaining low, he turned the device on and watched with excitement as something that had to be a Tasmanian tiger, stared at the lens intently and then bit off the camera. Turning the device off, he slipped it into his pocket and returned to camp.

Two weeks later an article by Mason Murray appeared in the mainstream press.

Alone with a Tasmanian Tiger.

When you think about being dropped in the wilderness with just a few tools, your first thoughts are focussed on creating suitable shelter, finding adequate sources of food and identifying activities or distractions that will keep boredom and loneliness at bay.

One of the contestants in the most recent game of Alone, had quite a different distraction altogether. In the middle of the night, he heard a low-pitched husky bark. He was all too aware that animals he'd trapped were disappearing. There were animal scats he couldn't identify. Then one evening when he was sitting at the water's edge fishing, he was sure he saw a brown animal, the size of a small dog, with distinctive tiger-like stripes, moving through the bush. Startled by this visitor, he headed off in search of a creature that's been considered extinct for nearly a century.

Following game trails through the bush with occasional clues from unidentified scats, he headed off deep into the wilderness. In leaving his assigned territory, he knew that he was risking disqualification from the competition he so dearly wanted to win. But the possibility of finding this almost mythical animal, was too strong a temptation.

For five days and nights he tracked the animal along the water's edge and deep into the bush before deciding that his journey was in vain. He returned to his camp and tapped out.

Even now, he still hears the animal's cry in his sleep...

AFTERWORD

Well reader, how do you feel?

Did you enjoy the journey into the Tasmanian wilderness and onto the high seas in the Sydney to Hobart yacht race?

I'd love to know what you thought of *Alone with a Tasman Tiger*. Reviews can be left in all the usual places and I can be emailed at janeellyson@gmail.com

BIBLIOGRAPHY

Song References

'In the Air Tonight' by Phil Collins. From the 1981 album *Face Value*

'Sailing' Composed by Gavin Sutherland of the Sutherland Brothers in 1972, best known as a 1975 international hit for Rod Stewart.

'A Beautiful Day' by U2 song. First track on U2's tenth studio album, *All That You Can't Leave Behind* (2000)

About Havana Syndrome

https://www.theguardian.com/us-news/2021/apr/29/us-unexplained-health-incidents-officials-washington

ACKNOWLEDGMENTS

The writing of a novel is only possible with the support of others. My thanks to my editor Jackie Bates, and my many colleagues, friends and family who encouraged me as I crafted this story and provided feedback on early drafts of Alone.

BOOK CLUB QUESTIONS

1. What was the hardest thing about being *left alone* for contestants?
2. What would you find the hardest thing about participating in a survival contest?
3. What ten things would you take into the wilderness with you?
4. Should Scott and Skye have made the decision to wait until the storm passed before crossing The Paddock in the Sydney to Hobart yacht race?
5. Should Seb have been disqualified from the Alone competition?
6. Should the competitors have formed attachments to the animals in their local area?

For example, Galina with Suupiste and Archie with Rooster.

7. What concerns did Yuri and Anya Orlov have about Yuri's involvement with the Russian government?

8. Do you think that the Thylacine, also known as the Tasmanian Tiger, is still alive?

9. Why has the Tasmanian Tiger captured the imagination of so many people?

ABOUT THE AUTHOR

About Jane Ellyson

Jane Ellyson has written six novels across the action-adventure and romance genres. Having lived in Europe and Asia, in addition to her native Australia, her stories frequently visit beautiful locations. She currently lives at Possum Creek, just out of Bangalow in northern New South Wales – well she would if she was real – rather than being the pen name of someone who would prefer to remain anonymous.

www.janeellyson.com

OTHER BOOKS BY JANE ELLYSON

Northern Rivers series

Over Byron Bay

Substitute Child

Roman Roulette

Missing in Myanmar

Nonsense in the North

OVER
BYRON BAY

POOR TIMING AND AGONIES OF
CONSCIENCE ARE EVER PRESENT IN THIS
SWEET LOVE STORY

JANE ELLYSON

BOOK 1 OF 5

Over Byron Bay (Book 1 of 5)

Melissa Bourne and Andrew Wyatt were neighbours in the country town of Bangalow in Australia. Friends, good friends were all they'd ever been. This situation suited them both until Andrew found someone else. Surprised at her jealousy and with an international job offer in hand, Melissa left the country. She accepted a job offer in Boston, met Jonathan Brinkley, married and settled into life in the U.S.

Five years later she returns to Bangalow for a visit with her father, shortly after the death of Andrew's mother. The two meet briefly at the funeral, and the day before she flies back to Boston providing an opportunity to rekindle their relationship and to recognise that their feelings for each other go beyond friendship. Melissa returns to the States in turmoil.

SUBSTITUTE
CHILD

DISCOVERY OF A BOTTLE PROMPTS A
WHIRLWIND JOURNEY OF ADVENTURE, LOVE
AND A SEARCH FOR IDENTITY

JANE ELLYSON
BOOK 2 OF 5

Substitute Child (Book 2 of 5)

A deckhand in France discovers a bottle with a letter inside. The bottle has floated all the way from Byron Bay in Australia to the south of France. The discovery prompts a whirlwind journey for Charlotte Wyatt into the world of paparazzi, European royalty and the criminal underworld.

Substitute Child is the story of a student travelling to the other side of the world to collect a bottle with a love letter to a brother she never knew and a journey to discover who she is and what she wants from her life.

WHERE'S JACK?

R·O·M·AN
R·OULETTE

MISSING FRIENDS AND THE MAFIA CAUSE
MAYHEM IN THE MEDITERRANEAN

JANE ELLYSON
BOOK 3 OF 5

Roman Roulette (Book 3 of 5)

Unable to leave Rome due to an air traffic controller strike, Charlotte accepts an invitation to a party on a super yacht. A friend disappears and then Charlotte becomes an accidental stowaway as the yacht heads for Sicily. Inadvertently caught up in the international slavery trade and forced to choose between several unbearable options, Charlotte embarks on a bold plan to save the women captured by the Monk, and in doing so, to save herself. Adventure/Thriller set between Rome, Naples and Taormina in Sicily.

MISSING
— IN —
MYANMAR

A SIMPLE REQUEST.
A JOURNEY TO A FOREIGN COUNTRY.
ALL BEFORE THE LIGHTS WENT OUT.

JANE ELLYSON
BOOK 4 OF 5

Missing in Myanmar (Book 4 of 5)

The Australian Charlotte Wyatt wasn't sure what she was letting herself in for when she agreed to be available for occasional information gathering activities for the Australian Securities Intelligence Organisation. Her first assignment comes at the end of a holiday in Thailand. Having just said goodbye to her boyfriend, who has taken a job sailing from Port Vila in Vanuatu to Bundaberg in Australia, Charlotte Wyatt is intrigued by the opportunity to go to Myanmar to gather information about a missing person.

With the help of a mysterious librarian, she finds the information she was sent to retrieve, and then, just as she's making plans to return, the lights go out in Myanmar and the military takes over. With a reluctant passenger, Charlotte runs checkpoints and dodges bullets, in a race to the border.

NONSENSE

— IN THE —

NORTH

SAILING, SMUGGLING, SPYING AND
AVOIDING SHARKS, SNAKES AND SPIDERS

JANE ELLYSON
BOOK 5 OF 5

Nonsense in the North (Book 5 or 5)

A too-good-to-be-true sailing trip results in Scott's disappearance from waters near Hamilton Island in Australia. Now considered by police to be an integral part of an international drug smuggling operation, Charlotte relies on a sympathetic police officer and an aboriginal tracker named 'Nonsense' to travel deep into Cape Conway, to disrupt a drug exchange and to find her Scott, improving their chances of a happily-ever-after. All the while helping plan her best friend's wedding.

Chic Charlie Series

A CHIC CHARLIE NOVEL

An Extraordinary WEDDING

PREPARING FOR THE BIG DAY...
THEN THE BRIDE DISAPPEARS

JANE ELLYSON

An Extraordinary Wedding

The run up to any bride's wedding should be wonderful with bridal showers, honeymoon planning and rehearsal dinners. For Charlotte Wyatt, it's not that joyful. Her fiancé is in lockdown, her mother doesn't like her wedding dress and her best friend can't be there in person on their big day. Also, Charlotte's entangled in a tricky situation with Saanvi, the bride-to-be of a client, who's taken refuge in Charlotte's fashion design studio while considering if they'll cancel their arranged marriage.

Then Saanvi disappears.

***

www.janeellyson.com